# ECHO OF ROSES

### Echoes in Time
### Book One

## Paula Quinn

Dragonblade Publishing, Inc. is an imprint of Kathryn Le Veque Novels, Inc.
P.O. Box 7968
La Verne CA 91750
ceo@dragonbladepublishing.com

Produced in the United States of America

First Edition May 2021
Trade Paperback Edition

*Dearest Reader;*

*Thank you for your support of a small press. At Dragonblade Publishing, we strive to bring you the highest quality Historical Romance from the some of the best authors in the business. Without your support, there is no 'us', so we sincerely hope you adore these stories and find some new favorite authors along the way.*

*Happy Reading!*

*CEO, Dragonblade Publishing*

# CHAPTER ONE

*New York City*
*July 2019*

THE SUN BROKE through the clouds and bright sunshine filled the loft where Kestrel Lancaster lived with her four roommates.

She didn't want to open her eyes. Her bed and pillow were too comfortable, and besides, it was Sunday, her day to rest. It had been Lilith's suggestion. Lilith observed the Sabbath and had talked Kestrel into taking off one day a week with her. Kes had been doing it now for the last year, and her rest days were growing more and more enjoyable. Rest for her meant no reading anything historical, no watching anything historical on her phone or television. No visiting museums or other historical societies. It was a day to meet her dad for dinner and live in the now, as another roommate, Jack, had put it. It was a day to take a break from her work, her passion, to stay out of her head and whatever century she was working on.

And whatever man had broken her or one of her friend's hearts this past month. Jack was having the same issues with the women he dated, so it seemed to be that people in general sucked and love wasn't real anymore.

She pulled her pillow over her head.

Brian McGill sucked the worst. Kes had talked with him on a dating site. They hit it off and met. Things were going smoothly.

At first, Brian was all romance and flowers. A month in, and his attention wandered to a girl he met at work, and that was the end at that. Before him, there were others, some a little more serious where talk of love was involved and then forgotten as if it hadn't existed. Because it hadn't.

She was getting older. Twenty-five and still no serious relationships. Men just seemed like something to pass the time. There was nothing substantial. And she wasn't alone. Her friends went through it, too. Like her, all four of her roommates had been cheated on. They'd gone through terrible pain. She'd watched them fall apart, cry, or stay silent holed up in their rooms, or try to get revenge by sleeping with a dozen more people. It was all too easy. Men and women could have someone else at the touch of a keypad.

Kes wanted no part of it anymore. She wished for a time when life seemed easier and the world wasn't so small. When objects didn't come before relationships and "love" wasn't so instant and so fickle.

The front doorbell was ringing. Ugh. Was no one else already up? She didn't see anyone moving around inside the loft. What time was it? She pulled her phone to her. 10:12am. Seriously? Who was at their door on Sunday morning? She got out of bed, put on her soft, furry robe and lumbered toward the door across the entire length of the loft. She didn't bother brushing her hair. It better not be Brian. She'd dumped him a week ago. She would never take him back. If it was him, she was going to let him have it.

She pulled back the heavy lock and opened the door after another angry ring.

"All right," she grumbled and rubbed her eyes.

A young guy stood on the other side. He stared at her huge blue-green eyes, then smiled.

"Can I help you?" she asked.

He said nothing. He kept smiling and handed her an envelope. "Um…would you like to—?"

Kes shut the door.

She hated being rude, but she wasn't in the mood for flirting or dating. She wasn't sure she ever would be again.

"Who was at the door?"

Kes looked up from the envelope at her friend and roommate Kim coming from her screened-in space.

"A letter was delivered to me from a company called ISOAP Corp." She carried the letter to one of the overstuffed sofas taking up room in the wide-open space and sat down. "Ever hear of them?"

Kim shook her head and russet curls sprang up and down around her neck. "Nope. Must be important if they're sending a messenger on a Sunday. Open it."

By now, Jack and Lilith had left their beds and gathered around the sofa. "Constantine went out early this morning," Lilith told her when Kes looked around for him.

Kes read out loud.

*"Ms. Kestrel Lancaster,*

*Your presence is requested at our office on this date to discuss a legal matter. We await you at your earliest convenience this afternoon.*

*Regards,*
*G. Green."*

Jack took the letter and pulled out his phone the way a knight might brandish his sword. He dialed the number on the letter and waited. There was no answer. "Closed."

"Not entirely if they want to meet with me." Kes frowned. So much for resting. Now she was going to have to travel to West Seventy-third because she was probably being sued by someone. Talk about raining on her parade.

"What happens if I'm being sued and I don't go?" she asked.

Jack and Lilith started typing on their phones.

"This information only applies to not showing up to court,"

Jack told her.

"Right," Lilith agreed. "What you have is just a letter *requesting* your presence. That doesn't mean you're being sued."

"What else can it mean?" Kes asked them and rose from the sofa. "I'm not going. I'll call tomorrow and find out what they want before I see them."

"If you go today, I can go with," Jack told her.

Jack was such a dear friend. Kes could always count on him. Kim and Lilith said it was because he was interested in her. Poor Jack. She wasn't attracted to him in the least. She tried to be. But she didn't want to risk their friendship.

She went to the far left corner of the loft where her bed was and fell into it.

Her phone rang. She reached into the pocket of her robe for it. She didn't recognize the number. "Hello?" Why did she pick it up? She wasn't even thinking about picking it up.

"Ms. Lancaster?"

She sat up. British accent. She had relatives in England, but she didn't recognize this man's voice. Her stomach tightened into a knot. "Yes."

"Mr. Green here from ISOAP."

"How did you get my number?"

"I understand my correspondence was vague. Set your mind at rest." *Rest.* "This meeting is in regard to an inheritance. That is all I can say over the wire. Can I expect you?"

An inheritance? What? "An inheritance from whom?"

"As I have already stated, Ms. Lancaster. I am not liberty to say on the phone. Bring a friend if you are wary."

"I…"

"Can I expect you?"

She sighed. "Sure. I'll be there in an hour—with a friend. Or two."

She hung up then called her dad.

"Hi, Dad."

"Hey, Kiddo, what's up?" came his dear, familiar voice.

She told him about the letter that had just arrived. She didn't tell him about Mr. Green calling her. She didn't want to worry him. Should she be worried? "Do you know anything about me getting an inheritance?"

He didn't know. He took down the name of the company and promised to see what he could find out.

She also didn't tell him she was going there and on Sunday. He would have a fit. But she felt in her bones that she should go.

"We still meeting at Martino's at seven for dinner?"

"Of course, Daddy. I wouldn't miss it."

Great. See you tonight, Kes. Love you."

"Love you, too," she told him and hung up.

She bit her lower lip and called out to Jack and the others that she was going and asked them if they would come with her.

They agreed, which meant it took two hours instead of one.

They finally made it into a large Uber and traveled uptown to West Seventy-third.

They arrived at a four-story building built in what appeared to Kes in the early twentieth century. The inside was decorated in art-nouveau style.

They were met in the lobby by a ruggedly handsome guy who had Kim and Lilith nodding before he asked anything. He brought them to the beautiful elevator built outside the walls in a cage-like design. Its steel gates were intricately woven in soft, curved lines.

When they reached the third floor, the handsome escort asked that her friends wait outside a set of thick, polished wooded doors. Jack, of course, insisted on going in with her, but hunky guy promised he could go inside in a moment or two.

"She is going to be asked a few personal questions. She might not answer truthfully if you are there. What has been left for her is very valuable. We need to guarantee that we are giving it to the correct person. You understand. Have a seat. There is no cell service in the building. If you would like to make a call, please leave the building."

Kes thought this guy wouldn't be out chopping down trees, but surprisingly in a courthouse somewhere deciding someone's fate.

He leaned forward and opened the door then stepped inside after her.

The office was nice. Too nice for Kes in her slim jeans, graphic T and Adidas sneakers.

She wore barely any make-up and her dark, chestnut hair was loose and wind tossed past her shoulders. She patted it. She couldn't believe she didn't bring a scrunchie.

He led her to a large Victorian-styled chair behind a beautiful wood inlaid desk, its surface as smooth as a lake on a windless day. There was nothing on it. Not a calendar, not a pen, paper, dust. Nothing. The walls were papered with a beautiful burgundy design with gold accents. The lighting was soft, golden. Like candlelight.

She sat and looked at Mr. Rugged. Why hadn't he introduced himself? "I didn't get your name."

He looked down at her and his smile softened. "You have extraordinary eyes."

"Thank you." She smiled. "You were about to tell me your name."

"My friends call me Luke."

She arched a dark brow keeping her smile intact. "Are we friends now?"

"Ah, Ms. Lancaster," another man greeted as he entered through a side door. "I'm Mr. Green. We spoke on the phone. Let us get down to business, shall we?" He pulled out a chair and sat on the other side of the desk.

He was older than Luke by ten, maybe fifteen years. Big and broad-shouldered in his tailored suit. His hair was cut somewhat short and though he was well groomed, there was something tousled and wild about him.

Right now though, he was all business.

"Yes, let's," she said and offered him a fresh smile.

He didn't smile back but lifted a briefcase onto the table. Had he come in with the briefcase? He opened it and took out a small stack of papers and a small wood box expertly carved with deer and a stag in a forest. That was all she could see of it. She wondered if it was old.

No. Rest. No history today.

"You are…" He buried his nose into one of the papers. "A historian."

"That's right. Umm, Mr. Green, why do you know what I do for a living?"

"It is my duty to make certain you are the correct Kestrel Lancaster. Now," he said as he shuffled more papers. "Is your father Charles A. Lancaster?"

She nodded.

"Grandfather Edward L. Lancaster? Great-grandfather Nelson—

Kes held up her hand. "Yes. Yes. Nelson P. Lancaster. I've looked them up."

"Ah, well, then, given your passion for research and history, perhaps you are familiar with your Aunt Eleanor Pendridge, the Duchess of Glastonbury."

What did he say? Kes sat forward in her chair. Duchess? Of Glastonbury? There was a duchess in her family, and she didn't know? "No. I…I don't know of her." She narrowed her eyes suddenly. "Is this a joke by someone at the Historical Society?"

"A joke?" Mr. Green repeated as if the words were bitter in his mouth. "I can assure you this is not a joke."

"So I'm really the niece of a duchess?" she asked, stunned.

"The great-great-great-niece."

"How come my father never spoke of her? Did she leave him anything?"

"I'm not at liberty to say." His dark eyes bored into her. "Let's get back to you."

He pushed the box to her across the shiny surface of the desk.

"Ms. Kestrel Lancaster, you are bequeathed the contests of

the box from Lady Eleanor Pendridge, Duchess of Glastonbury," Mr. Green said all legal-ishly. He pushed some documents toward her. "Just sign this."

"Only one signature?" she noted out loud.

"It's all we need. We don't like to waste time. It's very precious, you know."

She nodded.

"You may wish to open the box when you are alone," he added furtively. He closed the briefcase, stood up and left the room without so much as a goodbye. Luke went with him.

"Good day to you."

"You, too, Luke," she bid and set her eyes on the box.

Alone, she ran her fingers over it then picked it up. It looked old. Maybe early nineteenth century. Tiny ivy climbed a tower and swept over the battlements of a carved castle on the other side of the deer. What could be inside? If the box was this nice, what treasure must it contain?

She looked at the door. Should she get her friends? Mr. Green said to open it alone. Why?

She lifted the lid and looked inside. She reached in and lifted a blackened brooch with a classic stick pin out. What was this? She looked up at the door from which Mr. Green left. This was a joke then.

She laughed and moved to return the brooch to its box. Something stopped her. She looked more closely at it. It was too worn to make out the once raised design. Her heart began to pound like a drum. How old was this brooch? Where did it come from? A thousand questions about its history began to catalogue in her head.

Was it a bird...or a dragon? She rubbed her thumb across its surface and for one shimmering moment the brooch appeared as if it were brand new. It was silver and shiny as if on fire from within. The dragon designed on it curled itself around a yellow stone. But it was the tiny name forged into the stone that blazed the brightest.

She looked closely at it. "Pendragon," she whispered. This had to be a joke. The air glittered around her.

The blackened brooch dropped to the carpeted floor.

THE OFFICE WAS empty for a moment before Luke returned. He bent to retrieve the box and the brooch and slipped them both into his pocket. He stepped out the first door and faced her friends. Sometimes he hated this part of his duty, but his orders were clear.

"Miss Lancaster has been given her inheritance, an ancient brooch we believe is priceless."

"Great!" the male of her friends exclaimed. "Is she ready to go?"

"Of course, we don't want her to go home in an Uber. We had one of our private limoseams come around for her. She was—"

"What?" One of her pretty girlfriends quirked her brow at him. "You said limoseams."

"Did I?' He chuckled. What was it called! He couldn't remember!

"Did you mean limousines?"

"Yes, limousines." His smile widened on her. "I'm afraid I had a late night." He waited until her eyes glazed over a little bit. Then he added, "As I was saying, Miss Lancaster was escorted down the side exit by three of our men and will meet you at the car. Leave the building, make a right at the corner and you will see her."

Immediately, her male friend touched his phone and held it to his ear.

"No service," Luke reminded him. "You will be able to call her as soon as you leave the building."

He turned away when they hurried to the elevator and he entered the office. He shut the door and disappeared before they could return. As soon as the enchantment wore off, the entire floor would be gone.

THE SUN SHONE in Kes' eyes. Her mind couldn't understand what was happening. Where was Mr. Green's office? She was just inside an office in Manhattan. Now...now, men were shouting, alarming sounds that frightened her senseless. The smell of leather and blood wafted through her nostrils turning her stomach. She lifted her hand to shade her eyes from the sun and looked up at the most terrifying sight her poor eyes had ever seen. A man covered from his neck down in dark metal sat upon a tremendous, snorting warhorse. The man's hair was black and damp either with sweat or blood, or both. His eyes, like the heavens before a storm, held her still, though all she wanted to do was fall to her knees and scream. She felt the earth tremble beneath her sneakers and turned to see more mounted, armored men on horses...giant horses like his that ripped up dirt behind them, running toward her.

This wasn't real. It couldn't be. *Open your mouth! Scream!*

Her friends at the society must be doing this to her as a—her knees almost buckled. She opened her mouth as a horse was almost upon her. The red-stained blade of a sword swung over her head. It was blocked by another, slightly shorter blade. Sparks rained down on her head.

This wasn't happening! The sound of metal clashing against metal boomed and clanged in her ears. She covered them with her hands and shook her head. "No! NO!"

The man whose short blade had saved her shouted at her to get behind his horse and continued fighting. There were hundreds of others in the same dark armor that he wore, while significantly less others wore silver. This was no re-enactment group. This was a battle. Men were dead around her. She had...somehow...come to the middle ages. No! But they came close swinging their swords at her. It was real! She screamed as each new foe appeared, his snorting horse breathing its fiery breath above her.

Her dark knight fought all who came at her. He blocked every blow with a jab or a swipe across the belly or throat. He was quick and strong, and brutal. Kes didn't want to witness this, but she was thankful he was here protecting her.

His eyes, staring into those of his enemies were like glaciers and just as cold. He swung his blade as if he were swinging a baseball bat. Blood and guts flew. Kes screamed and wept. Oh, it was real. She was convinced of it when the blood of one of the savage knight's victims splashed across her face.

That was it. She couldn't handle anymore and fainted on the battlefield.

# CHAPTER TWO

*Bridlington, England*
*July 1485*

NICHOLAS DE MARRE, Earl of Scarborough, barely dodged a swipe that would have killed him. The bloody blade sliced a thin cut along his cheekbone. His opponent should be quite proud of himself, for rarely did anyone make him bleed on the battlefield. If they had, it wasn't because Nicholas was distracted.

Nothing distracted him while he fought. It was what made him so deadly. But he'd never seen a woman appear as if right out of the glimmering air just a few feet away from him. For she was not there one moment, and the next, she was. She was dressed...he didn't know how to describe her clothes. There was no time to examine them further. Or to ponder why her huge anguished gaze made his chest feel odd. He had to kill his way to get to her. She was terrified and screaming, holding her hands to her ears. When the Reds moved toward her with intentions on killing her, he rode into the fray and fought and killed for her.

She'd finally stopped screaming because she'd fainted. He had to dismount and pick her up. He wasn't sure if she was solid form or a vapor that would dissipate when he touched her. He was happy to discover that she was solid.

He tossed her over his shoulder and ran with her back to his horse. He heaved her over the side of the saddle and fought two more men on foot. He disposed of them with full, air-cutting power, killing them both.

He was tired. His arms were aching. He could hardly breathe. He'd been fighting in Nottingham for the last three weeks. On the way home for a few weeks of rest, away from fighting, he ran into a skirmish just outside Bridlington. About a hundred Reds against his seventy men. Thankfully, his men were making a quick end of their opponents.

He had a few moments to tear out of his armor, piece by piece and leave it where it fell from his body.

His heart thundered and his breath stalled when another man charged him.

Without his armor, he felt lighter, almost weightless. He swung with both hands and the victim's head flew from his body.

The fight was almost over. The Reds were retreating. His men could handle the few who were left.

He motioned to his lieutenant to meet him with the men at the castle. With his path cleared, Nicholas leaped to his saddle and left the field with the woman from the air in his arms.

What was he to do with her, he thought as he rode home to his fortress in Scarborough. The fighting was over for now. His side had won. He wasn't surprised. The White forces were trained well—by him. He didn't celebrate with them though.

The woman had nothing to do with his sober demeanor. He wasn't on this earth to make friends. He hadn't been for many years. He was here to keep the House of York firmly seated on the throne. But it wasn't. Not since King Edward died and his brother, Richard ruled. For nearly two years, Nicholas fought for a man he hated and a house he loved.

He looked down at the woman beginning to stir in his arms. Where had she come from? What were the strange clothes she was wearing? What kind of magic was at work here? Surely, she would be accused of being a witch. Was she? Ordinarily, Nicholas didn't believe in such things, but he saw her appear from nothing with his own eyes.

She was beautiful enough to be otherworldly. Her glossy,

sable hair fell in loose waves around her face and hung a little past her shoulders. Her nose was small and her lips, full and shapely. But her eyes had hypnotized him. They were large deep-set, vivid blue mixed with green, terrified eyes. She had secrets. She wasn't from around here. He would have remembered her if he'd seen her before.

She was beginning to wake up.

What had he done? What was she doing bouncing up and down in his arms while he rode home as if she were a prize? Why had he fought to save...her lush, black lashes were separating, revealing pools as fathomless as the deepest oceans.

"What...?" she choked out.

Her eyes, opening wider, mesmerized him.

"Where am I?" she shrieked, pushing off him, breaking the spell. "What's happening?"

He put aside her beauty and hardened his gaze. "You are in England. Why do you not know that?" He wanted to study her further, but she jerked way and almost fell. The terror in her eyes and in her trembling lips appeared authentic. She was a mad-woman then. That's why she wore such odd attire.

But how had she come out of the air?

"Are you...are you real?"

Poor woman. Pity really. "Aye," he answered.

"This can't be happening." She lifted her cautious, shaking hand to the small slice beneath his eye.

"You're bleeding," she whispered on threads of disbelief and shock. "You can't be real. That battle—"

He pulled back as if she had slapped him. "I will not have you poking at me."

She drew her hand to her mouth. He watched it. She wore rings on six of her ten fingers and her fingernails were colored light pink!

"I don't live in England."

He guessed as much since she spoke with a tone and inflec-tion he'd never heard before. It wasn't French or Spanish, or

Scottish or Middle Eastern. "Where do you live?"

"New York."

"*New* York?"

"Please, you have to help me."

"What is new about it?" he demanded. "And what is wrong with the York we have now?" His voice sliced sharper than any sword, but it had no effect on her.

"What…what year is it?" she asked as if her thoughts were a thousand leagues away.

His expression darkened. He didn't like being made to look a fool. "It's the year of our Lord, fourteen hundred and eighty-five. Who are you?" he demanded. "Where did you come from?"

"Stop the horse!"

She had grown quite hysterical. Her hands were shaking when she brought them her mouth.

Nicholas brought his mount to a halt. He didn't need this bother in his life. He had battles to fight to keep the York name alive. When he wasn't fighting, he had all the issues at home to deal with. Namely, his cousin Reg, Reg's wife, Adele, Adele's maid, Margaret, and Reg and Adele's four children William, Eddie, Charlotte, and Andrew. They were enough to make Nicholas swear off having children if he ever married.

"Let me get off!" she shouted again. "I have to get back!"

"Back to where?" he put to her, for she looked as if she knew.

"Home." Her eyes filled with water and appeared like the color between heaven and the sea. "I have to find a way home."

"Where?" Why was he asking? He had duties to see to at his own home. Mayhap after that—but no! He wouldn't keep her with him for so long. Not another person in his castle. He should have realized it on the battlefield, before he took her, but he was covered in blood and exhausted. He hadn't been thinking straight.

"Not where," she muttered. "When."

He arched a brow. Should he help her dismount? "When?"

"Twenty-nineteen."

He gave her a hard stare. "What does that mean?"

"The year of our Lord," she corrected, wide-eyed, "Two thousand and nineteen."

He wanted to laugh, but someone else's affliction was no laughing matter. He groaned instead. He hadn't meant to do so as loud as he had. But what the hell was he supposed to think?

He frightened her. She pulled away and tried to slide from the saddle. He didn't want her to fall so he hooked his arm under hers and lowered her down. He shouldn't leave her. He should take her.

He didn't want to coddle a madwoman—and he certainly didn't want to bring one home.

"Farewell then," he said and nodded to her.

She said nothing but looked around. She appeared faint. He closed his eyes.

"I don't belong here," she sobbed.

He opened his eyes and set them on her. "But here is where you are."

"No! No. I don't want to be here because, you see, I know how crappy medieval times were. There's...there's no Advil. No antibiotics. My phone—" She looked at him with a whole new horror in her eyes. "My father, my friends." She began to walk.

He kept his horse at a slow pace beside her. "Are you certain you were not hit over the head, Miss? Your family might not be gone. They might be close by."

"Look—"

He did, expecting that she might be about to show him how she had done it. How she'd come from the air.

"I know this is difficult to believe. I can't believe it and it's happening to me. But I...I got some letter in the mail this morning from a law firm telling me to go to their office in midtown. I got there and it was all very sketchy, but, you know, I went in..."

What in the name of all that was holy was she saying? It couldn't be a different language. Some words were familiar to him. Some were not. Mail? Office? Sketchy? What did it all mean?

"...and it changed and looked brand new all of a sudden. The air seemed to sparkle and then I was here...on the battlefield."

Sparkle? What was she saying?

She started up crying again. What was he to do with her? He couldn't leave her. She was very pleasing to the eyes. Her odd, blue trousers fit her long legs and shapely derriere quite nicely. She wouldn't last the night with all these Lancasters about. She'd be raped before morning.

"Come on, then, Miss," he grumbled. He held his hand down to her. She refused it. Very well then. He flicked his reins and rode away.

He was glad she didn't want to go with him. He'd saved her life on the battlefield. He'd done enough for her.

Still, he couldn't stop his thoughts from returning to her while he rode. The smell of her, her fear, her sweat, and...a hint of floral. The sight of her sprawled across his lap shook him to his knees. Nothing ever had before. He was glad he was sitting. She was long limbed but weighed little in his arms. Her skin was pale against his tanned fingers. Her hair was dark brown with traces of red. It fell loose around her face, cascading over her shoulders. She wore no adornments or knots and braids. He liked it. He thought of touching it. Her lashes left shadows on her cheeks. Her hose were thick blue fabric with some kind of metal button and a line of tiny silver connecting pieces from her groin to beneath her belly. Curious.

Where had she come from? How was what he saw possible? He didn't catch her from a side view. He hadn't blinked. He happened to be looking straight ahead—in her direction when the air changed, and she appeared. He saw her come to being.

He shook his head. Time travel? It was impossible. Laughable. She was mad.

And what were Advil and antibiotics anyway? What did her words mean?

He rode on for another ten minutes. While he went, he told himself that she had to have come from over the hill and he'd missed her. But why would she walk straight onto a battlefield and then become so terrified?

She said she came from the future. Two thousand and nineteen to be exact. He slowed his horse. It was over five hundred years from now. Is that how women clothed themselves in the twenty-first century?

He cursed under his breath for even considering the idea that she was telling the truth.

He spotted a group of men riding toward the direction he'd left her. His blood went cold. What if they came upon her? Mad or not, she'd been through much today. She likely wouldn't do well fighting off six men.

Muttering an oath, he turned his horse around. He'd saved her once today, and for what? So she could die a short while later?

After half an hour, he realized he couldn't find her. There was no sign of her.

"Woman!" he called out. He didn't know her name. Where had she gone? Had another group of men already come upon her? "Woman!" Damn him! What was he doing? Why did he care? He wasn't the caring type. Perhaps because he saw her come alive in the shimmering speckled air. He didn't know the reason. He only knew that she'd been through enough today.

"What in blazes is your name?" he said in a lower tone and turned his horse around yet again.

When he saw her stepping forward from his right, he almost let out a sigh of relief, but he held it in.

"My name is Kestrel L—"

"What is this?" another mounted rider asked. It was one of the men he'd seen earlier. Nicholas was thankful he'd come back for her.

Five more men rode forward, brandishing swords. They all pointed them at Nicholas.

"What strange attire you wear," the leader remarked on a snarl as he approached her. "But it will not matter when I strip you out of it."

"I'd rather be dead," she said, sounding as if she were close to it. "And if I'm stuck here, that's certainly the better alternative."

"Back away from her before I kill you all," Nicholas warned them on a deadly growl.

"Are you her husband?" one of them called out.

"If I say no, will you think you have a claim on her?" Nicholas asked, watching them closely. He was weary, but he was always ready to kill some Reds, if that was what they were.

"I'm taking her whether you are her husband or not," the leader promised with a lusty smile.

Nicholas' breathing changed the slightest bit. His eyes burned into the leader. "And I'm going to kill you whether you surrender or not if you continue to put me in a foul mood."

"Surrender to you?" The man tossed back his head and laughed. "Who are you but shyte on the bottom of my shoes?" He looked at the shield hanging from the back of Nicholas' saddle. "You're a White!"

Nicholas pulled his sword free and prepared himself to fight. "Not just any White," he told them, slowly moving closer on his horse. "I am Sir Nicholas de Marre, Earl of Scarborough. Defender of York. I just left the battlefield, where my men and I left over a hundred Reds dead." He held up his stained sword and snarled at them. "I would not mind killing six more."

The leader paled. Nicholas thought he might. "I—we have no quarrel with you, Lord Scarborough."

"Then what are you still doing here?" Nicholas asked.

He wasn't always so merciful, but the woman...Kestrel—an odd name, just like the rest of her—had seen enough death for one day. He did nothing when the six of them took off running.

Alone with her, he held out his hand. "You cannot remain alone."

She stared at him. "Your name struck fear into them. Are you famous?"

He shrugged and waved his hand at her. Elia was going to kill him for bringing the waif home.

"You said you were a *White* and a defender of York? You...you were killing Reds?"

"That is correct, Miss." He put his hand into his lap. "I can only hope that the blood draining from your face is the result of fear and the belief that you have traveled over five hundred years into the past, and not because you are a Red."

Her huge eyes rounded. "A Red? No. Do you see a red rose badge on me anywhere?"

He raked his gaze over her and shook his head, relieved that she wasn't his enemy.

"Do you still insist that you have come back in time from the future?" He was hoping she'd had a change of thought.

"Why wouldn't I?" she asked looking up at him on his horse. "It's the truth."

Her eyes were bloodshot from crying. Somehow, they appeared even bluer.

"A truth," he countered stiffly, "that could see you tied to a stake."

She gasped and reached for his horse's bridle. "Burned?"

"Where did you come from?" he asked. Was she a witch? Would she tell him if she was?

"I...fell and hit my head. I don't remember where I come from."

It was what he wanted her to say. But hearing her say it and seeing the tears it produced only trumpeted the fact that she was lying and afraid. Afraid of him. Good. She should be. He wasn't here to coddle anyone. He would see to it that she was taken care of, but that was as far as he would go.

"Come, I will take you home and see that you are cared for."

She went to him this time and he hoisted her up and set her down behind him. She straddled his horse and wrapped her arms around his waist.

She didn't speak to him again, but about a half of a mile in, he heard her weeping and he felt his léine growing damp.

He wasn't used to comforting women at such close proximity. What does one say to a woman who was not right in the head? A woman who believed she lost her family and friends? He covered her hands resting on his belly and with one hand he patted hers. Soon, he would be home and he could hand her over to Elia.

Soon, he wouldn't have to concern himself with her anymore.

# CHAPTER THREE

K ES DIDN'T CARE if her cheek was pressed to this man's back, or if she soaked his shirt. She was heartsick and petrified. She was here—in the middle ages. In the middle of a war, or to be more specific, the Wars of the Roses. She wept harder.

The Wars of the Roses were a series of wars for the English, fought between two rival branches of the royal House of Plantagenet. The House of—her heart skipped making her feel dizzy—Lancaster, and the House of York.

Not only was she here, but she'd landed on the enemy side, right in the middle of the action. She trembled remembering the dying men and this savage in front of her. If she hadn't been so busy screaming, and if he hadn't been killing men left and right, she might have thought him kind of beautiful to watch.

How was she going to get back? She would never make it here. Loving history was entirely different than living it.

Still, there were little things to be thankful for, such as this guy saving her life—twice. His name was well known if the leader of the six was any proof. He couldn't get his men away quickly enough. Nicholas de Marre. She didn't remember reading anything about him. But she knew what he meant when he spoke about the Reds and the Whites. Some historians disagreed about *when* the phrases were termed. But here was a white rose on the knight's shield.

She nearly leaped from her skin when the man's hand came

to rest on hers. He was offering her comfort. She took it.

She would have given anything to speak to one of her friends. Kim would tell her to go with it, relax and enjoy the adventure. Lilith would tell her to rest and trust God. Jack would tell her to fight, and Constantine would tell her to seduce and sleep with the knight and secure a place for herself.

Maybe they were all right when added up together.

Would she ever see them again? What would her father do when they found out she'd disappeared? He'd lost her mother fifteen years ago and now her. Would he give up, be alone for the rest of his life? Maybe the police would talk to Mr. Green and someone could figure out how to get her home.

Until then...oh, until then, what would she do? She wasn't a survivalist. If she didn't stick to Sir Nicholas, she'd be dead in a week. A little part of her felt as if she were losing her mind for calling him who he claimed to be and liking how it sounded in her head.

Sir Nicholas de Marre, Earl of Scarborough, from fourteen hundred and eighty-five.

How could all this be possible?

She opened her eyes and watched trees and bramble, hills and valleys pass. He was taking her to Scarborough. And then what? She had to make him believe her. Or did she? He'd practically called her a witch! They burned witches in the middle ages.

Was she supposed to forget her life? Never!

She sniffled and caught a whiff of pine and sea air. It was nice, refreshing. But there was another scent coming from him that drew her. She turned her nose into his shirt and her nostrils filled with the scent of woodsmoke and the faint undercurrent of sweat. No cologne or artificial aromas. Just the smell of a man. Pure, unadulterated pheromones.

It almost made her forget the painful ache in her inner thighs from riding.

He must have felt her breathing him in.

"What did you say your name was, Miss?" he asked crisply.

"Kestrel." She knew she had almost said Lancaster earlier. He may have picked up on it. She quickly searched her brain for a Yorkshire name. "Locksley."

"Well, Miss Locksley, you must stop all this weeping."

"I can't promise anything," she told him woodenly. "I'm mourning my life. Try a little compassion."

"I'm a warrior, Miss. Compassion will get me killed."

"On the battlefield, yes. But this isn't a battlefield."

Why was she arguing with him? Because she wanted an understanding ear. She wouldn't get it from him.

"Don't worry," she said, pushing off him and holding on to him with her hands on his shoulders." You won't see me crying again."

"You have a saucy mouth," he remarked, keeping his eyes fixed forward.

"You think this is saucy?" She laughed a little. It was the first time she'd laughed all day. She must be hysterical. "Wait until I haven't had my coffee."

"What is coffee?"

She shook her head, feeling hopeless. "It's a brewed drink made from coffee beans. It has caffeine."

"What is caffeine?"

"It's a stimulant. It makes you feel excited and energetic. Filled with vigor," she supplied.

"Hmm," he breathed. She felt the rise and fall of his shoulders. "So you like to be vigorous?"

"I like to be on my toes, recognizing the bullcrap when it comes. And it always comes."

He turned and her hands fell away from his shoulders. He gave her a hard look. "I do not understand this language you sometimes speak. What it bullcrap?"

"Lies. Betrayals. Crappy stuff."

He shook his head and turned again for the road. "Crappy stuff."

He didn't understand her use of slang, but it was her. She

wasn't sure if she could stop it or if she wanted to. Hopefully, she wouldn't be here long enough for it to make a difference.

"What do you remember about the moments before you appeared on the field?"

Did he believe her then? Her heart thrashed like waves against the cliffs. "My aunt, Eleanor Pendridge, left me a brooch. I went to some office to pick it up. I was looking at it. I…I rubbed the surface with my thumb and the brooch began to change. The air shimmered and the brooch appeared new and shiny. There was a name on it. I spoke the name and then I was here."

"What was the name?" he asked.

She closed her eyes and thought about it. She'd been thinking about it while he'd left her alone. "I don't remember. I've been trying to, but I can't. It was something very old and legendary. But I don't know what."

"If 'tis real it will come back to you, Miss Locksley."

"It is real. I don't know what to do to convince you."

"Other than disappear," he muttered, "there is nothing. But if you speak the truth, I must warn you, it sounds like magic was involved in getting you here. You would be best not to tell anyone else."

They reached the small coastal town of Scarborough while she was pondering the thought of being utterly alone. She thought on it no further when she looked around. She drew in a slight gasp. If she had to be stranded somewhere…oh, my. Everything was built along the curved coast with the aqua sea rolling over the golden sand.

Fishermen cast their nets in the deeper end, while women washed clothing along the shore. Children ran and laughed.

Kes took everything in. She was pretty sure this place was a resort in the twenty-first century. She would have smiled if she wasn't stuck in a nightmare.

They didn't stop but kept going upward toward a long curtain wall made of stone, to the tall, majestic, stone castle. It was built along the promontory overlooking the North Sea and protected on three sides by cliffs and the sea. They crossed the massive ditch by a great bridge.

They reached the outer gate and rode into the mile-long outer bailey. Every dozen or so feet, a tower separated the wall. There was a great tower, four small towers and three larger ones. The place was a gigantic fortress. There were two stables and lots of bales of hay around. There was a steepled church with two men dressed in brown robes standing in front of the wooden doors watching their entrance. There were plenty of men to defend the fortress with two garrisons instead of the usual one. The sounds of clanging and banging from various smiths drove through her head as they passed them. Tanners hung hides out to dry. There was also a great hall, two kitchens, and the castle.

Impressive. Was it all his?

People came out to greet him as he rode into the inner court.

Everyone was dressed in appropriate fifteenth century garb. Women wore lower front openings with squared necklines and laces pulled tight over different colored kirtles. Some had a panel inserted beneath the laces. It looked terribly uncomfortable. One woman hurried out in a long dress which she carried in a loop to allow the freedom of walking. The men wore linen shirts with wide sleeves pulled through their doublets. Their hose were indecently tight and brightly colored. Some wore pointed shoes while others sported thigh boots.

Sir Nicholas didn't wear a doublet, but a long, *tapered* sleeve shirt that was belted low on his waist. When he dismounted first, she noticed that he was, in fact, wearing hose. She looked and then turned away, blushing when he caught her.

"Come then, Miss. All will be well." He held up his hands to catch her when she fell into his arms to dismount.

His voice, with his sexy British accent was immensely pleasing to her ears. But more than that, it soothed her and made her less afraid.

She caught his scent and looked into his eyes. That was a mistake. His piercing gaze went straight through her. She was sure he could intimidate any man she knew, but he didn't intimidate her.

Everyone else did though. People were swarming about, coming closer. A stable hand ran to take the knight's horse. Others wore wide smiles. She didn't want to meet any of them. They would realize she was odd. Would their first thought be witch?

"Welcome home, my lord," said at least fifteen people.

"Why, where is your armor, m'lord?" someone called out.

"My lord, your face is cut!" called another.

"My armor is on the field," the earl answered mater-of-factly. "And I will see to my wound. I am in need of a bath though. Kenneth see to it immediately."

An old man nodded and made way for someone to whom his lord beckoned.

A woman stepped forward. Kes guessed she was in her late thirties, early forties. Her hair was gray with streaks of black (but not many). Another terrible thing about this century. No hair dye. Her hair was long and braided into an intricate set of knots in the back of her capped head. Her eyes were a changing mix of gold and green, and kindness.

"Elianora," Sir Nicholas said, "this is Miss Kestrel Locksley of Bridlington. She was hurt and has lost everything, including parts of her memory. See that she has some hot food and a bed for the night. Come to my solar later and we will discuss what to do with her tomorrow."

Kes' hands balled into fists. Sure, she knew better than a lot of people that this was how men thought back here in the middle ages. But was she going to have to become a subservient woman because she was here? No. She wasn't from here. She turned to him. "Am I not invited to discuss *my* future?"

Whatever power her eyes had had on other men in the past, was stopped cold when his gaze met hers. He was unaffected by her.

"You do not wish to rest then?" he asked coolly.

"I'll rest after."

"Very well. Elia, see that she is fed and then bring her to me."

"Aye, my lord," Elia responded and turned to walk away.

Kes didn't want to leave him. She hated herself for it. She didn't know him. He was just as medieval as everyone else, but he had saved her. He knew her better than anyone else here knew her.

He looked as if he wanted to say something. He didn't and walked away instead.

All right then. She looked after him for a second or two and then turned to Elia and followed her to a small side-house off the western castle wall.

"Where are we going?" Kes asked, fighting a feeling that she knew the answer.

"To the servants' quarters," Elia told her.

"I'm sorry but I think there's been a mistake. I'm not a servant. I'm a historian."

Elia laughed. "A woman historian?"

Kes closed her mouth. There were no cell phones here, but word traveled quickly through gossip. If she behaved out of place, they would notice.

"Are all the women in Bridlington so cheeky?"

"Yes, yes," Kes said with a forced short laugh. "It's just good-natured fun."

"Of course," Elia nodded then dipped her gaze over Kes' clothes. "What are these garments that you wear? Your shoes are especially odd."

Odd?

"Oh," she said quickly, with another laugh, "my father is an inventor. He often asks me to wear his pieces."

"Hmm," Elia looked her over some more, and then smiled. "That could be interesting."

"It is," Kes agreed. Had she done enough to veer attention away from her being odd?

"And your hair? Why do you wear it without braid or

adornment? Why, there is not even a pin in it."

Kes lifted her hand to it. "I've been outside for a day. My pins have fallen out."

"Poor dear," Elia cooed and ushered her into the house and into the kitchen. "You sit right down and let me prepare something for you to eat. Cook made rabbit stew earlier. It should still be…ah, aye, 'tis still in the bowl and still warm."

"Thank you," Kes told her. It couldn't hurt to be polite. "What is your position here?"

"I'm the head maid," Elia told her, filling her bowl, "and I would like to think, a friend of Sir Nicholas'."

What did one call the head maid these days? "What would you prefer I call you?"

"Elia. And you?"

"Kes."

They smiled at each other.

"Have you known Sir Nicholas long?" Kes asked her when Elia handed her the bowl.

Elia nodded and took a seat beside her. "His whole life."

Kes liked the head maid. She was easy to talk to.

"When he was seven summers, his family was killed by men who fought for the House of Lancaster."

Kes felt her blood leaving her face, her brain. Oh, no. This man hated the Lancasters with good reason.

"King Edward took him in and raised him. I had been his mother, Lady Johanna de Marre's maid. I became Sir Nicholas' maid after that."

"King Edward," Kes repeated. Which King Edward? There were so many. Oh, she couldn't think anymore. Her brain was exhausted. Who was king during this time? "I…my lord mentioned that I can't remember some things. One of them is the king." She smiled sheepishly. "Who is he?"

"Richard," Elia scowled. "Richard III."

The maid wasn't scowling because of her, but because of the king. She didn't like him. Did the earl feel the same way about his king? And if Richard III was king, that meant Edward the IV, his brother, had died. He told her it was fourteen-eighty-five. July.

"You haven't touched your stew," Elia declared. "Are you ill?"

"No. I'm..." She tried to think of something to tell her. "I'm just feeling a little confused." She spooned up some stew and cautiously tasted it. It was surprisingly good.

"My dear, has anyone ever told you that your eyes are quite beautiful?"

Kes smiled without giving her an answer. She didn't want to come across as being vain.

"How did you and Nicky meet?"

Kes stopped. She nearly choked. Elia leaped up and patted her back until Kes held up her hands. "I'm ok."

"Ok?" Elia asked, looking somewhat lost. "Does everyone in Bridlington speak like you?"

"Speak like me?" Kes' heart nearly burst out of her chest. "My father is from Wales."

"Ah," Elia said, as if being Welsh made all the difference. "I have never been to Wales."

Kes waved her concern away. "It's...'tis quite all right."

"I only asked about how you met because he does not usually bring women home. You must be very special."

"Special?" What would Elia say if Kes told her the truth. Would she laugh, or call her a witch...or believe her? She couldn't risk it to find out.

She yawned and slumped her shoulders. She had no one to confide in. She missed her family, her friends, her phone.

"Come," Elia patted her arm, "let me show you to your room. We can talk some more later. Just a short rest. Aye, dear?"

Yes. A short rest. Kes let Elia lead her to a feathered mattress in a small room, which was one of many in the servants' house. She had nothing against being thought a servant. Her problem was with having servants in the first place.

The bed was surprisingly comfortable. It was nothing like her bed at home, but it wasn't bad. Were all the servants' beds like this?

"There now," Elia said in soft, motherly voice while she tucked Kes in. "Do not let the earl frighten you. All will be well."

The earl didn't frighten Kes. He was the only thing in all this that didn't.

*All would be well.* It had to be. Maybe she would wake up and this all would have been a dream. She didn't remember falling asleep or worrying about anything before she did.

# CHAPTER FOUR

NICHOLAS WAITED IN the solar for Elia to bring Miss Locksley to him. He also ate supper there after his bath. Alone. It was how he liked it when he was home, especially tonight with the return of the last of his guard, men who'd fought with him on the field. Not all of them had returned.

Tonight especially, he needed to be away from all the noise and distraction of the supper table in the great hall where his cousin, Reg, and his family supped. Reg had already pulled him aside to ask him when he might spare another room to their family. Perhaps a separate room for Adele's maid, Margaret. A room for Reg and Adele and four rooms for each of their children wasn't enough. Adele complained that Margaret could not reach her quickly enough all the way in the servants' quarters.

Since Reg and his family were only supposed to be here for a fortnight three months ago, Nicholas didn't see any reason to encourage their desire to stay.

Nicholas didn't have many friends or family. One of them had been his Yorkist king, Edward—and Edward's two young sons. They were all gone now. He preferred to think of them as little as possible.

Nicholas reasoned that he wasn't more decisive about his cousin living here because he wasn't here that often. And because there certainly were enough rooms in the castle. There was even room on the grounds for a separate house for King Richard, who stayed here five months out of the year. Those were the worst times for Nicholas. The days when Richard was here.

Richard was King Edward's younger brother. He wanted nothing more than to be king. Upon Edward's death almost two years ago, Richard was given his wish. After that, hell ensued, and Nicholas' heart was forever changed toward his king.

"Good evening, Nicholas," Elia appeared at the door then stepped inside the solar. "Ah, I see you sewed yourself up again."

He nodded. Not in the mood to hear her chastise him. "Where is our guest?"

"Miss Locksley is asleep—and most curious."

"I know." He got up and poured them drinks. Should he tell Elia? She was the only person he trusted. But this was too enormous and too mad to share with anyone. "Where did you take her?"

"To the servants' quarters. What?" she asked in defense of his scowl. "You did not tell me otherwise."

He closed his eyes. He was surprised she was sleeping instead of shouting for him throughout the castle.

"She seemed concerned at first. She claimed to be a historian." Elia paused to smile at the thought of it. "She was quite afraid and tried to convince me of lightheartedness. Her speech is as odd as her clothes, her hair, everything! She had an answer for my questions, but she did not remember who the king was. Something is not right. Who is she?"

He shook his head. "I do not know."

Elia narrowed her eyes on him. "She choked on her stew when I asked her where you met."

Nicholas swigged his wine and set the cup down hard. He ran his fingers through his freshly cleaned hair and let out a frustrated sigh. Elia wasn't going to let up.

"I found her on the battlefield. She had wandered onto it—"

"What?" She threw her hands to her chest. "Oh, Nicholas!"

"Aye. I know." He nodded. "She looked terrified. I fought off a few Reds and tossed her over my shoulder. She does not remember much about her life. I believe she had been struck to the head. I tried to help her, but she refused me, so I left. But I returned and just in time to save her from six Reds out for evil. She has been through something. I do not want you to push her about what is was."

"Poor, poor dear," she agreed with a gentle smile. "Now, tell me what to do with her."

"Have her brought to a room in the east wing and get her some clothes."

"Is she going to be here indefinitely?"

It was a fair question. But the look he allowed to settle over her silently asked her to cease, for he had no answers.

"Very well, Nicky." She stepped closer and patted his arm. "'Tis good to have you home. I will see you in the morning."

Nicholas watched her leave. He thought about going to bed but when he left the solar, his feet took him to the servants' quarters.

He didn't know why he went, or what he would say to her. He should not have brought her here. If word of her spread, she would bring danger upon them. Especially if she ever met Richard and told him her story.

After questioning a few of the servants, he found her asleep in one of the rooms.

It seemed that tonight, he wouldn't be saying anything.

He didn't turn away from the door where he stood but watched her sleep for a little while longer. For a few of those moments, he let himself consider that she was telling the truth. That she traveled back here from the twenty-first century—as impossible as it was. Everything about her was different. What did she know about the wars, the throne?

No. He wouldn't want to know the future if her story was real. But...the princes in the Tower. Could she tell him anything about that?

His gaze softened on her. If her story was true, then she had indeed lost much in one moment. To be cast into a place that was likely barbaric compared to where she came from would be harrowing for anyone.

Then again, if her life right here in this century was difficult, she could have escaped through this fancy of coming from an easier time. If she kept it up, surely the cracks would begin to appear, and her story would fall apart.

Finally, he turned away and walked down the hall. She was not his concern. His moments of believing her were over. Her tale was imagined. She was a madwoman. He had to send her away. He would tell Elia in the morning. He made it around the corridor when he heard her call to him.

"Sir Nicholas?"

He stopped and turned slowly. "Miss Locksley."

She looked disheveled and dreamy from the bed she had just left. Even from several feet away, her eyes shone like jewels ringed in black, haunting, hypnotizing eyes that tempted him to—

"May I walk with you for a few moments?"

He nodded, not breaking their gaze. "Of course."

"I'm surprised to find you awake," she told him, catching up.

Did she know where he was a moment ago? "I waited for the last of my men to return from the field."

"Did they all return?"

"No," he answered quietly.

"I'm sorry to hear that." They walked for another moment before she spoke again.

"I realize that my story is very difficult for you to believe. I just wanted you to know that I will not ask your or anyone else's assistance with anything. I will find a way to get home myself. If I got here, I can get back."

He looked away and asked in a quieter voice, "What if there is no way back?"

"I refuse to believe that."

He glanced at her. It was best not to look directly at her too often or for too long. It was too easy to lose his thoughts to the way torchlight fell over her rich sable locks.

"What if you are supposed to be here? What if the brooch was given to you for a reason?"

"What kind of reason?" she asked.

"I do not know." He shook his head. What was wrong with him, going along with this dangerous game? It seemed as if her slightly floral scent was going straight to his head. "'Twas just a thought." He led her to a large wood and wrought-iron door. He opened it and they stepped outside onto the wall near the great bridge.

A soft wind blew her hair off her shoulders. He watched it, and the way her eyes widened at the sight of the sea roiling in the distance, the whitecaps rolling onto the shore beneath the bright full moon. He didn't know why he brought her here. Just that he loved the solitude and the scent of the briny air.

"Wow," she breathed out. "It's beautiful here." She turned to get a panoramic view.

He thought her heard her sniffle.

She was cold. He should have thought of that when he brought her outside.

"We can go back in," he offered.

"No. Really, I don't want to. Let's stay out here."

She wanted him to stay. It shouldn't matter to him.

"I told Elia to change your room. She did not know—"

"I didn't blame her. I hope she knows that," she told him quietly.

"Did you blame me?" he asked, staring at her while she stared at the sea. How was she more beautiful in the moonlight? He rejected his thoughts of her. He wanted no woman in his life to complicate things further. He could leave whenever he wanted. There was always a battle between the Yorkists and the Lancasters being fought somewhere. If the king was coming, Nicholas could leave. If Reg and his wife and children drove him mad, he could leave. If he died on the field, no one would mourn him.

She glanced at him. "Well, you are the lord here. They follow your rules, don't they?"

He nodded.

"You didn't give Elia any. I remember. I was there. How can I blame her?"

"'Twould be difficult," he agreed and set his gaze toward the cliffs. He liked how she thought things out in her head.

"Is all this yours?" she asked, spreading her arms wide.

He nodded. "And the king's. Richard lives here a few months of the year."

"Elia doesn't like him. Do you?" she asked boldly.

He studied her in the stillness. "Why would you ask me a question such as that, Miss Locksley?" Was Richard questioning his loyalty? Had the king sent her to tempt him into confessing what he truly thought of his liege?

"There's no reason," she said, trying to sound reassuring. "I was just curious."

"Curious," he intoned with a sneer. "You almost had me believing your wild tale and doubting my own good senses."

"What?" she had the boldness to demand.

"Did Richard send you?" he demanded back.

Her eyes opened wide and she reached the pinnacle of audacity by slapping his arm. "No, Richard didn't send me! What do you think he did, transport me from some vessel in space onto the battlefield? You saw me appear. You were looking straight at me."

He almost nodded his head but then shook it to clear his thoughts. "Space? What are you saying?"

"What are *you* saying?"

"You're clever."

Her lips parted, tempting him to let his gaze linger there. "I guess anything would be clever to a fool."

He wiped his thumb across his lower lip as if she'd struck him and drew blood. "Perhaps it wasn't a good idea for me to bring you here."

"Perhaps it wasn't."

Was that water in her eyes? She turned away too quickly for him to know.

"Miss Locksley, I did not mean for you to leave."

He was mad. Out of his mind. He wouldn't throw her out. Besides, he didn't fully believe Richard would have been clever enough to send her.

She stopped and looked over her shoulder at him. "Thank you." She turned and gazed out over the torchlit wall to the village. "Care to walk with me?"

She was odd and bold, and he liked it. Very much. But could she lead him to his demise so easily?

What demise? Must he always think like a warrior? Mayhap God sent her.

When he nodded, she continued on and left the inner bailey and then the outer. Nicholas followed her.

He wasn't worried about Reds on his land. There was only one way they could get in and that was through the village. He had guards stationed everywhere.

It was a quiet night.

"Why do you not tell me a little about yourself?" If she kept her story going, she would eventually create holes. The more he let her talk, the faster she would fall through a hole and he could pull back his good senses and get on with his life.

"Do you want the truth?"

"Aye," he said and helped her leap over a thin ravine. She laughed when she almost lost her footing.

He stared at her. He liked the sound of her. More and more, he found himself hoping she wasn't mad. But if she wasn't mad—

"I was born in New York in nineteen ninety-four to Charles and Cynthia...Locksley."

His hope was dashed to pieces.

"Why do you call York, *New* York?" he asked, going along with her while they walked toward the shoreline, beyond the village.

"New York isn't in the U.K. I mean in England. It's a place in a far-off land some will soon call the colonies, but I call America. It hasn't yet been discovered. Many English settled there and named land after their families. There is even a place called New England."

America. Not yet discovered. Her story couldn't be more farfetched. But if only it were true. What an honor to the House of York to hold a place in the future, in a distant land.

"I live in a loft on the Lower East Side with four of my good friends," she continued. "My mother died when I was a kid. My father never remarried. He's an archeologist. He's going to mourn me deeply, as I will mourn him."

He looked away, close to believing all of this with her. "You have my deepest sympathy."

When she touched his arm, he returned his gaze to hers. "Thank you." She offered him a slight smile.

"Where was I? Oh, yes. I love my work. I'm a historian, so I know about this period in time."

"Oh? What do you know?" He turned to her and watched her hair snap across her face like warpaint in the moonlight.

She thought about it for a moment. "I don't think I should say too much more. If I change the past in any way, it will affect the future."

"Hmm, I suppose it would." Nicholas didn't care if she told him anything that would *affect the future*. He was humoring her tonight. He thought about asking her if she left a husband behind, or a man she loved, but if she had, he didn't want to bring up the pain of losing anyone else.

He almost laughed at himself. Was her madness spreading to him? Or was he there long before she arrived? There were plenty who thought so. Even Reg and his family were afraid of him. His foul moods were usually accompanied by ghoulish sneers, and most prone to escalate when the king or his cousin were near.

"It's so beautiful here," she said breathlessly and walked ahead to get to the shore faster. She pulled off her flexible shoes and rolled up her blue trews—hose? He didn't know what they were. There was nothing like them here. He would have Elia burn them tomorrow. He stopped caring about her clothing when she looked up at him from her ankles and smiled.

"Get your toes wet, Sir knight!"

His toes? Without asking what she meant, he pulled off his boots and his knitted socks and tossed them aside. Then he stepped into the water. He realized too late that he'd forgotten to roll up his hose. No matter, wet or dry, he followed her direction.

"Haven't you ever wet your toes?" she asked, looking down at her feet. The tide pulled back out and she almost lost her footing. Her hand reached for him.

Now, she held his wrist with a clamp-like grip. She didn't let go, nor did she pay any attention to their touch.

"I usually keep to the sand," he told her, trying not to pay attention either. "This is why." Walking against the tide made his head spin a little. He reached out for her when he almost lost his footing next.

"We will go down together," she declared with a slight giggle.

"Nonsense," he challenged. "We will not be taken down by one foot of water."

"The trick is not to keep your gaze pointed downward."

"Where shall I keep it then?" He knew where he wanted to keep it.

"On me," she said after a pensive moment. "I will keep you on your feet."

"I do not doubt it."

Her gaze on him made him feel drunk on wine. Her promise, coupled with the slightest, bold tilt of her chin, convinced him that there was more to her than sewing and learning how to look like a decorative bird the way all the other delicate ladies did to find a husband. She looked like the kind of woman who might come from the future.

"What about you?"

He was already looking at her, so he raised his brows not

understanding what she wanted him to tell her.

"How did you come to be King's Richard's knight?"

Nicholas turned his eyes toward the distant waves. He never shared his life. Oh, Elia knew of it because she was there for much of it. Edward had known him well. No one else. He didn't fancy talking about himself. But she wanted to know. She was waiting to listen and, for some reason, he wanted to tell her.

"I was Edward's first in command. I brought him many victories. As had my father before he was killed, and his father before him. The de Marres have always fought on the side of the House of York. And they rarely lost."

"If I remember this part of history correctly, then you're right," she told him. "The Yorks were always victorious."

"Aye, because of my family."

"Who taught you to fight?" she asked and rubbed her arms.

She was cold. What should he do?

He wasn't a child. Why was he behaving like a peach-faced squire? He grinded his jaw and yanked her into his side. He put his arm around her and held her there. "I should have taken a cloak for you."

"It's…ok. This is…um…fine."

"You are freezing," he pointed out. "We should head back."

"Not yet," she pleaded softly. "I want to talk to you."

His mistake was to look down into her eyes. "Why do you not fear me after what you saw me do today?" He had no idea why hearing his words made his throat tighten.

"You did it for me," she answered softly, her breath warming his chin. "They were coming to kill me. Why didn't *you try* to kill me, too?"

"Why should I?" he asked. "You are not my enemy."

"I wasn't theirs."

"They likely believed you a witch."

"And you don't?"

He shrugged his shoulders and walked her to the shore. "I don't know what I believe about you."

"I wish there was a way to prove my words."

"To what end?" he asked. "What would you have me do? I'm going back to the field in a few of weeks."

She stopped walking and gave him a horrified look. "You are? I...I mean I don't know what I would have you do... I don't know what anyone can do. I may be stuck here for the rest of my life."

Her large eyes grew larger, more haunted. He thought she might begin weeping again. "Miss Locksley," he began with a scowl. He killed. He didn't comfort. He didn't know the first thing about soothing a soul. "I do not know if there is anyone to help you get back home. But it does not have to be so bad here."

"Oh, no?" she asked separating from him. "How often do you bathe?"

"I just had a bath earlier today," he told her with his brows dipping low over his eyes.

"And the time before that?"

His expression darkened. "You can clean up anytime you like right behind you." He pointed over his shoulder at the waves.

"What do you do for pain?" she asked. "Wine?"

"We have something stronger if needed," he defended.

"Whiskey?" she asked with a mocking twist of her pretty mouth. "We have pills. They are medicine all crushed up into a powder and made into a solid ball. I just have to pop it right into my mouth and swallow it and poof—" she snapped her fingers in the air. "No more pain. Advil. There are pills to help with just about every disease. What pain medicine is given to a woman in labor...the labor of giving birth?"

He had no idea. He was still trying to imagine the medical marvels she mentioned.

"Right." She chuckled. "No thanks. How do you communicate with friends or family far away?"

"I do not have any friends or family," he told her, meeting her softening gaze. "But I would think the same way I would get in touch with the king from the battlefield. Send a missive."

She nodded her worried head. "We have a slim box that fits into the palms of our hands. With it, we can see and speak to whoever we want, wherever they are in the world in a moment."

She had an ingenious imagination.

"Not only can our phones—that's what they are called—put us in touch with friends or family in an instant, we can check the news anywhere in the world, look things up, virtually visit anywhere—"

He let one corner of his mouth curl into a slight smile.

She shook her head at him and gave him a disappointed look. "It's all real. As real as you. But the world is a very different place."

"It sounds like a better place."

"No. Not in some ways."

"Like?"

"There are a lot of people where I live! There are almost two million in the city alone!"

He stopped walking and gave her a doubtful stare. Another crack in her fantastical story. "Two *million* in one city?"

"Yes. It's crowded."

"How big is the city?"

"The island that I live on is called Manhattan. It's a little over twenty-two miles long. It's surrounded by the other four boroughs that comprise New York City. Those boroughs also have millions of people."

"Where do they all live?" he asked, not knowing if he should keep going along with her or put a stop to this now. She sounded so convincing. She'd thought of everything.

"In buildings. They are tall, some are called skyscrapers. They consist of apartments, and each apartment has rooms, and a working bathroom. It's all very private. Everyone has a key to his or her apartment."

"Miss Locksley?"

"Call me Kes. Miss Locksley sounds old."

"I will call you Kestrel," he complied, somewhat.

"'Tis…different and, ehm, beautiful."

She smiled and tilted her head just a bit. "You think so?"

He nodded. Pity she was mad. She was mesmerizing. So much so that she tempted him not to give a damn what the state of her head was. "Why would you want to go back to *that*? It sounds nightmarish."

"Ok." She laughed a little, making his head real. "I know it doesn't sound so inviting. But we've adapted, and we don't mind the dense population."

He gave her a disgusted look. "I understand that 'tis your friends and family you miss, not necessarily all the rest."

"I miss everything," she corrected, sounding as haunted as she looked. "It's my life. It's who I am. I have to get back."

Nicholas didn't know how to answer her. None of it could possibly be real. She may as well have come here and told him she lived on the moon. It was impossible.

So was her appearing from nowhere before his eyes—in the shimmering air.

# CHAPTER FIVE

K ES LAY AWAKE in her new, more comfortable bed. She was thinking of the dream she'd had earlier in the servants' quarters. Sir Nicholas was somewhere—in another lifetime, watching her. In her dream, she had felt his gaze warming on her. The power and carefully leashed emotion exuding from him washed over her and woke her from her sleep.

She'd gone to look for him and found him walking away in a hall close by. Before she'd called to him, she took in the sight of him, his strong thighs and hard ass beneath his forest green doublet. When she'd caught up with him, it was no better. He hadn't shaved, but his hair and beard were clean. His hair was almost black. It was combed back and tied at his nape, accentuating the hard curve of his jaw and eyes like diamonds that cut deep into her, where her wounded heart was. He had a scar down the side of his left temple and a small scar across his jaw. He'd been cut in the battle and would have a scar from that as well. Despite it all, he was utterly, breathtakingly handsome, but he was tired. The dark circles under his eyes attested to it. The slice along his cheekbone, below his eye, had a few crude stitches in it.

They had spent a few hours together. He saw that she was fed and brought her to a good-sized chamber on the second floor. The bed wasn't bad for a medieval bed. It was made of wood, of course, with carved swirls traveling up its four posters and hangings draped from a frame suspended from the ceiling beams.

There were chests and two tables. One was larger than the other with a basin and an empty jug set atop it.

He'd promised to have her necessities brought in in the morning.

It had all felt too permanent.

She'd spent another hour, thinking about ways to find that brooch in the middle ages. She couldn't look it up on the internet. She had absolutely no idea where to even begin or how to get anywhere.

She cried as hopelessness of ever going home covered her. What would everyone think? Most likely that she'd been kidnapped by a sex trafficking ring. Did Mr. Green and Luke know about this time traveling thing? Of course they knew. They wouldn't sit around waiting for the cops. They were gone for sure.

No one would find her. She was stuck here.

Sir Nicholas de Marre barged into her thoughts. She tried not thinking of him, but everything else was so bad. He was the only good thing in all this.

Of course, he was a male so she couldn't trust him. She wondered if men were different in this century. She wasn't expecting Sir Galahad. Wait. What?

Her eyes opened wider. Pendragon!

She sat up in bed. The name on the brooch was Pendragon! How could she forget? She knew the legends of King Arthur Pendragon. But the name had completely eluded her.

Should she speak it? Should she say goodbye to Sir Nicholas first?

Why did she think of him before she left?

"Pendragon," she whispered, heart pounding. Nothing happened. She said it a little louder. Her shoulders slumped with disappointment when she remained in her bed.

She finally slept sometime later with the name Pendragon on her lips. All too soon, morning came and Elia appeared over her bed with three other women, who looked at least two decades younger.

"Good morning, lady. Am I correct in assuming that you had no knowledge that Lord Scarborough was planning to give you this room without telling me?"

"You are correct in that assumption," Kes told her. "But if this is an inconvenience for you, I don't mind moving again. This is, after all, temporary."

Elia's large, hazel eyes warmed on her. "I would not think of asking you to move again. I just wish he would keep me apprised of things. I went to the servants' quarters and you weren't there. No one had seen you. I was afraid you had run off alone. Nicholas told me that he found you on the battlefield, poor girl, and you didn't remember things too clearly. It would have been quite dangerous for you."

"I wouldn't just leave," Kes assured her gently. Was Elia so concerned for her already? They were strangers. But people were different here. She watched the three younger women scurry around the chamber, tidying up and filling the water basin and jug.

Elia issued a series of orders to the women, who were called Agnes, Caitlyn and Hilde and they left only to return with fresh linens, kirtles and overgowns, hair clips, and more. They then proceeded to brush her hair away from her forehead and secured a crespine toward the back of her head. They paid no attention to Kes' meager protests. When they were finished with her hair, they dressed her in a linen chemise, a kirtle of deep blue that fit her perfectly, and a wool dress with full skirts of lighter blue. The neckline of the dress was low, but the kirtle covered up what cleavage she had.

She had to stop the girls from pulling her laces too tight across her chest and stomach. It was hard to breathe. How did the women work and get anything done in these clothes?

"My, but you look enchanting!" Elia cried out when she hurried back into the chamber a few minutes later. "Mayhap seeing you will make Lord Scarborough feel better. He is in a foul mood."

Why would Elia think that seeing Kes would make the earl feel better? "Why is he in a foul mood?"

"He did not say," Elia told her. "But he has many reasons. You will find that he is most often quiet."

Kes was surprised at what she was hearing. He spoke easily enough to her last night.

"Since King Edward perished, God rest his soul, Nicholas has changed."

"Changed how?" Kes asked while Caitlyn slipped her feet into soft slippers with leather bottoms.

"Never mind that," Elia said, glancing at the other women. Perhaps she didn't want them to know. Kes would ask her later.

The pins in her hair pinched her scalp and she could barely inhale.

"Do you remember anything about your life yet?" the head maid asked her.

Would Kes forget it all? Tears filled her eyes and she bit her tongue to stop them.

"Oh, I would say you were noble born for certain."

"That's kind of you to say, Elia." She thought of her aunt, Eleanor Pendridge. "My distant aunt was the Duchess of Glastonbury."

"You remember!"

"Only bits and pieces."

"Well, come. Let's go find Nicky and tell him."

*Nicky.* It was a familiar pet name that almost made Kes envious when she heard Elia say it.

She almost laughed at herself. Who was she to feel possessive of him?

After three steps, she tripped over her skirts and almost landed on her face.

"No, no, dear," Elia caught her and corrected. "You must loop your skirts over your arm and carry it."

This must have been the fashion of the day. Kes had seen

other women carrying their skirts earlier.

The masses of wool were heavy as she walked down the hall. The stairs were a bit of a challenge, but she managed. Elia led them outside to the separate great hall in the inner bailey.

Kes stepped on a pebble that felt as though it went through her flesh.

By the time she stepped into the hall, two of the pins in her hair popped out and a few strands of hair fell around her temples.

The hall was enormous, with twelve rectangular tables seating at least eight people each. The noise was almost overwhelming. It was like hearing everyone in the world's voices in her head.

She spotted Nicholas at the head of one of the tables. He held a cup to his frowning lips and looked around. He grumbled something to the people sitting with him at the table.

Elia pulled her closer. "Lord, look who I have found, and does she not look lovely?"

He looked at her loose strands of hair and then at the rest of her with those cool silvery eyes until the backs of her knees tingled. He didn't say whether she looked lovely or not. In fact, he said nothing at all. Not even hello.

Kes glanced at Elia. She hadn't been kidding. He really was in a foul mood.

"Well then," the head maid said with a slight whip to her voice. "We shall leave you alone. Come, Miss Locksley, there is room for us at that table over there."

She tugged on Kes' arm to lead her away.

"Wait!" he shouted. When they turned to him, he looked at the empty place to his right and then at Elia. "Sit her there."

"I would rather not sit with you, Sir," Kes said. Every eye at the table fell on her.

Elia drew in a slight gasp.

Perhaps she shouldn't have spoken so boldly to the lord of the castle. She was in the fifteenth century after all. She felt a little faint at the thought of it. The laces of her dress were constricting her air flow.

She didn't want to faint in front of him.

The pins in her hair were making her itch. Last night, she'd had the slightest thought that it might not be so absolutely terrible here. She'd changed her mind. She hated it here. She wanted to go home.

She spun on her heal, ready to leave them all sitting there gaping.

"Miss Locksley!" he roared. Everyone in the great hall quieted and turned to look at him, and then at her.

She pivoted around and glared at him. He was on his feet. Two women at the table took hold of a small group of children and ushered them away. "Yes, my lord?"

He walked around to the empty bench and dragged it screeching from under the table. "Sit down."

She stared into his eyes from across the room. She was going to give him ten seconds to apologize and then she was leaving the hall and going back to her room.

*1...2...3...4...5...6...7...8...9...*

"Please."

She scratched her head. Another pin fell to the floor and sounded like a bolt of lightning striking in the quiet hall. She guessed his asking nicely was as close to an apology as she was going to get.

Besides, Elia looked like she was going to pass out. She hadn't moved. Where was she planning on sitting?

Kes took a step and almost fell into the table. She hoisted up her skirts and made it to the bench. She tried to breathe when she sat. He motioned for Elia to sit beside her.

So, he allowed his maid to sit at his table. Was she sitting in Elia's seat? At his right? She wanted to fan herself.

"Miss Locksley," Elia said. "I think you will enjoy today's—"

"I'm sorry," Kes managed. "Just give me a moment." She began untying her laces. If everyone was shocked a minute ago, they were probably choking on their ale as she pulled and tugged her way out of the contraption. Did women really eat with these things on? Her skirts were overly heavy in the warm hall, so she untied them and let them tumble around her on the bench. She knew wearing a kirtle alone wasn't considered indecent. Plus, she'd stopped caring. She needed air.

"What were you saying, Elia?"

Elia's blood had drained from her face. The angry earl was smiling.

It didn't last long, for another scowling man had turned his angry glare on him. "You drove my wife and children away with your temper."

Nicholas ground his jaw. "Reg, why do you not go after them?"

"I do not find you humorous," Reg protested.

"That is because I'm not trying to be humorous," the earl let him know. "I'm trying not to knock out your front teeth."

Kes turned to glare at him again. "Can we eat in peace?"

"Of course." Nicholas agreed and turned a fearsome smile on the other man. "Reg, you will stay silent or I will cut out your tongue."

Reg fumed but he didn't say another word. Who was Reg? How come Nicholas didn't mention him or his family last night? He and his family sat at the lord's table. They must be his relatives. They didn't seem like friends. She thought he'd said he had no family? She realized he actually hadn't said all that much last night. Not anything too deep, at least. They ate in silence, which was better than the previous conversation.

"Why are you grouchy this morning?" Kes asked when conversations started up again.

"What is grouchy?" he practically growled at her.

"Bad-tempered."

"I am not any different today than I am every day."

"Oh, great." She tossed him a fake smile.

"Am I going to have to ask you what your words mean all day?"

"You don't have to ask anything," she countered coolly. "In fact, you don't have to speak to me at all."

"Who are you?" Reg asked, looking like he may fall to his knees before her at any moment.

"I am—"

"She is my guest," the earl said through his teeth.

"Kestrel Locksley," she told him.

"Miss or Mrs.?" Reg asked. He wasn't a handsome man. He squinted and had a sharp nose. His fingernails were clean and there didn't look to be a callus on either hand.

"Reg," Nicholas warned.

"Miss," Kes answered at the same time.

"Her distant aunt was the Duchess of Glastonbury," Elia told them.

Nicholas' brow rose on Kes. "You did not mention that."

"Neither one of us mentioned our relatives," she pointed out, staring right back at him.

"Now you understand why," he answered, shifting his gaze to Reg.

Kes thought the earl a bit of a bully. Reg obviously could never fight him. He was scrawny. Poor man.

"Where are you from?" Reg asked her, ignoring the earl's barb.

"Damn you, Reg—"

Kes turned to the earl with an incredulous glare. "Are you kidding me right now?"

The earl aimed his angry, curious scowl on her. "What?"

"I can answer for myself." She turned back to Reg. "I think I'm from Bridlington, but I am having trouble remembering many things. We think I was hit on the head."

"Hit on the head?" Reg asked, aghast. "By whom?"

She shook her head.

His small eyes opened wider. "You do not know?" He turned to the earl. "You brought a woman into the castle who could be a Lancaster! Why, she could be here to kill us all. My wife and—"

"I assure you—" she tried.

"Reg." His voice was low, deep, like the waves outside, covering hers. "This is *my* castle." The sound of him made her heart tremble. "You seem to forget that, Cousin. Don't question me about who I bring in. If you don't like it, take your wife, your children and your maid and leave.

"As far as her being a Lancaster, those kinds of words could get her killed. If I ever hear them come from you again, I'll beat you senseless every day for the next seven days. Do you understand?"

"Aye," Reg said, surrendering without a fight.

A Lancaster. A Lancaster! He hated the name. They all did. Was she here for a reason as he said? Did it have something to do with her being a Lancaster? Was she supposed to confess her identity to him within the next few weeks? *Few weeks*. Forget it. Send her home right now because—

"Miss Locksley, I will see you out of the hall." He didn't wait for her response but rose from his chair and stood over hers.

She didn't know what to do. Go with him or stay here with Reg. At least Elia was—

"Miss Locksley!" he commanded.

She threw her napkin on the table and stood up. She had to keep reminding herself that he was a fifteenth century oaf and if she went too far, he could throw her out. Or worse. Did the castle have a dungeon?

She bent to pick up her skirts and dress, but Elia beat her to it. "Go now, Miss. I will take care of this."

"Woman, if you make me call to you one more time—"

Kes straightened and two more pins fell from her hair. "What?" she challenged with her hands on her hips. "What will you do?" She didn't care if threw her out. There had to be a villager around somewhere who would take her in until she could find her way home or flung herself over the cliffs.

"Are you ready now?" he asked, controlling the tone of his voice.

"I seem to be," she said, smoothing her kirtle with her palms.

When he offered her his arm, she looked into his eyes for a moment before she accepted it. She didn't know what she was looking for, but she found something different from what the men possessed at home.

Whatever was going on with him made his breath stop and his eyes shine from within.

Was it because of her, as Elia suspected?

What did she think if it was?

# CHAPTER SIX

"M ISS LOCKSLEY?"
       "Yes?"

They left the great hall and stopped outside the doors. She was dangerous, with her hair springing down her temples, Nicholas thought while his heart still pounded from the challenges she threw at him inside. In front of Reg.

Damnation, nothing had been so thrilling off the field in a long while now. She was dangerous and delightful, facing the beast head on, boldly and courageously. She said she was a distant relative of the Duchess of Glastonbury. He would send word to Glastonbury by the king's couriers and ask if there was a record of Kestrel Locksley in their books. Even if she did descend from nobles in Glastonbury, it didn't mean she was a Red. Glastonbury was one of the towns in Somerset that did not stand on either side.

"I'm heading to the stable. I have things to see to. The castle entrance is there." He pointed over her shoulder. "I shall see you at supper."

Did she appear disappointed? He couldn't tell. She definitely appeared to be fighting some desire. He glanced down at her hands. They were balled into fists. He stepped back.

"My lord," she called to him as he turned to walk away.

"Aye?"

"I don't like being ordered around."

That much was obvious, he agreed silently. "And I, Miss Locksley, am not accustomed to my every word being challenged."

"Disappointing," she said, looking him over. "I thought you could meet the challenge. I was wrong."

Damn it, he would not chase her. He would not! He'd lain awake all night promising himself that he would step back from Miss Locksley. Now, was the hardest temptation so far. She'd sparked his blood and he had to walk away. Why, after he had trained himself not to be distracted by women, not while there were battles to be fought, did this oddling capture his thoughts?

Was she putting him under her spell? It certainly felt as if she were. He'd known after hours of contemplation last night what he had to do. She was too volatile. Hadn't she just proven it? Shouting at him for all to hear?

Why did it amuse him? Why did he think her the bravest soul he knew?

She was dangerous. Aye. He had to detach himself from her. If that meant staying away from her, that is what he would do. He wouldn't throw her out. He was no heartless savage. Despite what was whispered about him by campfires at night, he was only a savage when he needed to be.

He reached the stable, saddled his mount, and rode out of the gate.

He was glad his mood had changed—thanks to her. He did have things to see to in the large town a mile away. Nothing pressing, but it was better than being here all day with her.

He remembered how she tore off half her clothes and it still brought a smile to his lips. She didn't care what others thought. She did what needed to be done and seared his blood in his veins while doing it.

He'd had to leave the hall before he made Adele a widow. He hadn't wanted to leave Miss Locksley there with Reg. He hoped she realized now that he'd tried to stop her from speaking to Reg because the man was a snake. Before long, Reg would have her telling him her bizarre story.

He rode to the town and hoped no one recognized him. He'd made certain to wear his trousers and worn woolen léine. He left his sword at home but was armed with knives in his boots.

He wasn't sure why he'd agreed to meet Thomas Walley, Earl of Malton. Nicholas had tried on several occasions to stop former Yorkists from giving their support over to the Lancaster side. But more and more Yorkists were switching. All because Richard was untrustworthy. Even when it came to his wife Anne's death last March, many believed Richard poisoned her so that he could marry his niece, Elizabeth of York, Edward's daughter.

Nicholas hated him for losing so many supporters, but he hated him most of all for what he'd done to Edward's sons.

King Edward IV had made his brother, Richard, the then Duke of Gloucester, Lord Protector of his two sons, the eldest being heir to the English throne. He wanted to declare Nicholas their protector, but he needed Nicholas on the battlefield winning his wars. Upon Edward's death almost two years ago, his twelve-year-old successor, Edward V along with the boy's younger brother, Richard, were lodged in the Tower of London to prepare for the boy's coronation.

Nicholas had gone to see them. He'd had a day off from the fighting and spent it with them. Young Edward had been anxious, but what boy of his age about to be crowned king of England wouldn't be? They'd laughed and practiced their swordplay with him. They spoke about their father and their futures. Nicholas loved them as brothers. He never expected such wretched betrayal from their protector.

Before the king could be crowned, the marriage of his parents was declared bigamous and therein invalid. The man who led these false charges? Richard. The children were declared illegitimate and banned from inheriting the throne. Richard III became king four months later. The worst part was the boys disappeared from the Tower the same day and were never seen again. The rebellions began soon after that and still continued. Richard had lost many of Edward's staunchest supporters including Nicholas.

Nicholas suspected Richard of killing the boys and it was driving him mad.

He fought for the House of York with the hope that the boys would be found alive. But his forbearance toward Richard was fading. Almost gone.

He entered the town and dismounted in front of a small tavern. He had a look around at the dimly lit interior. No one looked up from their drinks to see him—save for one man.

Nicholas went to him. "Malton."

"Scarborough."

Nicholas sat on the bench opposite the visiting earl. "You do not have much time. What is it you wished to speak with me about?"

Malton began to sweat a little and pulled at his collar. In the soft candlelight, he appeared wary, even afraid.

"I'm not going to hurt you," Nicholas assured him.

"Even if what I speak is treasonous?"

What could he say? He wasn't ready to turn sides just yet. Richard was the last male York. If this Henry Tudor, to whom the Lancasters gave their support, took the throne, what would become of the Plantagenet dynasty?

"You may speak freely," Nicholas promised.

"We have the support of many," Malton told him.

No matter how bad Richard was, the thought of betraying York sickened Nicholas. "And what are you prepared to do with all this support?"

Malton blinked his dark blue eyes. "Join us, Scarborough. We need you."

"I'm not prepared to do that," Nicholas let him know.

"Then you will fight against us."

Nicholas didn't want to fight them, but he couldn't help the tilt of one end of his mouth curling into dark grin. "That is more of a threat to you about me, than the other way around."

"Aye," Malton agreed with a rueful sigh. "We all know of your great skill and cunning. But you fought proudly for Edward. Things have changed. Richard is—"

"Careful," Nicholas warned softly.

"I need not say. In fact, I will say no more. I regret your decision, as I know the others will."

"Malton," Nicholas said, stopping him. "I will not speak of your treason to the king. I will wish you Godspeed."

The earl stared at him for a moment and then smiled and nodded. Nicholas didn't smile back. He watched Malton leave and then he ordered a drink.

His foul mood had returned with thoughts of the two princes in the Tower. Perhaps he should ask Miss Locksley...that would be admitting that she was telling the truth. She was from the future. She couldn't be, and he was putting it out of his mind once and for all!

He downed his ale, swiped his sleeve across his mouth and left the tavern.

On his way back, he thought about the missives he had to pen, some to Glastonbury—she had to come from somewhere. Her story of traveling back in time couldn't be true—and also to their supporters telling them of their victories these last few weeks. He couldn't wait to get back to it. Then he would be away from all the annoyances of Scarborough Castle, such as the king, Reg and his family, and now, the mad Miss Locksley.

He arrived home and went straight to his solar to begin his writing. He found it difficult to think. It wasn't due to Reg's children shouting and screeching. No. The halls were quiet. It was her. Beautiful, saucy-mouthed Kestrel Locksley. What was she doing now? Repinning her hair, mayhap. He smiled thinking of the pins dropping to the floor and tendrils of her hair falling around her face.

She certainly didn't seem to belong here.

He almost rose from his chair three times to go find her. He held back the urge. But it was there. He enjoyed being with her, thrilling in her boldness. She was the first person he actually wanted to spend time with in as long as he could remember.

But what would ever come of them? The poor woman wasn't right in the head. But the shimmer...the shimmering air. What did it mean? How could a logical mind accept this as true?

He put down his quill and rubbed his forehead. Her face appeared in his thoughts. Her eyes, as blue as summer skies, as green as verdant fields. Her lips were pink and plump and fashioned to be kissed. She wasn't one to be taken lightly. She didn't like it when he shouted or ordered her about, and she let it be known.

He found himself pacing in front of her door. Was she inside? What was he doing here anyway? What was he here to tell her? He knocked after he wore a path on the ground, but she didn't answer.

It was a sign for him to leave her alone. Maybe she was gone into thin air, the way she came. Would that happen one day while they were out walking, laughing, perhaps kissing?

He went back to his room and agonized over her for another hour. Why couldn't she just be from a neighboring village? Not from Glastonbury. Mayhap there was no distant aunt. She might simply be someone's daughter, sister. He believed she was of marriageable age. What if she was someone's wife? He ignored the knot his last thought tightened in his belly. Perhaps she was from a village or town close by, assuming she walked the entire way here, and lived in her own made up world in her head. He hadn't even checked with anyone!

He hurried out for his horse and caught her when she plowed into his chest and into his arms.

"Oh, sorry," she said breathlessly, looking up into his eyes.

Was she breathless over him? Or from running?

"I didn't see you," she told him with the slightest of smiles. "You can...um...let me go now."

She had a swatch of flour on her chin and on her cheek.

There was also some in her hair.

"What are you doing?" he asked, releasing her.

"Baking." She stepped away. "Elia sent me out to Robert, the chicken farmer, for eggs. I'm showing her and Cook how to make cupcakes."

"Cupcakes?" he repeated. How odd she was.

"I'll save you one. I don't know what flavor they'll be just yet. Cook doesn't have many ingredients to choose from. He would like supplies from other villages or towns further out. You would benefit from it, too."

He nodded and looked her over. "I'll see to what he needs."

"Thank you." A slight smile curled her mouth.

"How are you faring, Miss Locksley? You appear," he paused for an instant, thinking of the correct word, "well."

"I'm ok. It's hard not having my phone though. I miss texting Kim and Lilith. Poor Jack must be out of his mind."

He only understood about half of what she was saying. But he did hear one thing. "Jack?" he asked, feeling his foul mood stirring again.

"My roommate. Are you going out again?"

"Aye. I have some things to see to." He thought she liked being with him, as well. At least, until she'd heard his temper this morning.

She smiled and he had to look away to keep thinking clearly.

"A pretty girl, no doubt."

He shook his head and scowled, settling his gaze on her again. "No. No pretty girls."

He moved to step around her, but she caught his arm. "What has come over you since last night? Last night, you weren't half-bad. But today you're an ass."

His mouth curled into a woeful smile. Just when he thought she was softening again. His lips went stiff. "I have come to my senses."

Her soft expression grew hard. "About me. Fine. Just don't throw me out into the str—the road."

She let him go and stormed away. He wanted to go after her. To assure her she could stay as long as she needed. But first, he had to find her village.

What if he couldn't find any village that had lost her? He wondered about that on his way to the stable. What if no one had?

He searched every village and town closest to Scarborough, seven in all. No one knew anyone fitting Miss Locksley's description, and none had lost any of their women. Of course, there were more towns farther away from which she could have come. He couldn't check them all in one day.

For now, it pointed to her story being real. All the more reason to stay away from her.

He made it home in time for supper, but he had no intentions of going into the great hall. He did look inside the open door when he passed it. He found her immediately. She sat with Elia at a different table. She smiled and looked spellbinding doing it, but there was a deep sadness in her eyes. Was he the only one who saw it? Elia was a clever woman. She would pick Miss Locksley's thoughts to pieces, until she discovered the truth.

"Are you going in, my lord?"

Nicholas scowled and growled down at William, Reg's eldest son. He was twelve, just like young prince Edward, but nothing like the king's son.

"Are *you* going in?" he countered, gravelly.

"Who were you staring at?" the brat demanded.

"Get moving," Nicholas ordered. "Before I kick your arse all the way to your seat."

The boy hurried in, calling to his father and drawing all attention to Nicholas. Miss Locksley was already looking his way.

He felt his scowl growing darker, harder. Had she seen him watching her? There was nothing else to do now but go inside. He didn't want to eat with everyone, but it was too late now. He was here. And so was Miss Locksley. He gathered his wits and control and walked inside.

Boldly, she watched him. He lifted his hand to his hair, his chest. He became acutely aware of how he was walking. As he grew closer to his chair at the head of his table, he decided he didn't want to sit there with Reg and Adele. But sitting with Miss Locksley was a bad idea. No matter what her story was, it turns out poorly for him.

He yanked his chair from under the table and sat.

Adele lifted her hand to her head and then glared at him when her husband spoke. "Nicholas, can you not make your chair screech across—"

Nicholas pulled himself and the chair in, adding banging to the screeching.

Now Margaret added her hateful glare with her lady's.

Nicholas held up his cup for some ale, ignoring them and Reg's flaring nostrils.

"I will sit in my castle however I wish," he said quietly, calmly. "I will say what I wish and do what I wish, without worrying about offending any of you. You were not invited here. Have you forgotten?"

Reg looked at Adele. Whatever they spoke in their heads to each other worked because they nodded and softened their expressions.

Nicholas set his icy gaze on Margaret the maid while a server poured ale into his cup. Margaret was in her late thirties, never married, and wanted Nicholas in her bed more than anything else in the world. That was what she told him anyway.

His eyes sparked with a challenge. Would she say something about the noise he made? No. She remained quiet.

The ale was watered down. He would speak to the servers about it later.

He looked over to where Miss Locksley sat and watched her while she spoke to Elia and the others sitting around her. She seemed to be settling into her new surroundings. She was no longer crying and going on about the future. He hoped.

She should be sitting with him so that he could manage her

conversations. And keep her from the stake. He would speak to Elia about it later. He'd have to make something up. Even Elia couldn't know their guest's beliefs.

These responsibilities on his shoulders didn't bother him. He had strong shoulders. He was built for this. It was Reg, his only living relative, who hated him since they were children, but liked him enough as an adult to come for a visit and never leave that made his mood so foul.

He was sorry he'd come inside. Being in the same room with her was as bad as sitting right next to her. He was aware of her. He could see her through his side vision. His neck was beginning to ache from tilting in her direction.

The only thing that made supper quite extraordinary was an appetizing little cake with some kind of fluffy, stiff sweet mixture atop it. It was set down before him on the table. In fact, one cake was given to everyone at all the tables.

"A cupcake!" the head server called out and then motioned toward Miss Locksley.

She stood up. "A lemon and meringue cupcake," she announced. "It's a recipe handed down to me by my grandmother. Cook and I made enough for everyone."

A few people clapped. Most stared at her and then at her cupcake.

He held one up and examined it. The *meringue*, as she called it, was white and sticky.

"It's made with egg whites and sugar. And a little cream of tartar which, thankfully, your cook had. It's quite sweet.

"Ingenious." Nicholas didn't hesitate to sink his teeth into his. He sat back. He'd never tasted anything like it. "Delicious," he called out and ate the rest.

He couldn't help but smile at her again when after her first bite, she came away with meringue on the tip of her nose. Apparently, it was happening all over the hall, for laughter could be heard from every bench.

Nicholas ached to stand up and walk to her bench. But she

was hanging on the precipice of something and he didn't want to fall with her.

But finally, he jumped.

# CHAPTER SEVEN

N ICHOLAS STOOD UP, turned his feet, and marched toward her table.

When he reached her bench, he motioned for Charlie Mayfair, one of the guardsmen, who was sitting next to her, to move.

"Aye, Commander," Charlie said and left without another word.

"You didn't tell me you were a commander," Miss Locksley said as he sat.

He smiled. Slightly. "My fighting skills didn't prove that I was in command?"

"I was too busy screaming for my life to notice."

He shoved his finger into his ear. "I still cannot hear properly."

He had a look at her hair. It was tied back with chicken wire into a tail hanging past the back of her neck. That was it. No pins, no clips, no adornments, just—chicken wire.

"I was harsh with you earlier, Miss Locksley. Forgive me."

"What of your senses?" she asked with a playful arch of her brow.

He smiled softly and shrugged his shoulders. "They have abandoned me yet again."

She stared at his stitched cheekbone and then sank her gaze into his. "You're going to have a nasty scar from that slice. Who stitched you?"

"I did."

Her eyes opened wider. "You stitched yourself?"

He nodded and forced himself to look away. He stared into Elia's curious smile.

"How did you do it with no mirror?" Miss Locksley asked, tugging on the sleeve of his léine. "Are you crazy or something?"

"Crazy?" he asked darkly, not liking the sound of it.

She pointed to her temple and twirled her finger. "You know...nuts...mad."

"Mad, aye. I'm mad. I thought it might be you..." He smiled and shook his head. "...but no. 'Tis me."

"Oh gosh, what am I laughing at?" she suddenly lamented. She lifted her hand to her forehead and closed her eyes. "My life as I knew it, is over."

He looked around to see if anyone heard it. "Miss—"

"Yes. Yes, I know." She lifted her head and whispered. "I'll be quiet about it."

"'Tis for your own good."

He couldn't forget his results from today. No one knew her. No one had lost her. Kestrel. What kind of name was it?

"Oh! I almost forgot to tell you," she told him with excitement now etching her face. "I remembered the name on the brooch!"

"What was it?" he asked, swearing at himself silently for enjoying her company so much. He could sit here and listen to her for the rest of the night.

"Pendragon."

He raised a brow. "Arthur?"

"You've read of him?"

He nodded. "I have a copy of Monmouth's *Historia regum Britanniae.*"

He was sure her eyes just misted over.

"I have a library. You have not seen it?"

"No," she breathed, "I would love to though. I'm a historian," she leaned in and whispered to him. "I've never seen such an early edition. My heart is pounding."

He had the insane urge to grin at her and not stop. "Your cheeks are flushed."

They grew even redder.

He wished they were alone.

"I have many volumes that will interest you. No originals, of course, but I do know the king."

She laughed, and if they were alone, he might have laughed with her.

He had the servers bring them wine. They drank and she kept smiling when she caught his eye, or he caught hers. He didn't smile back. He tried to remain strong and in control, but he hadn't made it one day avoiding her, without falling under the spell of her eyes, or her voice, or the soft flush of her cheeks.

"Come." He finished what was in his cup and stood up. "I will take you to my library."

She practically leaped into his arms. "Ready!"

"Did you like your cupcake?" she asked him as he led her to the castle.

"I'm saddened that there were no more. I could have eaten another one or two."

"I'll bake more if Cook lets me," she promised.

"You will tell me if he causes you any trouble."

"He was grouchy when I started but he came around. We're friends now."

He was glad she was making friends, but if she trusted someone enough to tell them...

What if she wasn't mad? What if she was as sane as the town chaplain? If this was all real and she traveled through time—no. He simply couldn't fathom it.

He led her up the stone stairway to the second landing.

"Who taught you to read?" she asked.

"Edward had me instructed privately."

"Edward the king?"

He nodded.

"Elia told me he raised you after the death of your parents."

"Murdered," he corrected. "They were murdered by the Lancasters."

"Yes, of course. Murdered," she amended, shivering in her spot. "Was he a good foster father?"

"Aye. He was."

"Is Richard very much like him?"

His scowl returned. "Richard is nothing like him. I assure you, Miss Locksley—"

"Kestrel."

"If your story is true and you are a historian from the future, nothing you have read about Richard can compare to who he truly is. If you ever have the ill-fortune of meeting him, stay away from him."

He heard one of the guards outside shouting. "What is it?" he called to another running in the hall.

"'Tis a letter! A letter from the king!"

CHARLES LANCASTER TOSSED the letter onto his desk, followed by his glasses. He rubbed his bloodshot blue eyes. There were no leads on his missing daughter. She was gone, snatched away in the middle of the day without a trace.

Charles considered himself a civilized man but if he got her back, he was going to kill everyone involved.

What if he was the reason she was taken?

He looked at the framed photo of her on his desk and wiped his eyes. His beautiful girl. They were going to meet for dinner. Her friends called him long before their date. She was gone. She'd gone into a building and disappeared into an office. But there was no office. No fourth floor. Her friends had to have been mistaken. That's what the police said.

But Kes' father feared something much bigger was at work.

# CHAPTER EIGHT

"Y OU DO THIS every day?" Kes asked Claire, the laundress, while Claire turned clothes with a wooden wash bat in a giant barrel.

The news of the king's return in a week turned Nicholas' mood worse than before. He'd shown her to the library and left her there. She hadn't seen him again for the rest of the night.

"Aye, every day."

"For everyone here?" Kes asked, incensed while Claire rubbed the soiled garment with lye soap and continued turning.

"Aye."

Either the earl or the king was going to have to do something about this or the help was going to walk out. "I want to help you," Kes said and reached for the bat. Besides, she needed something to do with her hands. She was going crazy with the need to text! She had so much to say and so many to tell.

Claire stared at her and looked to Elia standing at Kes' rear. When Elia nodded, Claire handed over the stick.

"When was your last day off?"

"Day off what? M'lady, I really do not think—"

"I'm fine," Kes reassured her with a smile. "A day where you didn't come here to work? A day to rest."

"We do not work on the Sabbath. That is all."

"And is it just you laundering everything?"

Claire nodded and Kes fumed. What was the Earl of Scarborough running here? How could he expect one person to do all this? When she complained to Elia, the head maid informed her that Edith, the other laundress, had died of a fever three months ago.

"Three months!" she seethed.

"Oh, but, m'lady," Claire cried. "I do not mind doing it all. I do not want anyone else cleaning the castle garments and linens."

Was Claire crazy like so many others here?

"Why in the world would you not want help?" Kes asked beating a sheet. Then it hit her. Claire didn't want someone else handling *his* things. Nicholas' or someone else's. That had to be the case.

"You can keep the things you want to wash and dry and give the rest to someone else. You would be the head laundress. What's wrong with that?"

Claire grinned. "Nothing at all. I would like that."

"Then I shall speak to Lord Scarborough about it."

Elia came to stand close while Claire began to fold the other clothes she'd dried. "Do you presume that Nicholas does as you ask?"

Kes had to be careful. She liked Elia and didn't want to step on her toes. "He has avoided me all morning and yesterday, as well. But I will find him today and speak to him about this. He is an intelligent, compassionate lord—"

"He's intelligent, aye," Elia agreed. "But not always compassionate."

"He will do as I ask," Kes smiled at them both. "I have something to bargain with."

"Oh?" Elia raised her dark brow. "What is it?"

"A cupcake. I saved him one last night. Once he heard the king was returning, he left to his duties. But I hid one away in the hopes that he liked them."

Elia tossed her a furtive smile. "You are thoughtful toward him."

Kes shrugged. "He put a roof over my head and food in my

belly. An extra cupcake is the least I can do."

"Hmm." Elia gave her a curious look. "My dear, do you still not remember where you came from?"

Oh, Kes wanted to tell her. She couldn't. The threat of burning at the stake was very real here.

"I remember bits and pieces. I...I think I remember my father. I..." She sniffed and bit her tongue to stop her tears from falling. She hadn't meant to think of her father. "We were very close. He raised me. Still, I wish I would have called him more last week."

"Called?" Claire asked, listening while she folded.

Kes' blood drained. She didn't know where it went but it left her head, her face, her lips and made her feel dizzy.

"You are pale," Elia said taking her arm. "Here, sit."

"No. I'm ok." She looked up at Claire. "My father lives a few houses away in our village. We called on each other frequently."

"You will see him again, my dear," Elia promised. "If anyone can find them, 'tis Nicholas."

Oh, how she wished it were true. She wondered, while she turned the wash bat and scrubbed the castle linens, if Sir Nicholas, Earl of Scarborough, would go with her. Why would she want him to? He would never fit into her world with her friends.

That is if she ever got back. She'd asked every woman in the castle if they had a brooch with the name Pendragon on it. None did.

Elia was busy with Claire, so it gave Kes time to think about her brooding rescuer—and what he was doing in front of her door yesterday.

She had been returning from sewing in the public solar with Elia and some of the other women who lived here. She wanted to change and go help Cook in the kitchen. She'd seen her knight as she turned the corner in the hall. She'd backed away into the shadows and watched him. He looked tormented pacing before her door. What was he going through? She'd known he'd had a difficult morning. Was it because of her? Or something else? She had been tempted to go to him as he raked his fingers through his hair.

She hadn't because he was most likely no different than what she'd left behind. Maybe worse with his antiquated (to her anyway) ideas. She'd sworn off men anyway, at least for a little while. She needed a break after Brian McGill. What was she doing thinking of Nicholas de Marre in any sort of intimate or romantic way?

But seriously, who could blame her? He was a knight! In armor! He wielded a real, very big, very deadly sword. His naturally provocative smile was unfortunately almost nonexistent, but he'd bestowed it on her a few times now. It was only slight, but still dangerously alluring. If he ever decided to flirt with her, she had no chance against him.

Kes had learned that grapevines worked the same way in every century. And that kitchens were the best place to find them.

Her cupcakes had baked while she learned that Margaret, Lady Adele's maid, *fancied* Sir Nicholas.

Kes didn't think the feeling was mutual. Especially when the maid glared at him at his own table last night. The smile he aimed at her was more like a weapon. Its beauty was meant to entrap and paralyze while he landed the final sting. And the sting? It wasn't a word. It was him turning his attention away. He hadn't so much as glanced at Margaret for the rest of his stay there.

He didn't hate Kes, and the only reason she cared was because he was the proprietor of the roof over her head. She had seen him standing by the great hall door, as he'd stood before hers earlier. Did he have a problem with doorways? Or was it just hers?

Before he'd entered the great hall last night, he was looking at her as if he didn't come inside right away because of her. Why should she affect him in such a way?

He was a strange one, and hadn't she had her share of those?

Oh, but he hadn't brooded when he'd come over and sat with her. He seemed to hang on her words, and his library! It was filled

AULA QUINN

with treasures though she couldn't fully enjoy it. When he'd heard King Richard was returning, he'd said very little. Anger and…the source of his hatred etched his face and he'd left before she could ask him what was wrong.

She finished another batch of linens when she heard his voice outside calling Elia. She bit her lower lip when his footsteps grew louder. She didn't want Elia to get in trouble for letting her launder the clothes. She certainly didn't want to do it full-time.

Elia rushed out to speak to him and hopefully veer his path in a different direction.

But it didn't work. He stepped inside the wash house and looked at her standing over the barrel. He quirked his brow at her and gave her a curious look. "What are you doing?"

It was kind of hard to believe how good looking he was and how masculine he looked in hose. The more she saw of him, the more irresistible he became. She liked the size and shape of him, how he moved and breathed, how he remained still. She liked the way he was looking at her now, as if he couldn't figure her out.

"I'm helping Claire."

He turned to the laundress. It gave Kes another second to look him over. He wore a black léine, belted low on his waist, hose that stretched around the long, lean sinew of his thighs, and boots. His dark hair was pulled into a tight queue. His beard, trimmed.

"I know I already asked you this, but do you need help?"

"Aye, she does," Kes told him. "But not me. Claire, do you want to tell him your idea or should I?"

"You can," Claire said meekly in front of him.

"Very well. We think Claire should be head laundress. She likes things done a certain way. That is why she never asked for help before. Isn't that correct, Claire?"

"'Tis," the laundress admitted.

"She needs an assistant…an apprentice. Someone to help because honestly, Ni…" Kes caught herself in front of the others from being so familiar with him. She wasn't. "…my lord, this is backbreaking work, six days a week."

Nicholas blinked at her and then turned to Claire.

Everyone was quiet. Kes thought she heard Claire's heart pounding…or was it her own?

"Claire, is there a reason you did not tell me this yourself?" His deep voice fell like a sheet of velvet over Kes' ears. Poor Claire. The laundress obviously liked him and was terribly shy. Kes wondered if she could help.

She couldn't have him for herself since she was going to find a way home. There had to be a reason she was here, and she didn't think it had to do with her marrying a knight and not seeing him for weeks or months, or even years at a time. And then waiting to be told that he wasn't returning home because he'd had his head loped off. No, thank you.

"I did not want you to think me weak," Claire admitted.

Nicholas breathed in, stretching his léine across his shoulders. His silver gaze did not soften on Claire. In fact, his expression had relaxed a bit to one of indifference. "What I think of you should be of no importance. I am your lord, nothing more. I will send someone to you this afternoon to help with your tasks."

Without waiting for her response, he turned to Elia. "See to it."

"Miss Locksley," he said on his way out. "Come with me. Please."

She would have smiled at his courteousness, but she felt too bad for poor Claire.

She felt the laundress' eyes on her as she left the wash house.

"Are you feeling better since the news?" she asked, catching up and walking at his side.

"No. But 'tis a new day."

And what? Did he intend to spend it with her?

"You were quick and precise with Claire," She wondered what he wanted with her and if she would be able to get her mind off his foresty scent. "I guess you're used to it."

"Used to what?"

"Women falling all over you."

"No one falls all over me, Miss Locksley. They are mostly silent about what they feel, if anything. 'Tis how I prefer it."

So, there were no women in his life, and he wanted to keep it that way? Why?

"Why do you want to be alone?"

He shrugged his shoulders and picked a twig off a bush and put it in his mouth. "Less headaches."

"So you think women are headaches?"

"No," he said. "They just cause them. I do not have time to nurture a relationship," he quickly added when she scowled at him. "How about you? Did you leave behind a husband, a lover?"

She shook her head. "My last boyfriend cheated on me."

"Cheated?"

"He was sleeping…having sex with his dog walker while telling me he loved me."

When he said nothing, she frowned at him. "Please tell me that you don't think it's ok…I mean that you don't approve."

Oddly, he looked at her mouth while she spoke, and not at her eyes. Men always looked into her eyes.

"I do not think 'tis *ok*," he told her, then looked up. She was sure she saw a light spark in his eyes. "I would prefer it if you did not try to hide your quirks from me."

"My quirks?" she asked lifting her brows.

"Aye," he nodded, and there it was, that elusive, genuine, knee-melting smile. "I like them. I also wonder, when did he have time for *two* women?"

"His life is very different than yours." She thought of Brian, a top IT technician making seven figures and his easy life with the best of everything. "He doesn't even know how to fight."

Nicholas stopped walking and stared at her. "How can he not know how to fight?"

She was so tempted to smile at him but she didn't want to make him feel in any way inadequate, as if she smiled out of pity.

"Battles are fought differently. Men and women only fight if they join the armed forces."

"Armed forces," he echoed softly.

She understood the appeal of watching one's lips while they spoke.

"You probably would be in Special Forces," she told him, and then told him what she knew about such thigs. "But not Brian. He'd be the one making sure the generals stayed in immediate contact with their superiors online. It's technology." She finally laughed at his perplexed expression. "Most men and women don't join and don't get called to fight. Brian is one of them. There." She took in a gasp of air. "That's who I left behind. Before him, Tom Eddings broke my heart. At first, there's all this romance and then it fizzled into nothing and he decides he loves someone else."

"And these are the men you wish to hurry back to?" he asked, his smile fading into something curt.

"Are they any different here?"

He cast her a playful smirk. At least, she thought he was being playful.

"That depends on the man, I would suspect."

"Oh?" she put to him. "What about you?"

"I am not one for romance. But if I had a woman, I would put her first and not betray her."

She worried there might be hearts coming out of her eyes. Why did hearing him talk about having a woman make her mouth go dry? And why did she believe him?

Because it was hard to keep a clear head around him. He exuded virility with every move he made. She was especially weak against his accent and the soothing resonance of his voice.

Where was Elia? Why had Kestrel just gone off with him anyway?

"Where are we going?"

"Back to the castle. Elia doesn't understand how danger-ous 'tis for you to be talking to others—"

"What? So I can't talk to anyone?" She stopped and tugged on his sleeve to make him stop, too. "That's not ok with me. Am I a prisoner here?"

"No. Why would you be?"

"But you want to keep me locked up?"

"Locked *away*," he corrected as if that made all the difference. "Kept safe," he started over. "You do not seem to understand the danger of what you say. Word travels fast, even without your pone."

"Phone," she corrected. "Yes, I know. I've already heard about Margaret, the maid. But not to deviate, do you think I'm stupid and will tell everyone the truth about where I'm from? I'm the one who could be burned."

"But you do not have to tell them any truths, Kestrel. You have odd ways of thinking. Standing up to me and beating the laundry for Claire. I do not want tongues to start wagging about you."

"You don't think they'll wag if you *lock me away*?" she demanded. "You just don't want to be around me. You want to lock me away so you don't bump into me around the castle."

"That is not true," he defended.

"No? Are you planning on avoiding me all day today the way you did yesterday?"

"Am I avoiding you now?" he countered sharply.

"Until you get me to the castle where you can lock me away." She pushed out a feigned laugh. "Do you even get how that sounds? What's next? You hit me over the head with a bat and drag me to your cave?"

"Since I left the bat at the wash house, I would say that opportunity has passed."

She was quiet after that. He was clever and charming, and she didn't want to be charmed.

"I have no intention on hitting you with anything," he let her know when they reached the castle. "One thing you will find different here is me."

"Then don't lock me away. I'll be more careful."

He stared at her for a moment, thinking it over in his head. "Very well," he said finally. "But no roaming around alone."

"Then you'll have to stay with me," she said, knowing it was not what he wanted to do.

"I usually practice in the lists with the men at this time."

"Perfect! I'd love to watch!"

"You would?" he brooded.

"Yes. You don't really expect me to sit in a castle all day without anyone to even speak to, do you? I'll go nuts. I can't text and now I can't talk!"

He looked at her as if another eye had just appeared on her face. Then he shook his head as if to clear it. "There are many people to speak to inside the castle. You would not be alone."

"Like who? Cook doesn't like anyone in his kitchen. I didn't tell you, but he clapped my knuckles with his wooden ladle *twice* yesterday. I warned him that if he did it again, I would knee him in his nuts. He understood me then and let me make my cupcakes.

"Who else should I speak to?" she asked, ignoring his smile. "The maids and servants who all think you're wonderful? I'll make my own judgment on that, if you don't mind. And hearing it all the time gets boring, you know?" She didn't wait for him to nod. "I've spent more time with Elia in the last couple of days than I have with my closest friend in the last six months!"

"You are upsetting yourself, Miss Locksley."

"You shouldn't blame me," she said, sounding terribly sad to her own ears.

He stopped and set his worried gaze on her. "I do not."

# CHAPTER NINE

NICHOLAS DODGED A blow to his head and leaped to the right, narrowly avoiding his lieutenant's heavy sword. Charlie had come close. Nicholas couldn't let that happen again. It was because she was here, standing off to the side, watching him.

Ridiculous because why would he get his head swiped off for a woman? Also, this was one of his soldiers making him look bad. Nicholas should be driving him back into the ground. There was no mercy on the battlefield, and little on the practice field. Of course, it was practice and no one died. But it could get bloody.

He should never have sat with her last eve in the great hall. She'd utterly charmed him with her cupcakes and her breathless anticipation to see his library. He wished he'd enjoyed it with her, but news of Richard's return had taken precedence.

The king was a month early. It must be all this news about Henry Tudor's escape to France from his exile in Brittany. Things were moving. A battle was coming.

It was the perfect time to step away from the king, let him fight this battle without Nicholas. But that meant the end of the York line. Nicholas couldn't do it. He'd even advised Richard against fighting a losing battle. Hopefully, Richard would have a son. But until then, Richard was all there was.

Nicholas had to leave in a little over a fortnight. Would Miss Locksley settle in by then? Would she forget her past? Or rather, her future in *new* York and be safe here?

He swung his mighty blade. He didn't want to think of Richard or all the support the Yorkists were losing to Henry Tudor.

He wanted to show Kestrel Locksley that he could protect her.

Charlie came at him swinging his sword in one hand and a dagger in the other. Nicholas parried both strikes, grinding the steel of his blade down his opponent's, bringing sparks to life. Before Charlie had time to readjust, Nicholas brought his sword over Charlie' head and whacked the flat of his blade across his lieutenant's back.

Kestrel covered her mouth with her hand as Charlie landed close to her feet.

She offered his lieutenant a kind smile. "I don't think anyone would have seen that coming," she consoled. "He was hard on you. You did well against him."

Charlie grinned at her. Nicholas looked heavenward.

"Miss Locksley!" he called out. "My lieutenant is not a child. He is a soldier. He does not need coddling."

Her lips tightened. She was about to open her mouth. He stopped her.

"Perhaps I was wrong to have you watch us. If 'tis too difficult—"

"Commander," she said through her teeth, "you are the only thing difficult here. You sound like a petulant child—"

She stopped speaking and took a step back when he shoved his sword into its sheath and came toward her.

He didn't stop to say a word but bent forward and hoisted her over his shoulder.

"What do you think you're doing?" she shouted. "Put me down! You can't do this!"

"But I can," he corrected her. "You will not speak to me so in front of my men again."

"Oh, won't I?"

"No, you *won't*."

"I can't believe you're doing this to me!" She pounded on his back.

"You seem to have trouble believing things that are real and make perfect sense."

"Don't you dare take me inside like this! Nicholas! Don't you—" She pinched his side to get his attention.

He smacked her on her behind.

She fought him the entire way upstairs. Good thing his body was well honed, or she would have worn him out. He brought her to her room, dumped her on her bed, and left her alone, locking the door behind him.

He thought he'd have to listen to her wailing and crying all night, but she didn't utter a sound when he left her room and said very little to Elia when he sent her to Kestrel an hour later.

"She asked me to tell you that she has nothing more to say to anyone. She wishes to be alone."

"What?" he asked Elia, pacing in his solar. "Alone? What was she doing?"

This woman, more like a mother to him than a maid, gave him a hard look. "I heard about what you did, Nicholas. Why would you treat her that way? I'm sure you humiliated her and now you want to know why she lies in her bed with her head in the pillow. Here is the key to her room. I will not take part in locking her inside."

He took the key from her hand and started for the room without a word to Elia. He wasn't sorry. He couldn't allow her to fight and argue with him in front of his men.

When he reached the door, he drove the key inside the hole and turned. The door didn't budge. He pushed harder. Something was blocking it.

"Miss Locksley." He didn't shout. He wanted to wring her neck. "Kestrel! Open the door." He looked around. No one was in the hall. Yet. "I wish to speak with you."

Something smashed against the wood directly opposite his face. He moved back, then scowled hard at the door. "Fine then. Be alone." He strode away, glaring at Elia as he passed her.

His supper was served in his solar. But he couldn't eat. She plagued his thoughts. She'd turned things around like a brilliant tactician. He'd locked her in her room, and she'd locked him out. Somehow, he was the one being punished. He missed her company. Surely, she missed him, too. She'd told him she missed texting and talking—whatever the hell the first thing was. She believed she came from a place with millions of other people. She had to be lonely in her room all day. Why had he locked her away in the first place? She was no fool to tell anyone her story.

And why did his blood rush hot through his veins when she'd told him the name on the brooch. Pendragon. It was a name shrouded in magic and legend. Of King Arthur and his…knights.

He pushed his bowl away. Why did he have to be the one to see her on the field? Why had he taken her off the field and brought her to his home?

He thought of her in her bed, weeping. Was she weeping? He moved toward his door. He should try to talk to her, just to make sure she was well.

He found himself walking to the western end of the hall, where her room was. Did she still have the door barred?

When he came to it, he knocked and then tried the key. Still barred. "Have you eaten?"

"Go away."

She spoke. That was a promising sign.

"Kestrel, open the door. I wish to speak with you."

"And if I don't? Will you hang me from the window?"

He closed his eyes, gathering all his patience.

"I acted too harshly. How long will you be angry with me?"

Silence. Then she asked, "How can I be angry with an ogre for being an ogre?"

"Then will you open the door and have supper with me?"

He heard her moving about inside and moving something by the door. She opened the door and stepped out.

Her hair was loose and luxuriously thick, falling over her shoulders. Her eyes were bloodshot and round looking up at him with caution.

He felt ill because of it. He didn't want her to be afraid of him or to not trust him.

"Are you hungry?" he asked softly, not moving when she stepped closer, closing the door behind her.

"What did you have in mind?"

Her breath fell against his chin. He had the urge to put his arms around her and draw her in closer. "Some pheasant with roasted mushrooms in some kind of honeyed sauce."

"That actually sounds very good."

He nodded and smiled at her. He hated to step away, but he didn't want her to think he was going to jump on her at any moment.

He walked with her and called to a passing servant. "Have our supper brought to my library."

"The library?" she asked, looking up at him while they walked. "You really know how to charm a girl."

"I hope to prove to you that I am not an ogre."

"Beast, from *Beauty and the Beast* had a library."

"Who?"

She smiled. "It's a story from the eighteenth century written by Gabrielle-Suzanne Barbot de Villeneuve." She told him about the story, and he laughed to think of himself as the beast. She was most certainly the beauty though.

He liked the library. He didn't come here enough. Once he put some wood in the hearth and started a fire, it was cozy. There were books set neatly on shelves, opened on a chair, piled on a table. "What did you get to look at last night?"

"Monmouth of course. I was impressed to see some Christine de Pizan in your collection. She was innovative and challenged male writers of misogyny in their literary works."

He shrugged his shoulders. "I do not know about all that. I have only read *The Book of Deeds of Arms and of Chivalry*, so far. And for a book about warfare written by a woman, 'tis quite good."

"Hmm." She looked him up and down. "Maybe you're not an ogre after all. But I cannot come to any premature conclusions."

They ate, with Nicholas' appetite fully restored, and drank fine wine. They gave up their chairs for blankets on the floor. Her idea, not his. They read in front of the hearth from Monmouth's *History of British Kings*. There were many, according to this work, including Constantine, Vortigen, Uther, but Nicholas opened book eleven and read from chapter two.

> *"And even the renowned king Arthur himself was mortally wounded; and being carried thence to the isle of Avallon to be cured of his wounds, he gave up the crown of Britain to his kinsman Constantine, the son of Cador, duke of Cornwall, in the five hundred and forty-second year of our Lord's incarnation."*

"What?" Kestrel blinked and sat up straight. "Why did you read that part? *That* in particular?"

"I...I don't know." And he didn't. He'd never read past book six. "I just opened there by chance."

"No. There's no by chance. One of my roommates' name is Constantine. I wonder if he has a part to play in this."

"He is not here," he pointed out woodenly.

She stared at him for a moment and then smiled behind her hand.

"What?" he insisted.

"You're jealous."

"Ha!" he mocked. "I do not get jealous. And besides, we hardly know each other."

"It doesn't matter," she quipped. "You're jealous, and you were jealous this afternoon with your lieutenant."

"You have a lively imagination."

Her smile faltered. "Nicholas, you know I'm telling the truth about how I got here."

"Kestrel." He moved closer to her and leaned in. "Please understand how fantastic your story is. Believable as you make it sound, 'tis impossible."

"No. It's not impossible because here I am. I was almost six hundred years away and then I was here in a moment, in the middle of a bloody fight. How do you think I got here, Nicholas? You were staring right at me. Where did you see me come from?"

"A trick of the light."

She sighed. "You're not a stupid man."

"My thanks."

"You're afraid, I under—"

He laughed, but he was insulted. "What am I afraid of? The future?"

She shook her head. "That people will think you've aided a witch."

He stopped laughing. "I could lose the castle, my rank, and mayhap some other people who live here."

She covered her mouth with her hand. "I understand. I will be extra careful. I wouldn't want to cause anyone harm."

"Aye," he said softly, "You seem to have a very kind heart."

Her eyes seemed to grow rounder, bluer. "You have been very kind to me also."

"So then you don't mind being tossed over my shoulder?" he asked playfully—but his low, deep voice was evidence that she made him burn everywhere, especially in his belly.

"I mind it so much that if you ever do it again, I'll run a dagger through your heart while you sleep."

He felt his heart pumping. He heard it, loud, strong. He liked that she did this to him. His mouth hooked into a half-smile. "How will you get to me in my bed while I sleep?"

Instead of answering him, she looked into his eyes with a teasing glint of her own. "You might discover the answer to that if you're not careful."

He lifted his brow and let out a little laugh. "You tempt me to haul you over my shoulder and take you to your room."

"You had better lock me in if you do."

He laughed. He actually tossed back his head and laughed.

He hadn't done so since the night before he rode to the Tower to find the boys gone.

"May I ask you a question?"

"Of course."

"What's with you and Reg? He's your cousin, right? You let him and his family plus one, live here. I know he's a snarky little creep, but he really irks you. Why?"

His laughter faded. What could he say about his cousin? "His father was my only living relative after the attack. Reg was five and the master of his house. He was a jealous child and made my life miserable when I had to visit his family. When the king gets here, you will see Reginald de Marre disappear up the shoot of Richard's arse. He'll go quickly, so be watchful."

"If Reg was up King Edward's arse, would you mind?"

Nicholas gave her a scowl. She knew the correct questions to ask. "No."

She looked around his library and leaned in to whisper, "What did Richard do that you hold such strong feelings toward him?"

He sat up straighter and looked into the flames. He'd never spoken of it to anyone else. He wanted to tell her. "Edward had many children, mostly girls, one of whom is favored by Henry Tudor. His only two sons, Edward V and young Richard of Shrewsbury, aged thirteen and not yet ten, were very dear to me. Whenever I was home, I spent most of my time with them. I loved the girls as well. But I hardly saw them. My only consolation when Edward died was that his son would reign in his place."

The fire crackled and he blinked.

"Go on," she urged softly.

"Richard had them put in the Tower to study all the formalities of the coronation, which was to take place. I had been home twice in the months the boys were there. They had not been happy but they knew their duties and they did what their uncle, Richard, told them to do. None of us knew how hard at work he was at having Edward's marriage to Elizabeth Woodville declared bigamous and thereby having Edward's children declared illegitimate. Edward loyalists rose up in the streets against Richard. He had stolen the crown from young Edward. He had been named the princes' Protector and if what he had done wasn't bad enough..." He stopped to run both his palms over his face. "I went to visit them just a few hours after the declaration and they were already gone. They have never been found. I fear they are dead, and that their Protector is responsible, but I have no proof."

He was surprised to find a droplet falling to his cheek. Even more when he heard her sniffle beside him and then wiped her eyes.

"Are you going to tell me they found their bodies in the future? If so—"

"No," she said quickly, placing her hand on his leg. "No, I'm not going to tell you that."

Not that he believed her...fully.

"I think we should call it a night."

He gave her, and then the window a curious look. "But 'tis night."

She smiled. "Yes. It's just a figure of speech. It means, it's late and we should end our visit. Come on." She held her hand down to him.

He took it, wanting instead to pull her down into his arms. He was mad. He stood up and stared into her eyes. He didn't want the night to end. He ran the back of his knuckles over her cheek. "You are fresh air to my weary soul."

He wanted to kiss her. He ached to do it.

Someone knocked at the library door, interrupting his thoughts. It was Elia.

"Word has arrived that Richard lodges in Kirkham Abbey," she said coming inside. "He will be here by morning." She looked at Kestrel and smiled, then cut her gaze back to him. "I thought you would want to know."

"I do. Thank you, Elia." He tossed Kestrel a regretful gaze.

"We were just calling it a night."

Elia crinkled her brow, then smiled, getting it. Clever lady. "Walk with us back to Kestrel's room."

"Oh, dear. I'm afraid I cannot. Cook wishes for me to prepare a list of things he needs for the kitchen. Some of the guardsmen are going to Brompton and you said he could have a list drawn up."

"Aye, I did." Nicholas said and turned to give Kestrel a knowing look. As in, he knew she had something to do with Cook and his list.

He dismissed Elia to her task and walked Kestrel back to her room.

She was making changes everywhere she went, bringing a little piece of her future to the fifteenth century. People liked her. She'd even won over Cook.

But the king was different.

# CHAPTER TEN

KING RICHARD III arrived at Scarborough Castle with all pomp and circumstance.

Kes could tell by watching his entrance from the bridge wall, that he enjoyed lording over everyone. Even his wave was practiced and stiff as he greeted the villagers closest to the castle.

He rode on a majestic white stallion in trappings of purple. He wore his crown as he rode in with his private guardsmen of forty men around him. Kes was certain the crown made him more of a target. His men probably worked that much harder to keep him safe.

His procession, waving purple and yellow banners, moved over the bridge and through the outer gate. Everyone scurried to and fro, preparing this thing or that. Even Kes felt a little excited.

The only one who remained calm and together was Nicholas. Now, Kes knew better. For what boiled just beneath the surface of Nicholas' cool veneer, was fury, leashed and controlled. But for how long?

He stood against the wall, watching the king's procession growing closer. He said nothing but waited.

Kes had found him in the great hall at dawn. They broke their fast together but Nicholas said very little except that he'd enjoyed their time together last night. So had she. When he had opened Monmouth's *History of the British Kings* and began to read, she thought she might have found the man of her dreams. He read about Arthur and him going to Avalon to be healed. Was it all just coincidence? But a brooch with the Pendragon name on it had transported her over five hundred years into the past. Why did Nicholas read that passage in particular? What did it mean? She didn't know and neither did Nicholas. He had to believe her now. She believed he was afraid of such a tremendous truth.

How much should she tell him? Talking about buildings and modern marvels was one thing. She knew about the princes in the Tower. Their fates were common knowledge in the twenty-first century, as was the fate of the Yorks and the Lancasters.

She had to keep it all to herself. Changing this time in history could have terrifying consequences.

"Will he send for you?" Kes asked him as the king's carriage rolled by them and the king's gaze settled on his commander.

"The instant he is on his feet, if not sooner," Nicholas let her know. "Reg chases him, and he chases me."

"Why does he chase you?"

Nicholas pushed himself off the wall with a dark smile. "Because he needs me. He needs me to win against Henry Tudor when he comes. And I will win, but not for Richard. The Lancasters killed my parents. For that, I remain loyal to York."

What if she told him that Richard was killed in the Battle of Bosworth Field this coming August? No, no she couldn't. What if Nicholas did something to change that day and Richard lived? No. She studied history. She didn't change it.

But Richard did lose, and so did his army. What happened to Nicholas in that battle? Was he among the dead? An icy chill washed over her. She hadn't considered that Nicholas was going to die soon.

It was unacceptable.

"Come." He moved quickly through the crowd, away from the castle entrance.

"Where are we going?" It took a lot to keep up with him. She took two or three steps for his one.

Finally, he took her by the hand and pulled her away. She had to lift her skirts with one hand and use the other to hold on to him. She laughed at one point at the thrill of her feet lifting off the ground.

They didn't stop until they reached the shore.

He pulled his boots and socks free and stepped into the water. She smiled and did the same.

"Walk with me."

She nodded. She knew better. She wasn't an eighteen-year-old girl. Nicholas was so dangerous. The worst there was. He was irresistible, seemingly genuine. She had to keep a clear head, but it was almost impossible when she was near him, like now.

"Who should I say I am when I meet the king?" she asked him.

"Stick with what you have *remembered* already. Your name. You are from Bridlington. Your great-aunt was the Duchess of Glastonbury. Do not add anything."

"Ok."

"Try to use the same words everyone else uses."

"Aye."

He looked at her and genuinely smiled for the first time that day. "Aye."

"Will you get into trouble for leaving?" she asked as they strolled the shoreline.

"Not for long. He knows how I feel about him, but as long as I fight and win his wars, he will keep his nose up my arse."

"What if you don't win?" she asked quietly.

"I would have to be dead not to win."

She was quiet after that and took a few more steps with him.

"Does that trouble you, Kestrel?" he asked, bending to look at her when she kept her gaze forward.

"Yes, I mean, aye, it troubles me. We're friends. I don't—do not want you to get killed."

"I will do my best." He smiled at her.

She didn't want him to fight. Maybe he wasn't mentioned in the history books because he wasn't there. What if she found the brooch or a way back and took him back... rather, forward with her? She could trick him into going. So what if he hated her. He'd be alive.

She almost laughed and gave him a reason to believe she was a madwoman. She'd be lucky if she ever got back.

"Tell me more about your life, Kestrel. I want to forget duty while I can."

"What haven't I told you already? I live in a loft. It's a big open space—"

"You live outdoors?"

"No, I mean there are no separate rooms. It's just like one big room. We all have screens and alcoves for privacy."

"How many of you live there?"

"There are five of us."

"Two men and three women," he grumbled and scowled for all he was worth. Kes was impressed that he'd listened to every word she'd spoken, at least about her roommates. She suspected he didn't like the fact that she lived with two men. Did that mean he believed her? She didn't know why it was so important to her if he did. What could he do to help? The realization of it all sank in a little deeper. Chances are she was stuck here. The Earl of Scarborough was all kinds of good looking, and he seemed nice enough when he wasn't growling like a bear at his cousin or cutting men to smithereens.

But home was...home. It was everything she knew. Everything and everyone she loved. She wanted to go home. She felt the sting of her tears and could not keep them from falling.

"Do you think I'll get back?"

He looked at her, scowl fading, his expression softening. "I do not know. But if there is a way, I will help you find it."

She stopped breathing for a second. She wanted to jump into his arms. He would help her. He didn't need to believe her. She needed his help and he was giving it. "Thank you," she whispered.

He seemed ruffled. She remembered him on the battlefield.

He was a warrior fighting a war. He was confident and utterly savage, his hair flying into his face as he drove his blade into a man. Yet here he was with her, awkward and uncomfortable.

She liked him. She knew the dangers of getting involved, but she liked him. And now....she took a step forward in the wet sand and almost leaned against him when she lifted her face to kiss his cheek.

She felt his warm breath change against her neck becoming shallow and short. She withdrew at the same time an upward gust of wind blew her hair into his face. She looked up and smiled. "Where should we start?"

His breath stopped, and then he blinked and stepped away. He began walking back toward the castle. She felt awful but she didn't think anything could come of them. The one guy who might be decent and loyal had to be almost six hundred years in the wrong time. Great.

"The brooch," he said, turning when she followed him.

"You think there might be one here?" she asked with excitement.

"Or mayhap someone who knows about it."

"Like who?"

"I know a man in the next town who studies artifacts and, like you, history. He is the one who supplied me with most of my books."

"When can we go talk to him?"

"We?"

He looked at her with his sensual half-smile and set her blood rushing through her veins.

"Of course I'm coming, Nicholas. Even if this man knows absolutely nothing about the brooch, he's a historian. Do you really think I'll miss out on meeting him and seeing his collection? I only wish I had my camera."

"Camera?"

She told him what she knew of cameras and what they did. Nicholas was fascinated.

"Here, do this with your hand." She took it, trying and failing miserably not to thrill in the size of his fingers, the hard, callused skin underneath. She held his hand up, his arm out, level with his gaze, then molded his fingers as if he were holding a phone. "Look at the image you want to capture and then use your thumb to take the photo."

She hurried ahead of him then spun around with one hand on her hip. She pouted, then smiled, each time changing her *pose*.

He smiled with her and tapped away, capturing her in their invisible phone.

"We can take selfies, too!" She ran to him and pushed an imaginary button on the phone. "The lens is on you now—and me!"

She closed in and held her hand up toward the phone. "Smile!"

They took pictures of themselves, heads bent close. Was he turning his face to hers? Slowly, methodically, seducing her without abusing his power? She turned as his breath touched her ear. Should she kiss him? Of course not. But her heart defied her.

"My lord?"

Nicholas pulled away glaring at one of the castle soldiers.

"What is it, Barnet?"

"Forgive me, my lord," Barnet said nervously, "your king seeks you."

Nicholas was correct then. The king was summoning him. Should she go with him, or stay here with her life in his hands?

"I'm coming with you."

"This king can be very much like a weasel, digging where few have gone before."

She rubbed her hands together. "I can be a cat or a kitten. Don't worry. I'll handle him."

He aimed his half-smile at her. "I do not doubt it."

"Now, when do we leave to meet the historian?"

"Kestrel," he said, stepping around her to resume his trek to the castle. "I do not think—"

"Please." She remained close. "I want to go with you."

He stopped refusing and nodded. "Very well. We will go as soon as I can get away from Richard again. Be ready."

"I will be," she assured him.

They covered their feet again when they reached the end of the shore. While they walked the length of the wall, she captivated his attention by telling him what it felt like to look out the window of the plane she took to Scotland. "We were in the clouds. It was quite exhilarating."

He stared at her and shook his head. "If what you speak about is not real then the Lord gifted you with an extraordinary imagination."

"It's all real."

"I have never known anyone like you, Kestrel."

"Of course, you haven't," she grinned at him. "I'm not from around here."

Just before they reached the castle doors, he stopped her again. "I'm going to tell Richard that you are...that I am...ehm...in love with you. 'Twill keep his wayward hands off you."

In love with her? "Of course." She could have kicked herself for that saying again.

"Will he respect that?" she asked.

"He will fear me leaving his side. It always comes back to that."

"Aye," she said as the doors opened, and a man stepped out with an entourage of men all around him.

King Richard. She recognized him by the golden crown he still wore and the pompous tilt of his chin.

He watched Nicholas bow and Kes follow suit with a curtsey.

"I was wondering where you had disappeared to, Commander." He turned his sinuous smile on Kes. "Now, I understand."

She wondered if his irises seemed almost black because of the evil he had done in his life. She knew of most of the accusations against him, and there were many. They were grievous but unproven. Still, he was an unlikable man with all his airs.

"Your Majesty, may I present Miss Kestrel Locksley of Bridlington," Nicholas introduced her. "I discovered her near a battlefield in Bridlington. She had been injured and has lost most of her memory. I brought her back with me. Elia has been seeing to her. As have I."

"Dear Nicky," the king said, turning to Kes. "'Tis just like you to bring in strays."

Kes did her best not to let the king's insult rile her. "Sir Nicholas has been the perfect host."

"Oh?" the king asked curiously. "That is surprising to hear. He is not always a perfect host. In fact," he laughed as Reg joined them. "I have never known him to be a very good host at all."

"Mayhap," Kes countered sweetly, "'twas the guests who wore on this warrior's mettle."

The king turned to Nicholas, looking rather surprised. Kes wasn't being careful. She swore in her mind. Well, she wanted the king to know that his commander's feelings for her, when he admitted to them, were reciprocated.

"You have a tigress here, Commander. She does not allow a word to be spoken against you."

"Aye," Nicholas smiled at her. "Our feelings for each other have grown quickly.

"Quite quickly, indeed!" Reg balked. "Why, just the other morning they were shouting at each other over breakfast."

"Reg," Nicholas said on a warning snarl, "'twill be that you take your family and leave, or I cut out your tongue. Choose."

Reg's eyes opened as wide as Kes thought they could.

She wondered why Nicholas had let his cousin stay so long when they did not get along.

"Sire?" Reg entreated.

The king's face remained completely impassive. He looked at his commander, and so did Kes.

Nicholas' gaze pierced Richard's. His nostrils were slightly flared as he awaited the king's response.

Kes wondered what he would do if Richard overrode his command.

"Do as he says, Reginald," the king told him while he smiled at his commander. "Choose. I would forego my tongue if the choice were mine."

Seeing that no help came from that quarter, Reg began to weep. Kes looked away. She didn't want to witness any man's humiliation.

"Go weep to your wife," Nicholas ordered. "I will show you mercy for Miss Locksley's sake. But do not speak of her or me again. Do you understand?"

Reg nodded and then ran away.

The king peered at Nicholas as if he were reading him. Then coming to some secret conclusion, he gave his commander a pitiful look. "You should have thrown him out a long time ago."

"I need someone to take care of things while I'm away fighting for you."

"Take a wife," the king suggested, his smile widening when he glanced at her. "Then she can take care of things. Aye?"

Nicholas looked at Kes with bold impatience. "Aye."

Kes felt herself blushing. She couldn't help it. Worse, she couldn't help that she wished his words were true.

# CHAPTER ELEVEN

C HARLES LANCASTER SAT in the outdoor pub at a small, round, wooden table, alone in the shadows of twilight. He bid the server pour him one more drink while he contemplated everything he knew. His Kestrel had been abducted and it would seem through magic. He'd dug up enough to know certain things were true—and there was nothing he could do about it.

The server gave him a warm smile. He turned away. He didn't want intimate company. He wanted to mourn the loss of his baby, his only child.

When a woman recognized him and came to his table asking to hear his story, he settled in to tell her. Any opportunity he found to talk about his daughter, he took.

"I'm Noelle Upton, with TTN, The Truth in News. Your daughter's disappearance has become headline news. We understand there are no new leads. What's the most difficult part of this for you?"

"Not knowing if she's suffering right now is the hardest thing." He pulled her picture from his wallet and smiled looking at it. "If anyone has any information leading to her rescue, I will pay one hundred thousand dollars."

Ms. Upton smiled, reminding him of the sun and how pleasant it was to stand beneath its light. "The station will match that, Mr. Lancaster. Your daughter's disappearance is helping many eyes to open about crimes against women."

Charles wasn't sure he wanted to use his daughter's disappearance as propaganda. "Let us find her first, and then we can open more eyes."

He rose and dropped a twenty onto the table.

He was going to need help. He wasn't sure how far he could or should go.

For Kestrel, he would give up anything.

"WHERE IN YORK did you say you were from?"

Kes looked straight into the king's eyes and gave him a slight smile. "Not York, Sire, but Bridlington. I'm from Bridlington. I believe."

She lifted her cup and sipped her wine. She glanced around from where she sat at the head table, letting her gaze linger on the doors to the great hall.

Her knight wasn't around for help. The king had sent him away to spy out a rumor of a group of Reds close by. Thankfully, before he left, they went over everything she needed to know about her life if the king asked. Where she grew up and who her parents were.

"You are quite lovely," the king told her. "Your eyes are like gems in sea water."

She sighed inwardly. "Your Majesty is too kind."

"How is it that a woman like you is unwed? Are you a widow?"

"A woman like me, Sire?"

He grinned. "Well, you are not a fresh maiden, now are you? Twenty and two?"

"Twenty and five," she corrected with no coyness at all. "I remain unwed because I am...barren." Should she sniffle? Wipe a dry tear from her eye?

He laughed and leaned in. "Who cares about children? I

would marry you just to fu—"

"Your Majesty," she cut him off sharply, "do you think that crown gives you the right to speak to me that way?"

He gave her a hard look. "Aye, it does."

"No," she shook her head and went on boldly, "it does not." She was sure Elia was having a breakdown beside her (after Kes had begged the king to let her sit there). "And I think your commander will agree when we ask him upon his return."

He stared at her and Kes felt like someone was running their cold fingers up her spine. She had taken a bold chance, but there was just no way she could live with Richard salivating over her. Oh, he was angry. If looks could kill, she'd be pinned to the wall, bleeding out. She was a fool! This was the king in the fifteenth century! He would hang her!

"Perhaps 'twas a bit crass for your delicate ears," he admitted, sitting back in his chair. "I meant it only as the highest form of praise."

The chance had paid off. He *was* afraid of losing Nicholas' support.

Was this guy the father of all the future assholes out there?

"Of course, Your Majesty." She turned to Elia and rolled her eyes with exhaustion—and then realized that Reg was watching her. She held her hand to her head.

"I'm afraid I'm feeling unwell," she told the head maid. "Would you take me to my room, Elia?"

"Of course, my dear. Excuse us, Sire."

"No, wait. I will escort her."

The head maid sighed and took Kes' arm. "He will have my head and then yours if I leave her alone with anyone. Even you, Sire."

Richard looked down his long nose at her. "I suppose you are correct." He smiled suddenly. "And to show you that I mean no harm, I shall bid the lady good eve right here." He turned to Kes and bowed, wishing her good night.

She smiled and turned on her heel, anxious to be away from

him. She didn't want to be around the king without Nicholas. She was afraid she might tell him what a poor example of mankind he was. Nicholas would come back and find her hanging in the outer courtyard.

"Elia," she said, turning to her as they walked. The head maid was fast becoming Kes' closest friend. "The earl doesn't like him. I know that many Yorkist supporters have turned to the Lancaster side. Why does Nicholas continue to support him?"

"Because for Nicholas, the alternative is worse."

Kes looked down at her feet. Ah, yes, the other mountain blocking any path toward Nicholas. "Lancasters." Of which she was one. Of course, he never had to know, but she didn't want a relationship built on lies.

"Aye, Girl. Come, let us go to your room and speak there."

Kes nodded. They walked the long halls in silence until they reached her room.

"I will stay with you until Nicholas returns."

Kes appreciated that. What would Elia do if the king tried to get in? Kes didn't want to find out.

She showed Elia how to shove a chair beneath the door handle to make it almost impossible for anyone to get in.

"Now, as I was saying about Nicholas and the Lancasters," Elia said, sitting on the edge of the bed. She patted a spot for Kes to join her. "They killed his parents."

"Yes, he has spoken of it before," Kes told her.

"What you do not know is that they killed his sister and two younger brothers as well."

Tears colored the rims of Kes' eyes. His whole family.

"He doesn't speak of them or of what he saw. But I remember." Elia's eyes changed to olive green when she looked off into the distance as if she could see the past again. "They were good children, always obedient." She sniffed and pulled out a handkerchief. "They were happy." She stopped to wipe her eyes and cry a little. Kes hurried to her and rubbed her back.

"We were traveling to Leeds to visit with the children's

grandparents when we were attacked. They must have been following us. They knew who the de Marres were. Everything happened so quickly. I was young. Just nineteen. I was riding…closest…to Nicky." She wiped her eyes heedlessly. "They came out of the trees. At least fifty strong. They knew they would need that many to overtake Sir Albert de Marre when he was protecting his family. But he couldn't fight them all. I escaped with little Nicholas after they killed his brothers and we rode through the forest with the sounds of his mother's screams piercing the air, and our hearts. His sister and his father screamed after that. And then they screamed no more."

"Oh, Elia," Kes cried with her. "How horrible. I can't imagine what a nightmare that was for you. And for poor Nicholas. Of course it had the most traumatic effect on him. Seven is such an impressionable age."

She wiped her eyes and noticed Elia staring at her.

"Kes, when are you going to tell me why you speak the way you do? Who are you?"

What? What had Kes done to give anything away? For a minute, she was too shocked and frightened to say anything coherent. After a few attempts at speech, she stopped and closed her eyes. She prayed for help, and then began.

"Elia, you must not speak of this or tell Nicholas that I've told you. Do I have your word?"

"You have it."

It had to mean something, or Nicholas wouldn't trust her the way he did. Kes liked her and she was going to burst if she didn't tell someone other than him.

"He found me on the battlefield."

"Aye, he told me that," Elia said. "You wandered—"

"No. I appeared out of thin air, as he explains it. For me, I was in an office on the West Side rubbing a brooch left to me by my great-great-great-aunt, the duchess. One second I was there, in twenty nineteen. The next, I was here in fourteen eighty-five. In the middle of a medieval battle."

Elia was quiet for so long, Kes thought her story had put her asleep with her eyes open.

"Twenty nineteen..." she echoed. "You traveled through...time."

"You believe me?"

Elia nodded. "I suspect one of our merchants may be a time traveler, but I say nothing lest he be accused of witchcraft."

Kes' stomach twisted into a knot.

"And Nicholas saved you?" Elia asked, seeing her worried frown.

"Yes. Some men rode toward me with their swords swinging. They meant to kill me, but Nicholas stopped them."

"Did he stop all of them?"

"I...I don't remember."

"Think," Elia pressed softly, her gaze was serious. "Did any see what Nicholas saw and live?"

"Maybe." Kes' eyes opened with fear. "You think they will say I'm a witch?"

"They might, and if they know he cares for you, you become their greatest weapon against the man they could never beat before."

Kes' heart drummed hard. It felt as if it were thrashing in her throat. Why would she come all the way back here just to burn as a witch? No. Nicholas wouldn't let it happen. He'd killed everyone who'd seen her. She was sure of it.

"There now. There," Elia comforted. "I have said too much. I worry over things. 'Tis what I do." She wiped Kes' eyes. "Now then, continue with your story, dear one. Tell me, what 'tis like in twenty nineteen. You are very different from anyone I have ever known, especially for a woman."

Kes forgot about witches for a moment. "In my time, women are very different, I'm very happy to report. There is still a long way to go though."

"In truth?" Elia asked.

"I would not lie to you."

Elia smiled and nodded. "What does Nicholas think?"

"I don't know if he believes me, but he agreed to help me get back."

They remained locked away in Kes' room for the next hour, until they heard the guards outside announcing Nicholas' return. They unbarred the door and waited for him to come. Elia was sure he would. Kes wasn't as certain.

Elia proved to be correct.

He looked tired and anxious, but as handsome as any man had a right to be, dressed in his dark armor. His eyes glittered like diamonds under a charcoal sky when they told him about Richard. Actually, it was Elia doing all the talking while Nicholas unhooked himself from his armor.

She grew angry in the telling, like a protective mother bear. Something Kes hadn't had in many years.

"He told her he would marry her just to—" Elia pushed up on her tiptoes to whisper the word in his ear.

Kes never fought so hard not to smile. She wouldn't tell Elia that she'd heard the word a gazillion times.

When Nicholas clenched his jaw and drew his hands into fists, Kes smiled at him. "Listen," she said softly, coming closer. "Words like that don't offend me. He's a jerk. So what?"

"His thoughts of you are dangerous," her knight muttered.

Oh, would she ever stop considering him her knight?

"I must confront him."

"No," Kes said, reaching for his hand.

Elia stepped back.

His large hand in both of hers made her ache to bring his fingers to her face. "I cannot change anything, Nicholas."

"Just being here has changed things alre—" He stopped speaking and looked over at Elia, remembering that she was there.

"I told her," Kes whispered, then let him go and closed her eyes when he cursed under his breath.

"Would you truly keep this from me?" Elia asked, looking at him.

He ran both hands through his dark hair. "'Tis madness, El! And what if he hears of it?" He pointed to the door of the room.

"Are you suggesting he'll hear it from me?"

"No, but—"

"I will not say a word, Nicholas. You should know that," Elia brooded.

"She could help us," Kes suggested, getting Elia to smile again.

Nicholas held his hands to his mouth and then shook his head as if he simply couldn't take anymore. "Who will you enlist next, Kes? Cook? The laundress, the scullery maids?"

Kes blinked and then physically pushed him out of the way— and it wasn't easy, but he blocked her path.

"You're a jerk just like the rest of them," she threw over her shoulder at him and left the room.

She didn't really want to be alone in the halls with the king possibly prowling about. She realized it was foolish to leave her room, but she had to get away from Nicholas. Madness was it? She was getting sick and tired of hearing that, too. She didn't care how insane it sounded. Couldn't he just suspend what he thought he knew of time and trust that she was telling the truth? Elia had done it. Elia believed her. Kes was glad she'd told her.

"Kestrel, wait!"

She heard him but she didn't stop. She hoped she remembered her way to the wall. She'd taken a wrong turn yesterday and ended up in Reg and Adele's wing. Harrowing.

"Leave me alone, Nicholas. I'm off to find more people to enlist. Because, you know, I'm an idiot and can't look out for myself!"

"I never said that!" he defended, pulling himself out of the padding that had been underneath his armor.

She spun on him. "There are many ways to say a thing, you oaf!"

She refused to think about how good he looked in a léine that was just tight enough to stretch across his chest and shoulders.

She looked away and stepped through a door. She was hit with a cool northern breeze. She took a deep breath and shut the door in his face.

"Look, I really want to be alone," she told him when he came outside.

"Kestrel, 'tis been a long day. I did not mean what I said. Come now—" He put his hand to her elbow to urge her along. She slapped it away. His arm snaked out and coiled around her waist. He yanked her in and she hit his chest hard enough to lose her breath for an instant. She meant to scold him for his treatment of her, but he used his free hand to smooth her hair over her forehead as he leaned down to kiss her.

She didn't think about it. She wanted it. He wasn't as bad as the others, and with a little work—

His mouth molded over hers like a caress. His lips were plump and firm, and oh so teasing. He didn't need any help at all. He brushed his curious tongue across her bottom lip and angled his mouth over hers again, letting his hand on her back sink lower, to the top of her rear.

She felt everything in her go warm. Not a good sign. She liked it. She liked it too much. The gorgeous knight in dark armor knew how to kiss. She closed her arms around his neck and curled her fingers through his hair. She pressed her breasts to his chest and thrilled when he groaned into her mouth.

He let her go. She held on to the wall. He battled with himself over her. She could see it clearly on his face. Part of him wanted to pick her up and carry her to his room. She felt it in his kiss, saw it in his eyes. The other part wouldn't treat her casually. Did she mean more to him than that? So soon? Did she feel something special for him in return?

"Come with me," he whispered in the coming twilight.

Where would she go with him? Anywhere?

They hurried to the first stable. He saddled a different horse than the one he'd ridden all day. He untied his blanket and cloak from his horse's saddle and tied it to the new mount.

"We're riding?" she asked, pausing.

"Aye. Why? Are you afraid?"

"Yes. It's getting dark. We could run into a tree or ride off a cliff." She gasped and took a step back.

It wasn't too dark to see his smile. "I know the way. Trust me."

"Wow, you ask a lot on the first date, don't you?"

"The first date?"

"Oh please, don't make me explain that."

"Now you must," he said and fit a boot into the stirrup. He leaped up and swung his other leg over the side. He held his hand down and lifted her under her arm. This time, he set her down in front of him.

"Begin," he said and flicked the reins. He kept the pace at a steady trot.

Kes didn't like riding horses. It always hurt her inner thighs and horses sensed when their rider was untrained at riding.

He held the reins with one hand and curled the other loosely around her waist. She thought, with the warmth of his lap beneath her and his waist and chest behind her, this might be a really nice ride after all. It was better than clinging on behind him, crying her eyes out.

She told him about dating and kept it brief, but still he picked up her distaste for the subject.

"You have been hurt by men you have dated." He guessed. His voice resonated in his chest and echoed through her.

"Yes," she admitted. She didn't usually tell guys about herself so soon, but Nicholas wasn't just a guy. "In the twentieth and twenty-first century, most men slept—sleep around or cheat. There have been songs about how 'he done me wrong', sung by women since before I can remember. Women are beginning to take their lives into their own hands and, well, they are sleeping around now, too. It's very hard to find someone you can trust your heart with when his dic—" Her eyes cut to what she could see of him. Women didn't speak like that here, did they? It wasn't a question. She knew the answer. "—his penis is—"

"His what, my lady?"

"His penis," she said just above a whisper this time.

"Forgive me. I still cannot hear you."

"If I elbow you in it, will you understand then?"

He laughed behind her, a rich and resonant sound against her back, sending cascades of pleasure through her. He didn't laugh often. So to get him to relax his guard and do it was a grand accomplishment.

"Now you made me forget what point I was trying to make."

"You kept speaking of his penis."

She kept—"Nicholas!" she scowled for all she was worth and pushed off him.

He yanked her back. "Why are you so eager to return to that life?"

*Believe me*, she wanted to tell him, *if it were just about you, I'd work you until I won you and never look back.*

"I told you," she said. "My father will be alone. He never remarried but dove into his work. He digs up bones and studies them. I'm all he has. And I would be leaving my friends, my work as a historian. I would miss all of it."

"Aye. I understand."

"No, you think it's madness."

"And yet, here I am taking you to see my historian friend a half-mile away."

She turned and smiled up at him and ran her palm over his stubbled cheek.

He cupped her wrist and kissed her fingers while she whispered to him her thanks.

"But you are weary from your day already traveling. I hate to think you are exhausted and doing this for me."

"Why would you hate to think that?" he asked, leaning down so that his lips fell across her ear. "It would be showing you my intention toward affection. It should please you, unless…"

"Unless what?"

"Unless you don't share my affection."

"I do," she told him without hesitation. She closed her eyes knowing she was in trouble when he leaned into her, his big arm resting in her lap, his face inclined to her ear. "I'm not accustomed to your behavior," she admitted.

"I will help you grow accustomed to it," he promised. "For however long you remain here."

He almost sounded like he believed her—or he respected that she believed it. She smiled even though the idea of leaving him made her feel miserable. She snuggled closer to him.

"Kestrel?" he said in a low, husky, sexy voice.

"Yes?"

"I'm wearier than I thought. Speak to me and help me stay alert."

"Nicholas!" She began to turn to admonish him, but he held her still and dipped his mouth to her throat. "In truth, I like listening to you speak. Your words are colorful."

She smiled when he kissed her neck. "All right then. But it's you who must do the talking in order to stay awake and alert. My voice will lull you to sleep faster."

He tried to deny her, but she stopped talking and waited for him to continue. "Very well," he sighed. "What would you have me speak about?"

"Whatever you want."

He muttered under his breath, but he did as she asked.

So far, for a medieval man, he wasn't doing bad. Not bad at all.

# CHAPTER TWELVE

"I WAS THIRTEEN. I had been with Edward six years. I was with him when he fled to Flanders fourteen years ago. I was one of two people who knew why he left. Richard was the other. The king had fathered a son in Flanders with a woman he loved. He knew that if his enemies found out, they would have the boy killed. It has been done to others in the past.

"The Lancasters found out. I did not know how at the time. I still don't. Not for certain. I thought Edward had told someone else and it had slipped his mind. But they found the boy and his mother and killed them. I was with Edward when he found out. 'Twas one of the more harrowing times in my life. Edward was like a father to me and to see him so agonized day after day, night after night…I swore to him never to give my support to the Lancasters."

She believed him. He hated the Lancasters. He'd never stop. "Why are you telling me this particular story?" she asked him, filled with anxiety over who she really was.

"Because after spending the day around Richard, I know you are wondering why I still give him my support."

"You're right. I had been wondering that. I asked Elia. She told me about your family. You have my sympathies, Nicholas."

"I see you two shared many tales today," he said quietly.

"I like her."

"Aye. She is like a mother to me," he admitted.

Kes smiled at him. She didn't want to get Elia in trouble for telling her too much.

"So you think Richard had something to do with informing the Lancasters?"

"Mayhap," he told her. "Many accusations fall on him and there is never any proof. I have to wonder if he could have done all these terrible things or if he is just easy to blame because there is so little likable about him. All I know is that I regretted fighting for him after the princes disappeared. I've regretted it every day since. I try to remain loyal to the House of Plantagenet and I deny my regret because 'tis treason."

Kes covered his hand with hers. "Treason to a king who leaves a trail of death behind him on his way to the throne. Does he deserve your loyalty?"

What was she doing? She shouldn't be treading these waters. Not when Nicholas especially could change history.

"Let's talk about something else," she suggested before he answered and gave his hand a rub.

"All right. But this time, you shall tell me something about yourself," he insisted.

"But I like how your voice sounds rumbling into me."

He rested his forehead on the back of her head. "No. Begin."

"You're so bossy!"

"If bossy means threatening and unbeatable, then you are you correct."

She laughed. "It doesn't mean that. But wow, you're arrogant, too."

He sat up straight. "What is arrogant about knowing I'm unbeatable?"

She shook her head. "No one is unbeatable, Nicholas."

He bent to whisper in her ear. "I am, my lady."

"Now," he sat up straight and boomed in the quiet forest, sending critters scattering. "Tell me about you," he demanded, but in a much quieter voice. "Something no one else present or future knows."

She thought about it for a minute or two. She knew what it was. It knotted her belly and filled her days with guilt. Not these days, but the ones in her past...Nicholas' future.

"I have felt envious of people I know that seemed to have good relationships with the one they love. I told myself it was only a matter of time before they were in the gutter with the rest of us. I overcompensated by buying them extra lavish housewarming gifts, saying extra nice things to them, kissing their rears as if some of what they had would rub off on me."

She laughed awkwardly. "I don't know why I'm telling you this."

"We all need to lay down our burdens sometimes," he told her quietly, as if he understood. Maybe he did. Then he asked, "Would you ever damage one of your friend's relationships because of this envy?"

"No. Never."

"Then there is hope for you yet," he announced then drew closer all around her. "Though you had me worried for a moment." They laughed against each other's bodies. He moved his lips over her ear. "I can make you the envy of everyone you know."

"Oh?" she teased, almost purring at him. "How can you do that?"

He kissed her lobe. "By giving you a good *relationship*."

She wanted to giggle and then to cry. His words and his close proximity released a thousand butterflies in her belly. But was it wise to develop a relationship with him? What if she popped out the same way she popped in? What if she was here for good and some other woman came into Nicholas' life...or worse, he died in battle?

"I would like that," she heard herself say before she could stop it. A good relationship. Did it make going into the fifteenth century to find one worth it? "But I'm afraid. I know this century, and I don't want to be here."

"You will not be happy if you stay then." He lifted his arm off her and took the reins in both hands. "We should not push ourselves into something because of Richard."

"Is that what we were doing?" she had to ask. Was that all this was to him? She was madly attracted to him. Was he not to her?

"Where is the hope for us?" he asked her, sighing at the moon peeking through the treetops. "I never thought I would care about such a thing with a woman. I am twenty and seven. Not a young man."

She turned to look up at him, catching quick glimpses of him when moonlight shone through the trees. "You're young enough." Her breath warmed his chin.

"Young enough for what?" She could hear his smile in his voice, slow, sensuous. Then the treetops parted and she saw it.

"To possess the..." He heated her blood. "...stamina to do what you claim you can do."

"You tempt me to show you, Kestrel."

She wished he would. But he shouldn't. He couldn't, and he knew it.

"You pain me, lady," he whispered into her hair. "We are almost there."

He caught himself and pulled back on the reins. She was grateful because she wouldn't have done it. He was all-consuming and sensual. He made her laugh. He made her forget why she'd sworn off relationships.

Theirs would be tragic. No, thank you.

"Why did we come at night?" she asked, glad for the change in topic.

"Old Walter doesn't like to bring out his more precious items in the light of day where they might be seen by thieves. I stopped at his place before I reached home tonight. I told him we would be coming by tonight."

So, this Old Walter meets with potentially big customers like Nicholas in the cover of night? Not likely. It was probably because his fakes couldn't be examined well in candlelight. "How precious are these pieces and have you ever seen any?"

"I have seen a few. A fifth century Roman chalice set with an eyeball-sized ruby and inscribed *Majorian*."

"Emperor Julius Valerius Majorianus?" she asked, wide eyed.

He shrugged. "What do I know? I'm not the historian."

Oh, if only it were authentic. She had to see it!

"I have also seen a page he claims is from William the Conqueror's *Doomsday Book*."

A short burst of laughter burst from her mouth. She couldn't help it. It was a bit much. *The Doomsday Book*.

"You do not believe they are genuine."

"No," she answered though his was more of a statement of fact than a question.

"Nor do I, but he is the only man I know who may have heard of your brooch."

"It's not *my* brooch."

"Aye, 'tis," he insisted. "You said your aunt left it to you."

"She did," Kes said. "I signed for it. So, it's mine if I ever find it again."

She realized that if she ever saw the brooch again, she would only have it for a minute until she rubbed it and spoke the name *Pendragon*. And then it would belong to anyone who had been with her when she disappeared. Most likely that meant Nicholas.

She didn't mention it to him.

They arrived at Old Walter's home when the forest opened up and the sky was teeming with stars. In fourteen eighty-five, the stars could be clearly seen.

Kes was searching for constellations and almost missed the short, pudgy fellow stepping out of his doorway.

"My lord Scarborough, is that you?" he called out to them.

"Aye, Walter. I have with me Miss Kestrel Locksley of Bridlington."

They rode up to the door and Nicholas dismounted before his host. "You are looking well, Walter"

"As are you, my lord." He waited until Nicholas helped Kes dismount, and then smiled at them both while his stable hand took the reins. "Now, 'tis late, what can I show you?"

"We are looking for a brooch," Nicholas told him.

"I have many of those. Why did you not say so today when you were here? Ah, let me guess. You want to let her choose. What are you looking for, dear lady?"

"A silver brooch—"

"A woman who enjoys fine things," Old Walter complimented.

"'Tis an engraved dragon curled up around a golden stone. The name Pendragon must be on it but 'tis worn off and can no longer be seen."

"You are very specific," Walter remarked, narrowing his eye on her.

"Yes, I saw one long ago and I have always wanted it."

"Hmm," the old historian shook his head. "I do not think I have anything like that but come inside and we will look together."

She followed him and Nicholas into his home and looked around. There were a number of old items placed carefully on tables and shelves. Kes' heart began a heavy litany, battering against her chest. What was here? Was any of it genuine?

She saw a magnetic compass on a table. They came from the Far East in the seventh century. How did he get one? It was said King Alfred the Great had one.

"May I?" she asked Walter. Inside, in the candlelight, the old merchant had soft-looking pudgy pink skin and white hair. He nodded, giving her permission to touch it.

"That one was made in the year eight hundred and eighty-three, in the Han Dynasty."

Kes picked it up and examined it as best she could in the low, golden light. She was no archeologist like her father, but it appeared quite old.

Where would a cute little man like Water get his hands on an eighth century compass?

"The earl has told me you have quite the collection of artifacts. Perhaps while we look for the brooch, you would show me some items."

"Of course, dear lady. Anything you would like."

"Eh, just the brooch for now, Walt," Nicholas let him know. "Do you know of one?"

"Only one," Walter told them in a low voice. "'Tis said to be very powerful. Only one exists and his men are whispered to have it."

"Slow down," Nicholas said. "You're going too fast. What kind of power is it said to possess? And whose men have it?"

"Power too strong for mortal men to play with. And Arthur Pendragon's men are rumored to have it."

"But I thought they were myth," Kes said. "Arthur Pendragon isn't real."

"Now how do you know that, Miss Locksley?" asked Walter. "'Tis said he lived in a very ancient time. A time when some men practiced magic."

She remembered how the brooch glowed and appeared new, and how looking at the name Pendragon made her want to say it.

"Where did you say you saw it, Miss Locksley of Bridlington? 'Twas a man who had it, aye?"

She nodded.

"His name?"

"Mr. Green."

Walt smiled like any jolly old man would, but there was more wisdom in his smile than fancy. "You met Sir Gawaine. Then, you are not from around here."

"She is from Bridlington, Walt. Get it straight, aye?" Nicholas warned.

She'd met Sir Gawaine? *The* Sir Gawaine? Of Arthur's round table knights? No! It was impossible! Oh—wait a minute. She looked at Walt. It seemed the merchant knew more than he was letting on.

"How do you know him?" she asked, hope rising like waves before a storm. "Please, if you know him—tell me—" What was she doing? Walt was looking at her as if a curtain had just come up around her, revealing things she'd tried to keep hidden.

"Miss Locksley, how do *you* know him?"

"I don't…I—"

"Walt," Nicholas said on a low warning breath. But the old man held up his palm to quiet the earl.

"My lord," he said softly with a reassuring smile. "Mayhap I can help her."

Nicholas allowed him to continue.

He bowed his head and turned his kind smile on Kes. "When are you from, Child?"

Kes looked nervously at Nicholas. Walt knew? How should she reply? She'd looked to Nicholas because this was his time. But it was her life.

"I don't understand your question, good sir." Walt knew things. What if he knew she was a threat to history? He could have her stopped. "I was born in Bridlington twenty-five years ago. Delivered by my Aunt Lori and two maids."

"Very well," Walt said, his smile faded, letting her have her way. "You may look but I'm sure I do not have the brooch you are looking for."

He led them down a short hall to another room, this one larger than the first. There was some furniture in it but nothing extraordinary. But he wasn't done.

He rolled away a large rug then lifted a small door hidden beneath it. He stepped down onto a stairway leading to a cavernous basement. His guests followed.

Kes had to be dreaming. Carved into the walls were small shelves, and on each shelf was an artifact. There were chalices, jewelry, weapons, and a variety of other things.

Both men stopped upon hearing her gasp. She did it again at least four more times until they stopped a fifth time and waited while she examined an old gold cross. It was plain in design, about a foot high, a half-foot across and looked to be made of solid gold.

"From the Lindisfarne Priory."

Kes looked at Walt. Lindisfarne. The Vikings. "Did you retrieve it, Walt?"

He smiled but looked down behind his spectacles. "No, Child. 'Twas a trade."

She chuckled. "What did you give up?"

"The pearl necklace that fell from Anne Boleyn's neck at her execution."

Kes touched her fingers to her neck. "A good trade."

"I'm glad you approve," said the old merchant and led them to curtained off corner.

Here were all his watches, brooches, medicine boxes, spectacles, and other small items. "You may look through it."

They looked among everything, but there was no brooch that matched hers among his pieces.

"All hope is not lost. I may know a man who can get it."

"A one of a kind piece?" Kes said incredulously. "From King Arthur's knight? Even if this man could get his hands on it, he would charge more than I have."

"Tell him to get it if he can," Nicholas told Walter. "He will be well compensated."

"Nicholas, no!" she refused. "I couldn't ask that of you."

"I want you to have it in case charges come against you," he said, drawing her aside.

"If charges come up, you'll be considered my accomplice. You'll get into trouble, too."

"I'm not worried over that. I will die one day. I would rather it be saving you."

She wanted to kiss him. She wondered if Walter would mind.

"Very well, I will contact him in the morning," Walter told them. "If there is nothing else, I have a room if you would like it for the night." He smiled.

"No," Nicholas told him. "The lady and I are not wed. We will be leaving now."

"Oh, couldn't we stay just a little longer?" Kes asked.

"We will return," he promised. "'Tis late and Walt is weary from the day."

"Oh, of course! Forgive me!" She set down a small terracotta vase she was checking out. It appeared authentic, Greek, maybe.

"We shall return tomorrow." Nicholas told him and then made a path for her to take the stairs.

"Do you think he's a time traveler?" she asked Nicholas the moment they were back on the horse. "He seems to know much."

"Aye. He could be," he answered quietly. "Elia has suspected him for some time.

"Do you believe it all now?"

"It seems likely but still difficult to comprehend," he answered.

"You realize you're going to pay a guy to rob Sir Gawaine of all people."

"Aye, the *guy* will more likely swindle me."

"Imagine if he gets it," she said, leaning against his hard chest. "There's no guarantee it would work again or that it would send me back home."

"Aye, you are correct."

"I wish I could talk to Gawaine again." She laughed. "That sounds so insane."

"Do you wish to return that badly?"

"Yes," she told him softly. "Of course."

But she wasn't sure anymore.

# CHAPTER THIRTEEN

S EATED AT HIS table beside Reg and his wife, Nicholas remembered why he preferred battle over being home. Richard's return made a bad situation worse.

Nicholas growled in his seat when Reg slurped his oats and cream.

He looked at Margaret. She rolled her eyes at Reg and smiled at Nicholas. She didn't glare at Reg the way she had glared at him when he'd pulled out his chair the other night.

He turned away from her and looked toward the door. He wanted to be here when Kestrel arrived so she didn't have to be with Richard on her own, but Richard wasn't here either.

He tapped his boot under the table. Should he go to her room and get her? He wondered if he was beginning to care for Miss Locksley, or did he just enjoy her company more than anyone else's? He didn't want to care. If she had truly appeared here, she could just as easily disappear. If she was mad, could he still love her with her quirks? Could he stop himself from loving her either way?

Was it all true? He didn't want to say a resounding yes too soon. Mayhap they were all mad. It wasn't as strange as time travel.

What else did Old Walter know about Arthur Pendragon's knights and this brooch? He hadn't known that they were reading about King Arthur the night before. Nicholas would question him some more today. All this talk of time travel had Nicholas thinking if Kestrel truly came back more than five hundred years. If so, she knew if Richard defeated Henry Tudor when they faced off on the field. She most likely knew what became of the princes.

More importantly, she was eager to leave.

It stung when she practically told Walter what was going on, but she hadn't. She was clever enough to tell Walt nothing, though he'd hinted at understanding her plight.

"Are you waiting so eagerly for the king?" Reg asked. "Or someone else?"

Nicholas turned in his spot to stare at his cousin. "Do you want to be thrown out into the dirt today, Reg? Adele and the children may stay until you find them a place to live. We discussed your flapping tongue already, so I assume you don't care where you sleep tonight."

"Of course, I care, Nicholas," Reg whimpered. "'Twas merely a question I asked."

"Ah, if that is all 'twas, Reg, then my answer is someone else." Nicholas didn't look away but dipped his head and stared at him from beneath the ridge of his dark brow. He waited. He dared Reg to open his mouth again.

His cousin went back to slurping his breakfast. Nicholas was about to tell him he'd be wearing the food if he didn't stop, when he spotted the king entering the great hall. He made his way to Nicholas' table.

Could this morning get any worse?

He stood up when Richard reached him and gave over his chair. He put one leg over the bench at the king's left, beside Reg, and straddled it. He kept his back to his cousin and his face to the king. Better he sit between these two fools, than Kestrel having to.

"Nicholas," Richard said, "I understand you disappeared with Miss Locksley last eve. Where did you go?"

Nicholas set down his cup. He wouldn't tell him and put Old Walter in any kind of danger. No matter what else Nicholas told the king, Richard was likely to ask Kestrel when she arrived, and their accounts would not match.

There was only one thing left to do.

"What do you mean by questioning me?" he demanded in a low, deadly tone. "I do not give accounts to you about my personal life."

"I am your king," Richard replied with a haughty tilt of his chin. "You will tell me what I wish to know."

"No, Sire, I will not." Nicholas held his ground. "It is of no concern to you."

"I will be the judge of that."

Nicholas leaned forward, close to the king. "You will not be the judge of what I do. Henry Tudor is as close as France and is gathering forces. 'Tis only a matter of time before he comes."

And then what? What would happen to Kestrel?

"You will die without me, Sire." He let his voice and his words drift across Richard's ears. Nicholas wanted to tell him that if Richard wasn't the last heir to the House of York Nicholas would never fight for him.

Richard glared at him with dark, hollow eyes. "You threaten to leave me. That is treason. I could have you beheaded."

"Do it. And when Tudor slaughters you and seizes your crown, the moment before you die you will remember this with heavy regret."

The king appeared to be rethinking his decisions. "I want obedience from you, Commander."

"You will have it on the field. What I do in my private time is my concern. If you have me followed, I will kill whoever you send."

"You are barbaric," the king told him with distaste on his lips.

"I'm many things, Sire," Nicholas agreed with a glint in his eyes. "But I'm not your prisoner. I will not be treated like one."

He saw her finally arrive with Elia at her side. Did he want them to come closer?

He stood up and Kestrel stopped for a moment as if to catch

her breath.

He saw why she was late. Her rich, sable hair was pinned up all around her head. The long column of her neck was pale in the golden candlelight. Her eyes looked like two oceans of blue-green splendor. Her body was clad in an olive-green kirtle with an over-dress of undyed linen. Sewn around the neckline and cuffs were swirls of gold and dark green.

Had Elia made it for her? It seemed to fit perfectly.

"Ah, here is our cherished guest, Miss Locksley!" greeted the king. She smiled at him and came closer to the table.

Nicholas wanted to hold up his hand to stop her. But he only grumbled. She gave him a curious look and came near to sit opposite him. Elia slipped into the empty space beside her.

"May I be the first to tell you that you look lovely this morning," Richard said.

"Forgive me for being tardy." Her gaze was fixed on Nicholas.

How could he be angry when she looked so beautiful? Then he remembered Richard to his left and Reg to his right and his scowl returned.

He would have asked her how she slept, but Reg's children began to argue. Adele lifted her hand to her forehead and Reg began to slurp his food again.

Nicholas had been patient long enough. He lifted his hand, signaling to one of the servers. "He gets nothing else to eat or drink while I'm here."

"Aye, m'lord."

"You are done with breakfast, Reg," Nicholas told him. "You might as well leave."

Reg stood up and opened his mouth, but Kestrel began to speak first. With her gaze on Adele and Reg's brats, she began softly. "Perhaps if he doesn't eat anymore, he can stay with his family until they are done."

Nicholas' eyes opened wide and he stared at her. She smiled.

"Very well," he grumbled. "As long as he doesn't speak."

"You're generous, my lord."

She sounded like she was telling the truth. The wide grin she offered him made him smile back at her.

"This is all very interesting," the king remarked.

"What is?" Nicholas asked, not caring what the king saw between them.

"I have known you for over two decades, and I have never seen you give in so easily to any woman."

Nicholas smiled, looking at her. "She steals more of my heart each day. Imagine what I will do to the man who tries to take her from me?"

Her face went completely flush. He wondered if he should say these kinds of things just to keep the king away from her. What if she thought he meant them? Did he? Was she stealing his heart? Was it getting worse every day? Aye. Every day, he felt more protective of her, grew more impatient to see her, to be with her. The king was correct, Nicholas gave in to her every whim. He wanted to bury his head in his hands. How had he let this happen?

He looked at her. Aye, she was the kind of beautiful that wrenched at his guts. She was tall and elegant in an oddly awkward sort of way. When she looked at him, his heart rumbled with longing to make her his. When she spoke—ah, that was where she made him weakest. Her words, half of which he couldn't understand, the way she laughed, and made him laugh, all worked at capturing his heart.

"You steal more of mine each day, as well," she told him. "Imagine what I will do to any man who tries to take me from you."

Nicholas inhaled as if he were breathing her alone, and she was enough. He smiled on her fully. She was different. She was from a different time.

"I heard from Reg that you are quite bold," Richard said, watching her.

Nicholas turned his deadly glare on his cousin. That's it. He wanted Reg out today.

"But now, I have seen it for myself," the king continued. "What kind of hall do you come from that allows its women to behave so?"

Nicholas' belly knotted and his mouth went dry. Richard suspected something. But what? It didn't matter. That he suspected anything at all wasn't favorable.

Nicholas had to get her out of there.

"My father's hall is quite humble, Sire." Kestrel turned her smile on Richard. "As is our cottage. I was raised by my father. He was a great man because he never taught me that I was less than he was." When Richard continued to look displeased, she continued. "He lived in Wales for twelve years before he met my mother—"

"Ah, Wales!" Richard declared with a burst of laughter. "That explains it! The Welsh have odd mannerisms. Your father obviously taught them to you."

"Obviously."

"The fault is not your own," the king allowed.

"What a relief," she replied then set her gaze on Nicholas. "May we go for a walk, or even a ride?"

The king balked. "But you haven't eaten!"

"I'm not hungry."

"You will need a chaperone."

Nicholas turned his flinty gaze on him. "Elia will come with us. Come," he said to both women and stepped around the table. "Excuse us, Sire," Elia said and hooked Kestrel's arm in hers. They stood up and followed Nicholas out of the great hall.

"My heart is racing," Kestrel told them. "We just walked out on the King of England."

Nicholas glanced over his shoulder. "We are going to have to get more drastic."

"More drastic?"

"Aye. We may have to wed to turn his attention completely away."

"You're joking."

"I believe he is being quite sincere," Elia told her, leaning in to whisper.

Kestrel shook her head. "I won't marry you to be safe from the king. I would marry you because I love you. And only then."

If she loved him. Why did the mere thought of it make his muscles shake to have her close?

"Elia," he turned to look at her. "Find a place for Reg and his little army to live. Not too close. I will pay whatever is necessary. I want him out of here."

"Aye, Nicholas." Elia smiled at Kestrel. "I'm leaving you in the best hands I know besides the Lord's"

"Thank you," Kestrel told her.

Kestrel looped her arm through Nicholas' as Elia left. She smiled when he looked at her. "What gives, Nicholas? Why did you look paler when I mentioned love than I did when you mentioned marriage? Are you afraid of love?"

"Likely not as much as you are," he remarked with a slight, but playful smile. "I have not been in love in...hmm, I do not think I have ever been in love."

They reached the stable and he began saddling a separate horse for her.

"No." She stopped him. "I want to ride with you."

He nodded, liking the idea but finished saddling the horse. "You will ride this one out a mile or two, until we can no longer be seen from the wall. And then you will ride with me."

"All right," she gave in easily and let him help her mount.

She appeared anxious in her saddle.

"You can do it. Be confident. Help the horse trust *you*."

She smiled and nodded. "Are we going to see Walter?"

"We will see where the wind takes us." He took up his reins and smiled at her. "Aye?"

"Aye," she agreed happily, taking up her reins, as well.

They rode out of Scarborough Castle, past the walls and the small village. They rode on until anyone standing on the castle

PAULA QUINN

walls, looking over, could no longer see them.

And after Nicholas checked and double-checked to make certain they weren't being followed, he took Kestrel from her horse and set her gently between his thighs and against his chest.

After he secured her horse's reins to his, they set out again.

"Nicholas? About the things we said—"

"Aye, we were convincing."

She let out a breathless little laugh. "Yes. Very."

She moved around on his lap to settle in deeper. He wanted to hold her, caress her, protect her from every harmful thing.

"So, do you still doubt my tale is true?"

He drew her in closer with his hand on her belly. "If I accept it," he said against her temple, "then I must also accept that I could lose you at any moment."

He felt her tight gasp at his words. She turned in his lap and kissed his scruffy jaw. He dipped his head and took her mouth with desperate need that matched her own. They stopped riding for a while and just kissed and touched against a tree in the grass.

"What should we do?" she asked him while she rested in his arms under the tree.

"About what?" he closed his eyes and leaned his back against the trunk.

"Us," she clarified.

"I like us," he admitted, closing his arms around her.

"So do I. But if troubles come, I would rather you weren't associated with me."

"'Tis too late for that."

He peeked down at her resting on his chest and belly. She wrung her hands together. He wanted to kiss her again. "Did you worry this much in twenty nineteen?"

"Not on this level of seriousness. I thought worrying about paying the bills was hard. I—" She stared at him. Her eyes opened wider. "Nicholas, you believe me."

"Aye. Aye," he repeated more softly. "But I wish I did not."

"Why?" she asked, her voice as soft as a sigh.

"Because you want to go back."

More silence. He didn't push.

"But, of course," he said, "now I wish to know what will—"

"No. I can't—"

"You will, Kestrel," he insisted. "Was it ever proven that Richard killed the princes?"

"No, Nicholas. It was never proven."

"Were they found?"

She looked away and then tried to get up. He grabbed her wrist, stopping her.

"Please, tell me what you know."

Her big blue-green glassy eyes stared into his. She regretted having to tell him. "The bones of two small boys were found in the Tower in the sixteen hundreds. It was believed at the time that the bones belonged to the princes."

"No," he groaned, letting her go. "I had hoped…"

She drew him into her bosom and held him while he grieved the boys. His little brothers.

"Who did it, Kestrel?" he asked, withdrawing to look at her. "You must know."

"I don't," she promised.

"The people of the future sound very clever. Is there no way to tell who killed the princes?"

"Nicholas, we don't even know for sure if the bones belonged to them. They were buried after they were found. No one is sure where. There was no time to test them."

"Their graves were not marked," he said, tormented by the news.

"No," she whispered, sounding heartbroken for the poor children, and for those who loved them.

"I was not there for them," he said, telling her, and only her, his deepest regret while held in her arms. "I wish I had been. 'Twas why Edward did not make me their Protector. I was always away fighting for the House of York. I would seldom be here to help guide them. I could die at any time. But I did not die.

And those battles could have been won without me. Even if we had lost because of my absence, the boys would be alive today and Edward V would be king."

He felt the sting of his tears and let them fall. "'Tis my fault they are dead."

"Nicholas, that isn't true," she comforted. "Did their father love them?"

"Of course."

"And yet he made Richard their Protector?"

"He trusted his brother. So did I!"

"So, if he did this, then he fooled you all. Why would the thought cross your mind that Richard was busy having the princes declared illegitimate? No one suspected him of evil against the children. Not even his brother. There was no reason for you *not* to go fight and do your duty."

"Aye," he whispered. "Then to return and discover that Richard was the king and the boys were gone, I have pain and wrath deep inside of me toward Richard. Sometimes…I…I hope he dies in battle."

"Nicholas—"

"But that would be the end of the House of York. Everything I have fought for my entire life."

"Yes," she said in a low voice. "I understand. We should be getting back."

No. Back to what? Richard? Reg? Eating alone in his solar? He closed his arms around her waist. "What is the hurry, Kestrel?" He didn't wait for her answer but lay her across the crook of his arm and bent over her. "You are the only person with whom I care to spend my hours." His lips descended on hers in a kiss that curled her toes and set both their hearts to healing.

# CHAPTER FOURTEEN

K ES LET HERSELF relax against Nicholas' chest and closed her eyes on the way to Old Walter's. She knew the merchant probably hadn't found anyone to help them yet. She just wanted to go and have another look at everything. She also wanted to ask him how he came about owning such rare treasures.

It was a wonderful day for letting the wind carry them, as Nicholas had suggested.

The afternoon sun was shining brightly, drenching Nicholas' dark hair in light.

What better way to travel than in the crook of the rock-hard arms of a handsome knight, resting on his solid thighs and broad chest? She was tempted to pinch herself to make sure she wasn't dreaming all this. It was dangerous, sure, but she wasn't going to let that stop her from exploring whatever she could.

Was she ready to explore the heart of a warrior? Nicholas was offering it to her. Did she accept it along with loyal love to her alone? She didn't think he would cheat. If it had taken him his whole life to reach out for her, he wasn't going to reach out to anyone else anytime soon. And that was what she wanted. What she thought she would never find.

He'd opened up to her and let her comfort him—and then he'd kissed her senseless. Oh, he made her want to climb upon him and drive him mad with desire. But she finally had a guy who didn't push, didn't force. She didn't want to have sex with him...yet. She wanted to do things differently this time...since she had been given the chance. She wanted to get to know him first. And he seemed fine with that.

She was falling in love with him and ignoring all the red flags and warning alarms going off in her head. She heard nothing but the deep cadence of his voice. She thought of nothing and no one else but him whether she was eating, sleeping or convincing the scullery maids to demand gloves to protect their skin when scrubbing the floors.

But five days wasn't long enough to know a person.

Still, she knew he harbored hatred for Richard. In terms of fighting though, he didn't fight for Richard. So, none of this would change anything.

"I can almost hear you thinking," he said behind her. "Is it something you wish to speak about?"

She smiled like a satisfied cat. "How is that a scarred and hardened warrior would take note of such a thing and say something so thoughtful?"

He shrugged his shoulders. "If the men of your time cannot do something so simple as lend an ear, then you should leave them."

She smiled at his suggestion. "And go where?"

He bent his lips to her neck. "Stay here with me."

"But Nicholas, we hardly know each other." *You don't know that I'm a Lancaster.*

"What do you want to know about me, Kestrel? You know my pleasant moods and my darker ones. Ah! Here is something you don't know. I want to stop fighting soon and live out my life with a wife I love."

She leaned up and looked at him. "There you go talking about marriage again," she quipped.

"I must," he explained. "I see my children in your eyes."

How could this be real? How could this man exist here and not there? What if she never made it back. Would being married to Nicholas be so bad? She wanted to laugh. Um, no.

"How many children?" she asked warily.

"Six. I do not know. Eight!"

"Ha! You're nuts if you think I'm going through childbirth six to eight times with nothing to ease the pain but whiskey. We'd have to live in the future for that." She grew quiet and thought about it. She did want a lot of kids. "Would you travel to my time with me, Nicholas?"

"We do not even know if you can get back—"

"But if we find a way, would you come with me?"

"Aye... if you left, but living among millions of people does not sound suitable for happiness and raising children... Let us see what Walter says, aye?"

She nodded against him. She didn't want to leave him, and it was insane! She didn't fall for men in five days! Maybe instead of just accepting everything that happened, she should fight a little. She had no right to ask a fifteenth century knight to step into the future with her. How would he ever grow accustomed to the bright lights, the quick pace, the sometimes rude people one met on a normal day? What if he killed someone and went to prison for the rest of his life? Prison in her time was probably better than prison in his, but it was still prison.

They remained quiet for the remainder of the trip, but the silence was becoming familiar and comforting. They leaned into each other, listening to the other's breathing.

They reached Walter's house after noon. Now, in the daylight, Kes fell in love with the house. It was much bigger than she thought and covered in ivy and other flowering vines. It was at least four stories high with huge windows, their shutters thrown open.

Kes blinked, looking up. Was...was that a bird that just flew out of one of the windows?

"Come. We will talk inside." Old Walter led them indoors.

This time, they followed him into a large, well-lit hall and were invited to sit at a long trestle table. Ale and black bread with jam were served by a man just a bit younger than Old Walter. His name was Jonathan, and there were two middle-aged women called Edith and Margery.

Kes looked at the large bowl of bread set before them and ate, and the smaller bowls of jams. Not exactly a healthy afternoon snack, but she went with it.

"How is the king this fine day?" Walter asked.

"He is well. Have you given any further thought to what you told us last eve?" Nicholas asked. "It all sounded very odd."

Walter smiled at him and then flicked his gaze to Kes. "It is very odd, is it not, Miss…ehm, Locksley?"

Her blood drained from her face. She nodded. It was all she could manage as fear overwhelmed her. Why did he say Locksley as if he knew it wasn't her real name? Her gaze flicked to Nicholas. He was watching them both.

"Are you a native to this time, Walter?" she asked him, tired of playing these silly games.

"What do you mean?" he asked in all innocence.

"How do you come by all these artifacts? Do you acquire them yourself?"

His smile deepened. "Of course not. I get them from the same sort of men whom you have secured."

"Secured?" she echoed then looked at Nicholas when he spoke.

"Have you found someone already?"

"Aye, and I heard from him just before you arrived. He—"

"How?" Nicholas asked. "How did you hear from him so quickly? Is he right in the village?"

"My lord, 'tis better if—"

"Walter," Kes interrupted, "please answer the earl's question."

"Very well. He is a frequent *traveler*."

"What kind of traveler, Walter?" Nicholas demanded.

"A time traveler, my lord."

Kes felt relief like a flood wash over her. Nicholas didn't look happy. In fact, he looked ill.

"My lord," Walter said to him, "I trust now that you care for a traveler, you will say nothing."

"I'm not a traveler, Walter," Kes told him. "I was brought here against my will and dropped into the middle of a battlefield!"

"I see," said the old merchant. "From when?"

"The twenty-first century."

Walter gave her a pitying look. "This must be extremely difficult."

She nodded. "It is." Her gaze found Nicholas rubbing his hands down his face. "But the earl has made it quite nice."

Walter looked at Nicholas and then at her. "Are you prepared to go back?"

"Yes," she said with the slightest hesitation.

"All right. Here is what we know so far. The brooch is in the hands of Arthur's knights in another realm, as I had thought. They are searching for him, waiting for his return. Some say the brooch was crafted by Morgan Le Fey or even Viviane of the Lake to guide her to Arthur, her only love. 'Tis rumored that both sisters loved him, so we do not know who crafted the pin. 'Tis also rumored that Arthur cast his own spell on the brooch, using it to show folks the path toward true love. After being burned several times while it hung from a *witch's* cloak, the brooch—"

"It was charred and blackened," Kes told him on the barest of breaths, realizing how many people had been burned as witches.

"The nine sisters decided something must be done, but the brooch could not be destroyed. They cast further spells around it so that the instant it was used it would return to the hands of the Round Table knights."

"This is getting crazier as we go," Kes mumbled. "Those people aren't even real."

Walter shrugged his shoulders. "The saying goes that sometimes there is truth in legend."

"I haven't heard that saying," she told him. This didn't sound right. She wasn't into magic and sorcery. Sure, it took some kind of magic to bring her back, but all this Lady of the Lake nonsense was too wild—even for her.

There was another answer. What if whatever she was experiencing *now* wasn't real? What if she hadn't traveled back in time but was lying on a hospital bed somewhere in a coma, fantasizing about this dark knight?

She settled her gaze on Nicholas. What if he wasn't real?

Panic seized her. She wanted him to be real. How would she ever know? What if she recovered from whatever had put her in that hospital bed, and opened her eyes and that was it? He was gone forever? No! Her knees felt weak. She reached her arm out to him.

Nicholas.

He came quickly to her side. "What is it?"

"Are you real?"

Why did it feel like it mattered more than life or death? "If he isn't real, let me wake up now," she prayed out loud.

"Kestrel." Nicholas closed his fingers around her arms. "Look at me! I am real."

"How do you know?"

"Miss Locksley, he is real," said Old Walter. "As real as everyone in your day, say... a month ago."

He's real. How could this be happening? How could she be falling for a man who could be dead soon when he returns to the battlefield?

She felt like a fool for reaching for him like some needy child. She realized she liked him close because it was the only time she felt safe.

"Forgive my outburst," she asked them. "I don't know what came over me. I think this has really been too much."

"Of course," Walter assured.

Nicholas stared into her eyes. He wasn't buying it. He knew there was more. How could she tell him she didn't want to begin something with him that would end if she could get home—or woke up.

She eyed Walter. "How well do you know this traveler? Or about traveling?"

"Well enough."

"What are the chances of going back to my time and not three hundred years too far? I don't think the twenty-fourth century would be to my liking if what's happened so far is any indication."

"Ah, but you were looking for a brooch, my dear. Not a way home."

"Are you saying there are other ways home?" she asked.

"There could be, but we haven't been looking!" Walter threw up his hands. "All right. Well, I will let him know to stay away from the other realm, for now."

"Why did I even get the brooch in the first place?" Kes asked. "What do I have to do with Arthur Pendragon?"

"Well," Walter looker her over. "You are obviously not King Arthur, but you must have Pendragon blood in you."

"My great-great-great-aunt was a Pendridge."

"Ah!" Walter smiled. "Pendridge / Pendragon. Same thing."

Kes' mouth fell open. "Are you telling me that my distant aunt was a Pendragon?"

"If there is an aunt," Walter said.

"But why did she send the brooch to me?"

"We do not know who wanted you to have the brooch. Unfortunately, as I understand it, the brooch is not functioning properly, hence your landing in the middle of a battlefield."

"So she may not return to the day she left. Or to the same century," Nicholas pointed out. "There is no guarantee."

"If our friend can even procure it, but aye, that is correct," Walter admitted.

"That is not good enough," Nicholas told her. "If you are going back for your father and your friends, I will not have you lost and never returned."

"Yeah, I wouldn't like that either," she agreed. "There's a lot to think about."

"Aye," he nodded, looking a little...relieved? "We should go."

She nodded and then called back to Walter when he asked her what he should tell his contact.

"Tell him to look for other more foolproof ways to get me home."

Nicholas stopped and turned to her. "Kestrel." Her name came on a deep, throaty groan.

"Yes?" She closed her eyes, unable to stop her heart from banging and her entire body from going stiff. She knew he was going to say something that he didn't want to say. She could see it written clearly in his storm-filled gaze, shaping his lips, shortening his breath.

"I think Walter's friend might just find a way to take you home and..." He shifted his body and held his hands, as if in prayer, to his nose and mouth. "...I return to duty in a little more than a sennight. I do not want to be pining over you then, so I will say farewell to you now. Walter!" He turned to the old merchant. "May she stay here?"

Walter nodded.

"What?" Kestrel hadn't anticipated this. She thought he was going to tell her he was hurt that she was so desperate to go home. She would have told him she was a little less desperate than she had been the day before. But this? "That's it, then? I don't even get to say goodbye to Elia or any of my friends?"

"Friends?"

"Yes, Cook, Claire the laundress, Hilde and Caitlyn, the girls from the kitchen." She tightened her lips. "You're just like the others."

"No. I am not," he said with an angry thread in his voice. "Am I wrong for not wanting to get to know you more, hold you more..." He paused while Walter left the room. "Kiss you more, so that I can watch you *choose* to leave?" He shook his head. "No. You will do well here. You are away from the king, and from me. Walter will get you home. I cannot continue on with you knowing how badly you want to leave. Understanding why you

138

want to go does not help. I am beginning to feel too much for you. I cannot go into battle with a such a heavy heart."

Kes couldn't be angry with him. He was right. She didn't want to cry, but her eyes stung, and her vision blurred with tears.

"I'm selfish, Nicholas. I don't want you to go."

"I do not want you to go either," he told her.

Did she have a future with him? Would she give up her past for him?

He took her hand and brought it to his lips. He kissed her knuckles and closed his eyes.

She wanted to kiss him, to feel his arms around her. She did nothing and said nothing as he left Walter's house and her life.

# Chapter Fifteen

KES STARED AT the beautiful bronze vase in her hands. It was of the Pala Dynasty, eighth to twelfth century. The workmanship was exquisite. It looked brand new because when it was taken, it was. There were other treasures, like Mycenaean pottery, and anthropomorphic iron figurines from the Mesopotamian era. There was so much, she could stay here for another year or two to catalogue everything.

This was her dream come to life. History, telling its stories of the people who lived in it. It was more than any historian or archeologist could ever hope for. She wished her father were here to see it.

And with that, came thoughts of home, and with that, came thoughts of Nicholas.

She thought he'd come back. It had been three days and he hadn't returned. At first, it broke her heart. It still did. She missed him but he was doing the right thing.

He'd been kind enough to send over her dresses so she could change clothes.

It still shocked her that she had grown attached to him so quickly. But why not? He was there for here during a traumatic experience in her life. He was thoughtful and kind toward her. It shouldn't surprise her that she wanted to be with him. She had to stop. They weren't meant to be together. What did a stupid brooch know?

According to Walter's contact, Mr. Roldan Simeon, a traveler who, after being cursed by an old hag after he'd tried to rob her in the woods, learned to use the curse to his advantage. He flitted around time snatching this piece or that and delivering it to his traders.

"I have many traders spread all throughout time," Mr. Simeon told her that afternoon in Walter's sitting room. "Your century gives me the most business." His eyes were hooded and veiled by long, black lashes. She couldn't tell if they were dark blue or brown in the candlelit room. He looked to be around her father's age with long jet black hair tied into a ponytail behind his head and a black beard.

"Time travel isn't something natural, allowed to us by the Omnipresent One Himself. Imagine the upheaval we would cause."

"What about you?" Kes asked. "Don't you change time?"

"No. I cannot leave one place or appear in another with any living thing or any object that would alter time, like a phone…or a magic brooch."

She looked away. So, he couldn't help her. But really, was she so disappointed?

"I can carry some goods but not people or animals or plants. I steal objects. I can be in and out of a place in a moment." He snapped his fingers and disappeared.

Kes gasped and blinked, then turned when she heard his voice behind her chair.

"For you." He handed her a hammered gold cuff encrusted with a tiger's eye scarab. "From Cleopatra. Don't worry. She will never miss it."

Kestrel looked at the bracelet. You just stole this?"

He nodded and grinned. "Easy as…what is it you more modern folks say? Cake?"

"Pie. Take it back. I don't want you stealing for me."

"Oh, but asking me to steal the brooch is different?"

"It's not stealing if you're going to give it right back. Plus I signed for it so it's technically mine."

"True," Mr. Simeon agreed with a short laugh.

"Please take the bracelet back to Cleopatra."

He took it back and disappeared.

He reappeared in front of her a few moments later. "I like this view better." He hooked his mouth into a friendly half-smile perhaps meant to lure her. She wasn't interested. Even if she wasn't mourning her loss of Nicholas, and even if almost all the guys she'd dated cheated, she wouldn't be interested in Simeon because he was her father's age and because he tried to rob an old woman. He didn't know she was a witch or whatever she was. He did it because he was a piece of crap.

"Mr. Simeon, what else can you tell me about me getting back home? If you're here for any other reason, I will tell the earl and he can withdraw his payment."

"Eh, no." His smile faded. "No other reason. Now, where were we? Ah, yes, your brooch. I can tell you what I know about it. 'Tis protected by the impenetrable force of Sir Gawaine and the other brothers of the table. Even if there was some way to get my hands on it, and believe me I would love to, they will know someone used it, and once they figure out it was you, well, I don't know what they would do. Do you still wish me to learn more?"

Kes certainly didn't want to stay here without Nicholas in her life. He'd said he cared and then dropped her as if she had the plague.

"Yes, and Mr. Simeon, a question please before you go."

"Go on," he said, forgetting her in exchange for his finger-nails.

"Why me? What do I have to do with King Arthur? Why did the brooch come to me?"

"That's three questions."

"Should I pick one?" she said with irritation staining her voice.

"It doesn't matter. The answer will be the same for all. I don't know why the brooch went to you. There may be no reason at all. But I do know the knights will find out it was you, and you will no doubt tell them it was me who stole the brooch. I will find you another way." His smile was riddled with deceit. "I like a challenge. But there is a rule. You must go back exactly as you came. Nothing new in your hair or on your fingernails, else it will not bring you to the time you left."

She nodded and he left. She sat alone in the solar for a little while wishing Nicholas was here. But he wasn't. He stayed away and she grew angrier with him each day.

The next afternoon, Elia came for a visit, escorted by one of Nicholas' soldiers. She brought news of Cook's gratitude to her for a cartload filled with vegetables, spices, and some beef all the way from Scotland. All Kes' friends were well and wished her well.

"Nicholas has been unbearable." Elia let her know. "Walking around growling at everyone like a wounded bear. Even the king has left him alone."

"It was his choice to go."

"Because you are choosing to go, Kes. Why should he risk his heart and his life when he must return to battle?"

Kes lifted her hands to her mouth, but she still gasped. "Oh! He is returning to that horror." She returned to a seat by the hearth. "I had put it out of my mind."

"'Tis always difficult to see him leave," Elia agreed.

"I can't stay here, Elia," Kes told her. "What would I do here?"

The pretty head maid smiled softly. "Hopefully, raise his children. From what I have seen, 'tis a difficult endeavor."

Kes groaned. Oh, children. There weren't any contraceptives back here. Nothing like morphine or whatever they give to delivering moms. "How do they do it?"

"I do not know how they do it anywhere else, but here, all the women come together as a family and help her deliver."

"That sounds nice. Still painful though," Kes sighed. "And my father—he probably thinks I'm dead or kidnapped. I'm all he had left, Elia. I don't think he would want to go on anymore."

"I'm sure he is stronger than you think."

"He's already lost my mother." Kes hugged herself and stared into the flames of the hearth. "I miss him so much."

"Why do you not tell me about him?" Elia said and sat in the chair opposite her. "It will help you remember him."

"I don't want to remember him," Kes cried. "I want to see him."

"There now, I'm sure you will. He sounds like a very strong, determined man to raise a daughter on his own."

"He was. He is." Kes let her know. "And patient."

"Ah, a most important trait to possess."

"Yes," Kes agreed. She liked Elia. They got along well from the very beginning. "He is quite handsome, too, Elia. Perhaps a few years older than you."

Kes told Elia about her father and her roommates. She didn't remember much of her mother, just the memories her father had built for her over the years. She had learned to love those memories as they were all she had. Many times though, Elia had made her feel like a daughter.

"I will miss you, Elia."

The maid's hazel eyes filled with tears. "And I will miss you, Kes."

They both smiled and wiped their eyes.

"Now, tell me. How badly is he suffering?"

Elia threw herself back into her chair and gave Kes an exhausted look. "He has never been this bad. I found a place for Reg and his family to live and they have been moving their things out. All the coming and going is driving him mad. He is somber and brooding all the time. The servants tell me he is awake all night walking the outer walls. I must tell you, Kes. I have never known him to be so affected by anyone."

"He will forget me."

Elia gave her a hurtful look. "I think he feels more for you than he will admit."

Kes left her chair and wrung her hands together. "I wish he hadn't left. They always leave, Elia. It seems time doesn't change anything."

"How is he supposed to fight and stay alive if losing you is fresh on his mind?"

Kes' shoulders sagged. How could she blame Nicholas for staying away, or Elia for understanding why he did?

Well, she understood, too, and it was time she stopped acting like a selfish brat. She couldn't have Nicholas and then be done with him when it was time to go home.

She swallowed her tears and squared her shoulders. "I understand, Elia. Please tell him that. He's doing the right thing. I'm being selfish." She took her friend's hands and swallowed back her tears. "Don't tell him though that I miss him more than breath if I was suffocating."

Elia smiled at her and pulled her in for an embrace. "'Tis easy to see why he is mad over you, Kes." She withdrew, sniffed, and looped Kes arm through hers. "Look, 'tis a beautiful day. Let us take a walk outdoors. 'Tis stuffy in here."

Kes nodded. She could use some air. "I will tell you what Walter's friend told me about the brooch. And Elia," she told her on a soft breath, "he can disappear and reappear. I've seen it. He left and returned a minute or two later with a gold cuff he'd just stolen from Cleopatra!" She nearly squealed her softly spoken words.

Elia stopped and her mouth opened into an O. Then, a breath before she said, "Cleopatra? How? How can he do it?"

Kes told her about his curse and everything he told her about Sir Gawaine and the brooch, and about the Pendridge name meaning Pendragon.

"Do the knights think you or Nicholas is…"

"No. They're searching for their…" the thought of Mr. Green's company letterhead invaded her thoughts as if to drive the truth home. ISOAP. In Search Of Arthur Pendragon. "If they thought they'd found him, they would have acted upon it. Celebrate. Something." She shook her head. "I don't even know if I was supposed to *land* here. I think it was a mistake and that's why I appeared in the middle of a battlefield.

"Unless," Elia pointed out with a growing look of horror on her face, "the brooch is their way of eliminating an enemy and they sent you to that field to die."

"Elia," Kes said calmly. "It doesn't make any sense that Arthur's knights would be sending people to their deaths. No. They're looking for him. I may have Pendragon blood, so I may be a key."

"I hope you are correct. I would not want to fight Sir Gawaine."

Kes cast her a surprised look mixed with emotion. "Thank you."

Elia nodded.

"But you would lose." Kes smiled and then they both laughed.

After that, Walter had tea made for them and brought to his gardens, where the ladies sat under the sun.

"'Tis lovely here," Elia said, looking around.

"Yes, and there are even more treasures inside." Kes knew the fruit-bearing trees and the multitude of flowers spread out around her with shy butterflies pausing above them were beautiful, but the artifacts inside were priceless to her.

What if she didn't go back? What if she stayed here and catalogued Walter's pieces? She could learn to embroider, maybe have exercise classes for the girls, learn to play a new instrument, have children.

No more father, no more roommates, or phones, or traveling, credit cards, dentists. The list went on. She leaned back in her garden chair and sighed to the sun. These things were difficult to give up.

But why should she give up her life when Nicholas was going off to fight and could be killed?

"How long will he fight for York?" Kes asked.

"However long they take to win."

"And if they don't win?"

Elia's eyes opened wide and changed from golden to green. "You know, do you not?"

Kes nodded. Oh, she would burst if she didn't tell someone. "Richard will be defeated by Henry Tudor."

For a second or two, Elia's look of horror returned. And then it disappeared. "Mayhap 'twould be for the best," she whispered.

Kes wondered if Richard had any allies. Maybe Reg.

"Elia, you have to promise not to tell Nicholas. If he does something to change what will happen, it could change the entire future. Oh, I shouldn't have said anything—"

"I will not tell him, Kes. You have my word."

They left the gardens together and then parted after finding Elia's escort. They promised to see each other again before Kes left…if she left.

Kes didn't expect to see Nicholas at the door two hours later.

## CHAPTER SIXTEEN

HOW WAS IT possible that he could look better than an oasis at the end of a dry desert? There were circles under his eyes. He looked like he hadn't slept for days. But his eyes were alert, piercing and powerful on her when she greeted him.

"What are you doing here?" she asked him, stepping outside as he dismounted.

"Edward's daughter, Elizabeth, arrived this morning to visit the king," he told her, staring at her long enough to make her fidget.

"Oh," she said dreamily. "You look good."

He exhaled as if he'd been holding his breath for a long time, then smiled slightly. "So do you. We should take pictures later."

"Yes," she laughed softly. "So what does Elizabeth—oh, she's Elizabeth of York! Right."

He quirked his brow at her and nodded. "Aye. What is said of her in the future?"

Kes remembered that Elizabeth was Edward's daughter, sister to the two princes. Nicholas loved Edward and his children, including Elizabeth. "Historians believe she was very well loved by everyone who knew her."

He smiled more fully, looking genuinely pleased by her news.

"And it is said that she and Richard were lovers."

His smile faded. "Aye. It seems to be true."

"She will do well."

"Married to whom?"

"The victor of your war."

His smile deepened on her. "I do not want to know about anything but you," he told her on a raspy voice and came a little bit closer.

She held her breath. She missed him. She missed how he smelled and how he looked and how he moved. She wanted to tell him.

"Come back to the castle," he beckoned. "Richard will not find any interest in you now. He will be leaving with me to return to Nottingham. You may stay until you return to your time."

"But what about—"

"Forget everything else and just come back with me."

She remained quiet but she couldn't forget everything else. He'd been right to stay away. But he hadn't done it just because of Richard. He'd left her at Walter's and stayed away because he wanted to forget her.

"Does this mean you're no longer worried about getting to know me more or—?" She remembered where he'd gone with this originally. So did he apparently because he stared at her with a subtle smile that made her knees weak.

"Nothing has changed." His voice was low, like a rumble as he leaned in closer. "I still want to hold you and kiss you. Mayhap more now than before."

Her heart beat so frantically she was almost sure she would pass out if he kissed her.

He came close, but Mr. Simeon appeared. In fact, he appeared right beside her.

He didn't stay long. Kes estimated it took less than one second for the sharp blade of Nicholas' dagger to slice a thin line down the traveler's cheekbone, and then Simeon was gone.

"Nicholas, no!" Kes shouted and held out her arms to stop him. She looked around—and then she looked at the man she'd realized she was falling in love with a minute ago. He appeared horrified, wide-eyed. His hands were shaking.

"What kind of magic is at work here?" He looked around also, but his eyes were searching for witnesses, not his victim.

"He's—"

Mr. Simeon appeared again, holding a white cloth to his cheek. "You cut me," he said, sounding more mystified than angry.

"He didn't mean—"

"I meant it," Nicholas corrected her. "He is fortunate I did not kill him."

"Um, Nicholas," she turned her face away from Simeon and said on a whisper that grew louder as she spoke, "I would use caution. He can disappear and reappear behind you an instant later with an axe and bash your brains in."

"'Tis all right," Simeon told them, hearing her. "I wouldn't kill a man with such skill, especially one who is so generous with my payment."

"Ah," Nicholas frowned. "Walter hired you to help take her home."

The traveler nodded and wiped the blood from his wound. "I am Roldan Simeon, a colleague of Walter's. No one has cut me before."

"Sir Nicholas de Marre, Earl of Scarborough, Commander of the king's army."

"You are very quick, Commander."

"As are you," Nicholas allowed. "Now tell me what you are. A witch?"

He said the last word as if it were poison on his tongue.

"I'm not a witch, but I was cursed by one to travel through time for the remainder of my existence. To never settle down or enjoy relationships."

Nicholas shifted his gaze to her while Simeon spoke. She wanted to look away from the fear she saw in his eyes. Fear for her. And from the sadness that he was going to lose her to the future.

"You can move through time," Nicholas asked him.

"Yes. As I said, 'tis a curse. Thank you for your sympathy."

Nicholas ignored his jab. "Are you going to take her back?"

"You mean forward, don't you?" Simeon flashed him a toothy grin.

Still paying no attention to him, Nicholas gazed at her. "Am I too late? Is he taking you home, Kes?"

"He's trying," she told him and turned to Simeon. "Is there any news?"

"Yes," said the traveler, making her heart accelerate again. "As I suspected, the brooch is impossible to get. It has been returned to the Lady of the Lake. And as skilled and adept at thieving as I am, I'm afraid no one has ever gotten into Avalon who was not invited."

So, that was it then? She was never going home?

"As discussed," he continued, "I cannot take you. You need a conduit, an instrument like the brooch. Rest assured, I am searching for one."

"You have our thanks," Nicholas told him. "If you must speak to us again, we will be at Scarborough Castle. You will use every caution not to let anyone see you appear or disappear and think you a witch. If you are careless, I will not be. I will kill you before you can escape. Understand?"

"Maybe I should just stay here," Kes interceded on Simeon's behalf.

"No." Nicholas softened his tone when he took her hand. "Come back with me. A little bit of time spent with you is better than none."

She agreed. Was it a mistake?

"Well, I will see you both again…eh…with discretion. Right now, I have a lock to pick and a diamond necklace to steal." Simeon didn't wait for their reply but disappeared before their eyes.

"Nothing is safe with him," Kes shook her head looking at the empty space.

"There was no shimmer," Nicholas noted.

"No," she agreed and started back for the house to retrieve what few possessions she had. Mostly, her two dresses. "Do you think it's a good idea to go back to the castle?"

"Aye. 'Tis a good idea," he said as though he had no concerns whatsoever.

"Goodness," she smirked then laughed a little. "What exactly did Elia tell you?"

"She mentioned that you missed me, and something about suffocating. I cannot remember."

She gave his arm a little slap. He grabbed her wrist and pulled her in close.

"I feel the same way, Kestrel," he said against her lips, "'Tis as if I'm dying of thirst and there is no water for my parched throat."

He ran his fingers over her temple, her cheek. He looked into her eyes as if something vital to him was there. He kissed her, softly at first, breathing her in. As his kiss grew deeper, his arms closed around her.

Oh, if there was any magic at work here, it was his touch, his kiss, his embrace. She never wanted to leave him, and maybe she was never going to.

The brooch was gone. She didn't want to take a chance and use just any old vessel to get home. She might step into a nightmare. She was most likely going to live out the rest of her life here.

She broke away from his kiss, his steel embrace with just a gentle shove.

"What is it?" he asked.

"My father. My friends. The people I work with. I probably won't ever see them again."

He said nothing but looked down.

This wasn't his fault. She smiled and took his arm as they stepped inside Walter's house. "I'm glad you're here with me, Nicholas. You've eased the shock and drew my attention to you. You're the only thing that could keep me from going mad at all I've lost."

"After you mourn," he said in a low voice when they saw Walter coming down the corridor to greet them, "maybe you will find room in your heart for a new family."

Did he mean him and the children he wanted to give her? Or him and the people in the castle? Maybe it didn't matter.

"My lord," Old Walter greeted. "'Tis good to see you back so soon."

Soon? Kes thought. It had been days!

"Thank you, Walter. I will be seeing to Miss Locksley now."

"Of course, my lord," the old man said with a smile. "It was a pleasure having her stay here. She is welcome anytime. Anytime at all."

After she gathered her dresses, she set them all down again to hug Walter. "I'll come back and visit."

"I would enjoy that!" he exclaimed when she withdrew. "I will have a feast made in your honor!"

She laughed. "Who am I that I should be honored?"

The old merchant smiled looking at her. "A very dear friend to us all." He turned to Nicholas with a slight sigh. "She informed all the servants that they should have two or three *breaks* a day, where they could roam the grounds and do as they pleased—"

"Without damage, of course," she interrupted.

"Because they live here."

"Yes." She widened her smile on her new dear friend. "If they learn to rest and play here as well as work, they will love it here more." She turned to Nicholas, who was watching and listening, and smiling with them. "And if they love it here, they will give it their best care."

"She is wise, my lord." Old Walter put his arm around her shoulders and turned to Nicholas.

"Aye, Walter. She is many things."

When they were outside and alone, she took his hand as they walked. He looked down at their entwined fingers after a moment. "Did you want me to follow you?" When she shook her head, he looked at their hands again.

"I just want to hold your hand while we walk, Nicholas."

"I have seen some people do it," he admitted.

She laughed and swung their hands back and forth between them.

He pulled her closer as they reached the horses and coiled his arm around her neck. "You are changing things," he said.

He was right. She hadn't even thought of it that way. What was she doing? She wasn't Norma Rae, starting unions for better rights for workers. This was the middle ages! Things were supposed to be this way!

But...couldn't she just help make things a little better for people if she could? "Yeah, I'll let up on that a little."

"I will put you in charge of grievances." He smiled and helped her up into her saddle. "Temporarily, I mean."

She lowered her gaze to his lightning streaked eyes, his quirked lips. She made him happy again. He didn't have to say it. She could see the difference from when he first arrived all over his face. He tempted her to toss every hope of getting back to the future right out the window. "Nicholas," she said softly, meaningfully. "If the brooch is gone, so is my past." She swiped a tear away for her father. "I don't trust anything else to get me back home—unless there are a pair of ruby slippers around that I can click three times and go home, I'm staying."

He looked a little confused, probably about the slippers but looked off into the distance and nodded. What else could he do? Jump up and down with happiness that she would never see the people she loved again?

She watched him leap up into his saddle and turn to her. "What about these magical slippers? Where did you hear of them?"

Her smile returned. "They aren't real. They're from a book I read when I was a child."

"Tell me of it. I like listening to you."

Kes thought that was the nicest thing anyone ever said to her. She happily obliged and began telling him the story, and then broke out into song.

She was enjoying herself so much that she didn't realize Nicholas had stopped his horse and was watching her, grinning from ear to ear at her singing or the song. She didn't know which.

She told him the rest of the story and how she was sure some of the characters scared the crap out of little kids.

They took their time riding back. He seemed very interested and taken with the story. That was probably why he noticed the change in her mood at one point.

"What is it?" he asked.

"Just another song," she told him and looked forward at the road.

He rode a little closer. "What is it about this song that makes you sad?"

"Nothing, I—"

"Sing it for me," he requested.

She cut her gaze to him and doubted she could refuse him anything. She began to sing it and when she was finished, tears were streaming down her face.

He remained quiet while she wiped her eyes. She didn't mean cry over it. It was just a song about a rainbow but the yearning in the melody revealed Dorothy's desire to go home.

Kes knew what he thought. "Nicholas, please understand—"

"Kestrel," he said in a low voice, staying close by her. "I understand. Do not fret over what I may or may not be thinking. If you do not find a way home, you will have lost much. I understand the pain of that. Though I was only seven summers when my family was murdered, I had lost everything, too. Even after Edward took me in and treated me like his own son, I mourned."

Her tears started up again and flowed more freely.

After a moment of him shifting uneasily in his saddle, he pulled her into it with him. "I should have known you would do anything to get back into my lap. Look at you." His deep, luxuriant voice enveloped her and she smiled in spite of what she felt. He pretended to hold a phone and snap a photo of her. She posed on instinct alone.

"Should I have screamed for help to prove to you that I can resist your oafish charm?"

He laughed, looking stunned at her insult, and then he grew more serious, more sensual. "You cannot resist it. Oafish or not."

She leaned into his chest and closed her eyes. "It's you who can't resist me," she countered with playful sigh. "It was you who insisted I sing a song that was obviously making me sad. You knew it would make me cry and then you could have me where you wanted me."

"Woman, I can toss you back into your saddle as quickly as I dragged you out of it."

"No, you can't," she challenged. "I'm not moving." She swung her leg over the saddle and sat sideways on him. She turned her body and wrapped her arms around his waist and chest. He was as hard as armor, but there was only flesh beneath his léine. She pressed her face close to his chest and held on.

Instead of acting out his threat and pushing her away, he slowed down the horse and leaned in, closing his arms around her and resting his face in her hair.

"Do not move from me, Kestrel," he pleaded. "Stay just where you are. For you are mine. I will give you everything you have ever wanted if you will stay where you are."

"I'll stay," she breathed against him. Where else would she go? What other man in the fifteenth century might have done the unthinkable to her, knowing she had no family, no one else here? What other man in any century was like her knight?

"I want to stay where you are, Nicholas."

He loosened his hold and smoothed back her hair. "The last few days without you have been agonizing. I cannot remember what I did with my days before you." He slipped his fingers beneath her chin to tilt her face to his. "I don't know how I would live without you if you left. But I would figure out a way to live." He kissed her mouth softly. "I will do everything I can to help you find a way home, until or unless this becomes home for you."

She closed her eyes and parted her lips to receive him when his mouth covered hers. His tongue pushed through the barricade of her teeth and swept inside her, stroking and caressing, branding her like a hot iron.

She was his. Yes. This was what she wanted. To be swept off her feet by a knight. She wanted him and nothing else.

# CHAPTER SEVENTEEN

"**N**ICKY!"

Nicholas smiled and stopped on the wall, overlooking the village and the water beyond to wait for Elizabeth. He was glad she was here at Scarborough Castle. He missed her. He missed her father, her family…her brothers.

"Nicky, are you off to think and brood, or would you mind some company while your lovely Miss Locksley helps Cook prepare *berjes*."

"Burgers," he corrected gently and held out his arm to her. Although she'd grown to a woman of nineteen years, he would always see her as a pudgy-faced little girl with golden hair and inquisitive dark green eyes. She'd always been out of breath from running here or there and her cheeks were always red against her alabaster skin. In that, she had not changed.

"Is something on your mind, Lizzie?" he asked her as she took his arm.

"I received a letter from mother last night. I thought you should know. Henry Tudor has landed in Wales. He is amassing forces."

"How many men?" Nicholas asked. Heart pounding. Battle. It was what he lived to do and did well. His blood coursed quick through his veins.

"Mother says five thousand men."

"With our reinforcements in Nottingham and Leicester we

outnumber them."

She quirked her perfectly shaped brow at him. "You will remain loyal to Richard then?"

"Of course."

"He has lost many supporters."

"I know," Nicholas told her.

"He is fortunate to have you, Nicky."

Nicholas didn't want to tell her that Richard didn't *have* him. Let her think someone remained steadfast to the man she loved.

"Henry plans to hit hard and fast."

"You would use your mother's information against her?" Her large olive eyes grew rounder and filled with tears. "I cannot help that I care for the king, Nicky."

"I do not condemn your heart, Lizzie. I just want you to be happy."

"But Henry is my betrothed. He pledged himself to me when my father died." She swiped tears from her eyes. "I haven't seen him in quite some time. Two years actually. He was kind to me, but shy. I cannot help feeling like prized cattle awaiting the winner."

"I know, Lizzie."

He could imagine how difficult this was for her. She'd been around Richard often. The king was able to charm her and win her heart. She barely knew Henry. Now her fate was about to be decided. It was frightening being so out of control.

"Your life is difficult, Lizzie," he said, looking into her eyes. "But you are up to it. Aye?"

"Aye," she agreed with a smile. "So what are you going to do about Richard's enemy?"

"I have yet to decide," he lied. He wasn't about to tell her how he would be victorious in the battle at Bosworth Field. "And let us not tell Richard any of this news yet. Let me take care of it."

She nodded but tried to hide her disappointment over getting no answer by looking away.

Nicholas decided to drop the matter. She'd given him valuable information. Now the rest was up to him. He could spare time to those he loved.

"What do you think of Miss Locksley?"

She grew exuberant instantly. He felt her powerful intake of air against his side just before she moved away. "Oh, Nicky, I adore her! There's something so, I do not know, genuine about her. Do you know that since you brought her here yesterday, instead of learning to embroider with her teacher, she was finding ways of being helpful to the staff?"

He wasn't shocked by this behavior. Since her first arrival, she'd been doing things to help the servants. They loved her. They loved her more than the man who did little for them, if anything. Soon, maybe even now, she would have power here.

"She has also turned one of the storage rooms into an *exercise* room. We ladies are to strip down to our chemises and do what Kes does. Like touch her toes and jumping up and down while spreading your legs and clapping over your head. Kes says it helps keep us in *tip-top shape*."

"Tip-top shape, eh?"

"She is unlike anyone I have ever met," Elizabeth continued excitedly. "Where did you say you found her?"

"Outside of Bridlington. She'd been wandering around hurt and remembered little about who she was. I brought her here to convalesce."

"Dear Nicky, ever the knight, always stopping to help a poor soul."

"'Tis my duty."

She smiled and leaned her head on his arm. "Have Miss Locksley's memories returned since she's been here?"

"Some of them have," he answered as if it were all true.

"Is she wed or betrothed?"

"No."

The lady he considered his little sister smiled as if she'd just discovered some hidden truth. "That's good news for you. Is it not?"

"I had not—"

"Her eyes are...mesmerizing, like fathomless oceans." She looked toward the waves and smiled. "She is adored by many of the men and accepts hundreds of accolades a day over her eyes."

"Hmm, is that so?" Nicholas asked her, senses piqued, honed to fight anyone for her. "What are their names?

She laughed. "I'm not so foolish as to start a battle over a woman. I want peace above all else. Whether 'tis from Richard or Henry Tudor, makes no difference to me in the end. I will do what is expected of me and always carry the white rose for my father."

"As will I," he promised.

"Oh, the sun is moving across the sky so quickly." She pointed to the sky. "I promised Elia I would sit with her this afternoon and tell her about what it was like in the care of the Earl of Oxford this past year. The de Veres are very kind and thoughtful, and Richard still has their support. We shall speak more later. Aye, Nicky?"

"Aye," he agreed and watched her run off.

So, Henry was coming with his army of five thousand. Nicholas thought of all the passionate Yorkist lords who had turned their backs on the House of York because of Richard, and he cursed them and Richard. York needed them now.

He would fight for York. He had to.

He would return to Nottingham, but not for a few more days. He'd gather the rest of Richard's army in Leicester and send Henry running back to Brittany as Tudor had done after his failed attempt to usurp Richard two years ago.

Nicholas would discuss it with his men later. Right now, he found himself smiling as thoughts of Kestrel filled his head.

He'd been smiling since he'd returned to Scarborough Castle with her yesterday. She was back, back in his great hall, in his kitchen with Cook and the scullery maids, back in the laundress' and the seamstress' rooms.

He thought about her new *exercise room*. She was going to

have the women strip down to their chemises and jump up and down. The men were definitely going to have to stay away, else, who in blazes knew what would happen?

Why was he still smiling?

Now that she had settled it in her head that she was staying, she was determined to keep busy here. He was glad, but he wasn't as sure as she was about Mr. Simeon not finding another way. She said she wouldn't take it, wouldn't trust it. But what if after a month here, she decided she hated it? And Simeon found another way? Would she go then?

He hadn't wanted to open his heart to her. But he seemed to have no control over the matter. She made him happy.

He soon found himself returning indoors—to the kitchen to find her. He'd been away from her long enough since parting with her after breaking their fast. He'd done some practicing in the field with a dozen or so of the men, washed up and changed his clothes, and then spent some time with Richard going over what they would do about Tudor. Now, with this fresh news, they should speak again.

But not now. Now, he wanted to be with *her*.

He leaned against the doorway of the kitchen and watched Kestrel as she bent to the oven and removed a tray with a thick towel. There were what appeared to be rolls on the tray. They smelled wonderful. So did the flat circles of meat cooking in a pan over the fire. Cook used a spatula to flip the circles and set off an eruption of pops and sizzles from the pan.

Kestrel and Cook didn't say much to each other, but they were working well together, moving about the kitchen without getting in each other's way.

Nicholas was astounded, since Cook was a mean bastard who didn't like anyone in his kitchen.

Kestrel spotted him and smiled. "Oh, I'm glad you're here."

He liked her greeting. He—

"You can help us cut the bread." She used her knife to motion how he should cut the rolls, and then she proceeded to slice a large pickle into disks.

"Unfortunately, it was really hard and time-consuming crushing the beef in a mortar and pestle, but it's not a burger if it's just one big slab of meat, you know what I mean? We could only make six. We have no ketchup. But we used a variety of different pepper, ginger, wine and stock to cook the burgers and I think they're going to be good."

"The smell of them is making my mouth water," he told her. "Or mayhap 'tis you," he added as she passed him.

She tossed him a slow smile and then instructed Cook to deposit a small amount of shredded cheese onto the center of each patty.

"Bring the pan here, Cook," she directed a few moments later. Shockingly, Cook obeyed and held the pan in the thick towel while Kestrel lifted a patty of meat and rested it on the bottom half of a roll. She did the same five more times and then set about placing slices of onion and pickle on top of the bubbling cheese. She covered each with the top half of a roll and told them to dig in. They only had three left. One was for Elia, one for Elizabeth and an extra one for Nicholas if he wanted it.

They ate in the kitchen, gathering Elia and Lizzie to them. Nicholas picked up his roll in both hands and took the first bite. He thought his knees would give out at the pleasure in his mouth. Lizzie sliced hers in half and took a dainty bite, then another. She finished hers after Nicholas finished his. Elia and Cook were quiet, eyes closed after every bite.

"This is delicious," Elia complimented. "Can we have it again tomorrow?"

"The mixture of spices and stock we used work well," Cook told her with a rare smile.

Kestrel smiled and took another bite. "I'm surprised they came out this good. I wish there were potatoes to make French fries."

They all gave a her a confused look.

"Potatoes?" asked Cook.

"French fries?" asked Elizabeth. "Are you friends with the French?"

"They're not really French," Kestrel explained. "At least I don't think so, but I'm no culinary chef."

Nicholas took his second burger and cut a half for Lizzie. No one else wanted seconds, so he was free to eat the rest.

He watched her talk and laugh with the others. For a moment, he didn't think anything could be better than this. He was here with her and others he loved and cared for.

When they were done, he took Kestrel's hand and pulled her out of the kitchen.

"Come. I want to be alone with you," he said in a low voice, while entwining their fingers.

She smiled. "Dessert?"

"Aye." He stopped before they left the castle and pulled her into his arms. "Something decadent." He gave her a quick, passionate kiss then flung open the castle doors.

They hurried to the stable and saddled Nicholas' horse. They would ride together. They weren't going far. He knew of a secluded inlet about a mile west of the beach.

He was tired of there being someone around every single time he tried to speak to her. Scarborough Castle was crowded. Everyone meant well, but they all wanted time with Kestrel. He didn't blame them. She was spirited, more vivacious than most. She helped everyone with one thing or another. She had told him, even though he hadn't questioned her, that treating the people who worked so hard in his castle fairly would benefit him in the long run. But he believed Kes, as Elianora called her, liked when folks around her were content and happy, and treated fairly.

Nicholas thought he was fair, but she still had grievances. He didn't mind hearing them. If making others happy made her happy, he would see to it that whatever he was doing wrong, he corrected.

"Now I see why Elizabeth was so loved," she said softly,

leaning back against him.

He loved riding with her this way and tightened his arm around her waist.

"She is kind and thoughtful," she continued. "Nothing like I expected royalty to behave. Who raised her?"

"Her mother, three nursemaids…and me." He smiled remembering little Elizabeth following him everywhere.

"And you," she echoed with what sounded like a smile. "I thought as much."

"She was a pest. She cried if she saw me and I left her vision without her." He laughed and shook his head thinking of it. He'd put it out of his thoughts, as he'd put everyone out since Edward died.

But since meeting Kestrel, he felt the emotions he'd suppressed, unless he was on the battlefield, boiling to the surface. She made him want to speak to her of things no one else knew about him.

"Edward's wife, Elizabeth Woodville—who was, in fact, his true wife, despite what Richard had the judges believe—she did not like that the king had taken in his captain's son and his nurse and was raising the boy as his own." His voice grew deep with melancholy. "But Edward would not give me up. He gave me every advantage he gave his children and I used every one and became who I am, who I became for him, for my true father, and for myself.

"Once, when I was about ten and four and thought I knew all there was to know, I snuck out of the castle—we lived at Windsor at the time—to pay a visit to a certain pretty milkmaid, called Bridget…or Emily…" He paused, shook his head as if to get the names out of it, and continued. "She sought my attention and I intended to give it to her."

Kestrel turned and looked up at him. She lifted her brow and the corner of her lips beneath but remained silent and let him continue.

"Edward's daughter Lizzie was five summers old. She had

spotted me sneaking away and followed me. Unaware of her presence, I didn't know she'd taken a wrong turn and was lost."

"Oh, no, Nicholas," Kestrel uttered.

"We did not find her for two days. Her mother did not sleep but wept every day. Her father searched for her. I was allowed to go with him. I thought it might have been me she was after, so we went in the direction of the milkmaid's house. We branched out in every direction. 'Twas I who found her. She had fallen into a ditch and was crying when I came upon her. She never wanted to be out of my sight again after that."

"You do give off a certain feeling of safety," Kestrel told him, then looked around.

"What are you doing?" he asked.

"Making sure Elizabeth isn't following you again. Where are we going anyway?"

"Just around that bend and you will see," he told her.

They rode a little farther and when they rounded the bend, he felt her gasp at the sight of the waterfall just off to the left. It wasn't anything very high or leading into the ocean. It was more like a secluded pool, almost as blue-green of Kestrel's eyes, and surrounded by trees and brush and blooming vines.

"Nicholas, this place is…"

"I know." He hadn't been here in years.

"Have you brought many girls here?"

He shook his head. All at once, he wanted to tell her everything about himself. "None. I had no time for courting. There were never-ending battles to be won. Edward and Elizabeth had had more children, so when I came home, I spent much of my time with them. What was the point in losing my heart to someone when I had to leave again so soon?"

She nodded, looking worried. "You're leaving in a few days,"

"Aye."

"I will miss you," she told him then sat up when he did.

He swung his long leg over her and dismounted close to a huge basking rock.

He squinted his eyes and then held up his arms to her. "Feel like going for a swim, love?"

Love?

# Chapter Eighteen

K ESTREL LOOKED AROUND at the lake surrounded by rocks and trees. Water dropped in a frothy white column emptying into the misty basin from a cliff bathed in sunlight. A family of falcons flew around it, soaking in the spray.

Only a man like Nicholas would know of a place like this. Only he would thrill her just by being with her. No other man would do. But she couldn't be in love with him in less than a fortnight. Could she? She'd sworn off men, of which, he was one. Sooner or later, the jerk side of him would rear its ugly head.

Still, if she was staying, and it seemed as if she was, she didn't want him to leave her. Needing him for safety wasn't the only reason she'd consider staying with him.

She watched him, drenched in sunlight, begin to strip down to his bare and very fine ass. She didn't have time to admire his long, shapely legs or the scars lacing the masculine flare of his shoulders. He bore scars everywhere, but before she could begin to take them all in, he dove from the basking rock into the water. Should she follow? Naked? Sex would complicate things. And she didn't want them to be complicated.

She walked to the edge and smiled at him wading in the blue water. She began to undress. She knew she didn't have some voluptuous body with which to bewitch him. She was thin and rather "stickish". She could have saved for some breast surgery, but she figured a guy should love her for who she was—a woman comfortable with herself. Not because of her boobs.

She pulled off her overdress, and then her slippers while he waded in a small circle, eyeing her beneath the shadow of his brow when he came around again.

She stepped out of her chemise and stood on the basking rock in her bra and matching panties.

He looked surprised and very happy at the sight of her in her underwear. She didn't think the lace would last much longer. It wasn't meant to be washed every night. But the pair was all she had.

Today, it would serve as a swimsuit.

She dove into the glittering water and swam to him when she came up.

"What is this?" He slipped his wet finger under the shoulder strap of her bra. He seemed mesmerized by the elastic.

"It's called a bra. It supports my boobs."

He looked into her eyes and smiled. "Your boobs?"

She nodded, cupped them both, and then swam away. He swam after her and caught her by the foot.

Laughing, she let him pull her close in his arms. His gaze was warm and his smile, sensual. He didn't say anything, he just looked into her eyes and dipped his head to cover her mouth with his.

His lips ravished her with mastery and hunger, claiming every inch of her mouth with subtle curiosity. He didn't try to grab her breasts or squeeze her ass like so many others—but he wasn't like any of the others.

That didn't mean she should let herself succumb to his raw sensuality and passionate kiss.

His arms closed tighter around her as his kiss deepened, becoming more needful. His mouth broke away and he slipped one hand behind her head, cupping her neck with his long, broad fingers. He tilted her head back, spilling her liquid locks over his hand, and exposing her throat to his ravaging mouth.

She ran her palms over the sleek muscles in his arms. He felt like solid rock, yet he molded to her like a caress.

He kissed the column of her neck and then flicked his tongue and teeth against her pulse.

Her nipples hadn't been this tight and hard in her life. She thought he must be able to feel them pressed so closely to him.

She could easily lift her legs and wrap them around his hips. He was big and strong. He could support her. She wanted to. She wanted to feel his hardness against her. She wanted to pillage him a little, too.

But she didn't. This wasn't her time, where people *hooked up* and it didn't mean anything. If Nicholas got her pregnant and then died in battle, where would she go? What would she do? Her father wasn't here to help. Neither were her friends. She had to try to keep a clear head.

Thankfully, he wasn't trying to pull her out of her panties—though the thought of it made her heart accelerate. She was able to break away without a fight from him.

If he'd given her a fight, she would have left. Finding a place to live in the fifteenth century wouldn't be as hard without a baby.

"Nicholas," she said with a worried frown. "I don't want us to have sex."

"Ever?" he asked with a disheartened look of his own. "Or yet?"

"Yet," she reassured, even as his disappointment reassured her that her wishes would be granted.

Now! she wanted to beg.

He nodded and began to swim away, then sank when she leaped on his back. She squealed with laughter when he rose up, lifted her in his arms, and flung her into the small waves.

She came back up laughing and swiped back her hair. "Let's swim to the falls."

He was up for it. She didn't doubt he would be. There didn't seem to be much that frightened him.

When they grew near, Nicholas said something, but she

couldn't hear him over the water crashing into the basin. They swam into the frothy mist and kissed some more.

"You are beautiful to me, Kestrel," he whispered with his mouth pressed to her ear.

"And you are beautiful to me, Nicholas," she answered, but she wasn't sure he heard. He took her hand and pulled her away.

They swam back to the rocks and Kes heaved herself up first. Nicholas followed and disappeared behind a bush to pull on his breeches.

She was glad for the bright sun to warm her almost naked body. She might try to get a—he reappeared, tying the laces over his abdomen and seemed to take up all the space, all the air.

Shading her eyes with her hand, she couldn't help but traverse his tall, strong physique from foot to crown.

She'd known he was cut from stone when she'd touched him but seeing him was a feast for her eyes. His long chiseled torso glistened with drops of water dripping from the hair slicked away from his face. Droplets fell from his sparse beard to his hard belly, where a thin rivulet flowed beneath his breeches.

She wanted to fan herself.

His mouth quirked into a scandalous smile when he saw her staring at him. She felt his gaze rove over her lounging on rocks in her bra and panties. His smoky gray eyes were almost chilling as they pierced hers. She lowered her lids to break the power they had over her.

In her century, they would have likely acted on their desire by now and been intimate. Many other guys would have tugged the barrier of her panties and tried to get inside. But not him. He'd stopped when she asked him to stop—though it wasn't what she wanted to do. It was what she *had* to do.

But, oh, to kiss those wet muscles…

"Do you want your kirtle?" he asked, breaking his spell.

She shook her head. "I thought I would work on my tan."

He chuckled lightly. "What?"

When she sat up and explained, he looked just as perplexed.

Her heart felt as if it had burst and flown off into all directions when he sat down next to her. She didn't know how to get it back—or if she even wanted it back.

"I forgot how much I missed this place," he said, looking around.

He said he had come here with Edward's family. Did he want to talk about them? He brought up Henry Tudor instead.

"So you are definitely going back to fight?"

"Aye," he told her softly and lay back on the rock. "I must."

She looked down at him strewn across the rock. She swallowed and fought the visions in her head of leaning down and kissing him. "Why must you?" she pressed instead.

He opened his eyes and looked at her staring at him. "What have your history books told you? Do I die? Is that why you do not want me to go?"

"I don't know what happens to you, Nicholas. You aren't mentioned that I can remember, but then again, I didn't study this period in depth."

He looked so insulted she almost felt sorry for him. But this was serious business.

"You would rather me tell you that you died in battle?"

"'Tis a good way to die."

She let out a sigh and collapsed beside him, close beside him, like half her body was on top of his. She pressed her cheek to his chest.

"I don't want you to die, Nicholas," she breathed against him. "Richard is the last of the House of York. You are fighting for him if you are fighting for York. If you no longer trust or value his authority, then you should not possibly give your life for him."

He was quiet while birds called out to one another around the echoing white noise of the waterfall. Then he said, "I never thought to go against the House of York. The men of my family have fought for it for centuries. How can I be the one who turns?"

"And if he had something to do with the death of the princes?" she asked. "How can you be the one who doesn't?"

She knew what she was doing. Changing history. She didn't care. Not when it came to Nicholas. She didn't want to lose him. He was all she had.

"Does he win or lose, Kestrel?"

She sat up. "You said you wouldn't ask."

He sat up next. "I will know if I live or die by if Richard wins or loses."

He gave her the slightest of smiles, but she was sure he wasn't happy about what she was asking him to do.

She hadn't planned on it, well, not until Mr. Simeon had advised her that the brooch was impossible to steal and could not be transported.

She hadn't wanted Nicholas to return to fighting when she'd had hope of going home. Now it was worse. The two sides were about to meet at the Battle of Bosworth Field, the famous battle that ended the War of the Roses.

"He dies," she told him on a whisper. Would she be punished for telling? Did she just eliminate her entire family line or someone else's?

"I see," he said, his voice sounding like a hollow drum. "So 'tis the end of the House of York."

"No, Nicholas," she corrected gently. "There is Elizabeth."

"She doesn't want to marry Henry."

"He will make her happy." She might as well tell him everything.

"And me," he said, breaking through her thoughts. "I die then."

She shook her head and ran her fingertips across his jaw. "No. Maybe you don't fight for him and that's why he loses."

They sat together, silent for the most part. Kes knew what she was asking Nicholas to do was difficult, seemingly impossible, but she believed it was the only way he would stay alive. Because as he said, if Richard died, and Nicholas remained loyal to him, Nicholas would have to be dead also.

She wouldn't think on it. That's what she told herself. But she couldn't help it. Especially since he was being so quiet. "What is it?" she asked.

"Nothing. We should be going."

She was sorry she'd upset him. They were leaving and soon it would be the end of another day with him home. Was that it? Would he not even talk about it with her?

Before, he had no one who was waiting at him for him...well, not including Elia. But now he had a woman who—who what? Was in love with him?

Had she let her feelings go so wild and rebellious over him that she hadn't guarded herself? That was the worst thing. Not guarding against something you should have seen all along.

She should tell him. She would. Later. She would ask him to take a walk with her and she would tell him exactly how she felt. She thought he felt the same. She hoped he did.

"Nicholas?" she asked, peering through the tree line. "Who is that?"

He stared at the figure approaching. He grew a bit closer and they both said the name at the same time. "Simeon."

"Clever to land in the trees where no one will see," Kes remarked.

Nicholas remained silent, watching the traveler coming closer.

"Mr. Simeon," Kes greeted. "You are unexpected."

"And unwelcome I am sure."

Kes smiled. He wasn't so bad once she got to know him a little better. "Not at all."

"I didn't want to take the chance of being seen appearing in the castle. I have news. I think we should—"

"Tell it," Nicholas demanded.

Kes was sure the time traveler had met many fearsome men and women in the times and places he'd been, so it was surprising that he obeyed without question. "I had hoped to gain some insight on why the knights gave you the brooch."

Kes' heart thundered in her chest. "It was my great-great—"

"No, it wasn't. That's what they tell you to make you come get the brooch."

"But why me?"

"I visited Camelot and found the knights discussing you."

"Camelot is real?" she breathed.

Simeon sighed and looked around. "It's not what you would consider real. It's on a different realm."

Before she had a chance to cast him a look of confusion, he continued.

"They didn't simply decide to give you the brooch. It had been fashioned for Arthur to wear as a sort of beacon to help Morgan Le Fey and the others find him when he left Avalon. Seems he left with more powers than he first had, but that is another story. He didn't want to be found so he tossed the brooch away with an enchantment of his own. He overrode the first spell under his, the brooch was to be a beacon for *others* to find love."

To find love? Kes looked at Nicholas, who was looking at her.

"But the thing is old and worn down and has been damaged by fire. Because of this, it malfunctions. Sir Kay was quite upset to learn that you landed in the middle—"

"—of a battle. Sir Kay?" Kestrel swallowed then smiled. Was this all a dream?

"Yes. He's quite the swordsmen," Mr. Simeon said and turned to look at Nicholas. "I doubt even you could beat him if he came here."

Nicholas didn't look ruffled when he asked, "Why would he come here?"

"Because Miss Locksley has told you things about the future that you should not know."

"How do they know what I've told him?"

"They are monitoring you," Simeon told her. "They must. It's their fault you are here. They're responsible if you disrupt time. They will have to send you back or the gap they left in your time will grow"

"Are they going to come here?" Kes asked, instinctively moving closer to Nicholas.

"I don't know. I didn't know it was you they were speaking of for a long time. I wasn't listening to much of what they were saying as I thought it pertained to someone else. But it was you."

"What do you mean?" she asked.

"Perhaps we can speak alone?"

"No," Nicholas refused. "We will have no secrets between us."

"You my speak freely, Mr. Simeon," Kes assured him, not having any idea what he was about to say.

"Very well," he gave in. "They called you Kestrel Lancaster."

"What?" Nicholas demanded.

Kes' heart felt as if it were giving out.

"'Tis a mistake!" Nicholas boomed. "She's no more a Lancaster than I am."

The dream just turned into a nightmare.

"Sir Lucan said they checked, and double checked that they had the right person. Miss Kestrel Lancaster. They found you in New York in twenty nineteen. That is you."

She could feel Nicholas' eyes on her, but she didn't look at him. She couldn't.

"Kestrel?" Nicholas asked.

"Yes?"

"Is it true?"

She couldn't lie. Not anymore. Somehow, he would find out the truth and she would look worse.

"Are you a Lancaster?"

"Yes."

# CHAPTER NINETEEN

NICHOLAS STOOD BY the window of his solar the next afternoon and looked outside. The sun shrank away from the thick, charcoal clouds that looked like gloom come to life. Lightning lit up the sky and made the hair on his neck stand up. Thunder shook the castle walls reminding those inside how meager their lives were.

He grabbed his sword and left the solar. He wanted to be out there, in the force of nature, feeling its power coursing through him. He felt the rage and white-hot anger of betrayal. He needed a way to release it before it overcame him.

He headed for the doors above stairs. The doors that led to the wall and the bridge, and ultimately, the coastal village.

He flung open the door and walked out into the rain like a storm unto himself—one even more dangerous than the one he was stepping into.

She'd betrayed him. All this time…all this time knowing how he felt about them. His mortal enemies!

She'd tried to speak to him. She'd even had Elia and Elizabeth try to speak to him for her, but he wasn't interested. She'd lied to him about something so important. She was his enemy. She tried to say she was afraid to tell him the truth, but no. She didn't tell him because she came here with a purpose—to convince him not to fight for Richard. Well, he would not only fight, he'd win for the House of York and then he would throw Kestrel Lancaster out.

He strode to one of the practice fields, his hair dripping around his face from the pouring rain, his boots sinking into the soggy earth.

He wanted to fight. He might ride out to battle a few days early. For now, swinging at a post would help.

He wasted no time smashing his blade into the hard red oak post. How could he have allowed himself to fall for her? She seemed so innocent of it all. Who did she answer to? Or was it more complicated than that? Had Richard won the battle at Bosworth Field and the Lancasters from the future sent Kestrel here to change history?

He was tired of these maddening thoughts of time travel and being able to change history. It wasn't right. And what about King Arthur's knights? Would Sir Gawaine come here and try to take her back to her century?

Just thinking of it made him feel like he'd accepted the fact that he'd gone quite mad. King Arthur? Camelot? Magic? Gah! All of it was exasperating.

He smashed his blade into the hard wood post from the right, the left, from above and below. He struck hard and fast, swinging, jabbing, ramming. He fought with savage desperation. He imagined Gawaine or Lucan in front of him, trying to take her. He cut deep into the oak, his blade slicing through. It took him some effort to yank his sword out of the wood, but he did so with a deep grunt.

She was a Lancaster. They killed his family. And now he had fallen in love with one.

He shook his head and water flew outward. He couldn't see from the rain falling constantly into his eyes, but he hit the post with every strike.

He fought against the hard wood for another hour and finally collapsed against it.

Her plan had almost worked. He'd considered abandoning Richard when Henry arrived.

He wanted to hate her. She'd lied. She'd let him fall for her, his enemy. Did she laugh behind his back at what a simpleton he was? At how easily he'd succumbed to her coy smiles, and hooded glances.

He wanted to hate her. But he couldn't, for he loved her with all his heart. He doubted he would ever love anyone as much as he loved her. That's why her betrayal pierced so deeply.

What kind of twisted fate would bring his true love into his arms only to discover she was from the House of Lancaster?

"Nicholas?"

He heard her voice and closed his eyes as the rain pelted him.

"What are you doing here, Kestrel?" he demanded in a loud voice when she came closer. "Go back inside before you catch a fever."

"What about you?" she called out, still approaching. "Come inside with me."

"No."

"Nicholas, look." She knelt by him in the rain against the post. "I'm getting tired of this. Come inside and talk to me or I'll stop trying and put you out of my thoughts and my sight for good."

"You threaten me?"

"It's not a threat. It's a promise. If you want to argue about it, let's do it inside."

"I will go nowhere with you, Lancaster," he let her know.

"Fine then!" she shouted, straightened, and pounded away. "Have it your way, you pigheaded fool!"

He swiped the rain from his eyes and rose to his feet as she ran off. He held the hilt of his sword in both hands and swung it one last time into the post, as hard as he could. The blade cut through the wood and stuck.

He left the sword there and stormed away after her. He entered the castle a short while after her, dripping wet and ready to battle.

"You are correct about one thing, Lancaster," he told her as she removed her soaked, muddy slippers. "I'm a fool. A fool for falling for you."

She froze but her eyes burned with blue-green fire. "And I, *knowing* that you hate Lancasters am an even bigger fool for falling for you, so don't feel so bad."

She padded off in her bare feet, hurrying away before he had a chance to reply.

He kicked off his boots and without drying off, pounded up the stairs behind her.

"There!" he argued. "You said it yourself. You knew how I felt about Lancasters—" he lowered is voice and looked around to make certain Richard wasn't anywhere in earshot. The king wouldn't take kindly to having a Lancaster in the castle. "—and you kept it from me."

She spun on her heel on the last step and stared at him. "I kept it from you because I didn't want to be here alone, and I knew you'd never keep me with you if you knew."

"You are correct," he said, his gaze level with hers. "So you kept it from me and tried to convince me to betray Richard."

She rolled her eyes heavenward and turned around to leave. "Forget it."

He blinked. Forget it? Discussing this on the stairway wasn't wise for many reasons.

He cut off her path in two strides and pulled her toward the solar. "You want to talk. Let's go talk."

Why? Why was he speaking to her? He'd promised himself he wouldn't. Staying away from her was safest, but here he was, telling her how he felt, asking for explanations. What did it matter? In the end, she was his enemy.

"I don't know what else to say, Nicholas," she told him when they entered the solar and he closed the door behind them. "None of this was my of my doing."

"Save for deceiving me, you mean."

"Nicholas," she said, refusing to sit down. "One instant, I was in an office building in New York City and then I was here, over five hundred years in the past, in the middle of a battle. You saved me. I will never forget it, no matter how far into the future I go. I quickly grasped what I was in the middle of. Historians call it the War of the Roses. You were from the House of York, and I, I was your enemy because of my name alone. I was too afraid to tell you."

"Were you ever going to tell me? Or did you think your secret was safe? How could anyone here know your true identity, aye?"

"Yes, but...I would have told you if things between us had grown more serious."

Her words stung a little. "More serious than love?"

Her expression softened on him. "I didn't realize it was love. I..." She paused and seemed to try to keep herself together. "I have never really been in love. Love seemed very fragile and I chose to stop believing in it."

He was tempted to smile at her, but he didn't give in. "It doesn't matter what we feel."

"Why not?"

He gave her a hard look that usually silenced his men but didn't seem to affect her in the least. "We have been fighting this war for many years now. Our side has almost proven victorious. Am I to forget..." He thought of his family. "...everything, toss it all aside for a Lancaster woman?"

"No one is asking you to forget," she said gently, making him miss being with her every day. "And is that all I am to you? A Lancaster woman?"

He wanted to go to her and tell her how much she meant to him, to sweep her up off her feet and kiss her senseless.

"Nicholas, I may not even be related to the Lancasters of today, there are so many descendants removed."

"But you are a Lancaster. I grew up hating Lancasters. It has been the one constant in my life. But 'tis more than that. You did not trust me enough to tell me."

"What would have changed if what you said before that is

true? You hate for the sake of hating. Perhaps you are not the right man for me." She headed for the door, but he blocked her path.

"Get out of my way, Nicholas."

He didn't move for a moment. "Do not go."

"I must. It's for the best."

He did as she asked. What was there left to say?

He closed his eyes when she left the solar and slammed the door shut behind her.

He wouldn't go after her.

So, that was it then? There was nothing more between them. He covered his face with his hands.

No. No. His heart refused to give her up, but his head forbade his legs to move. "Kestrel," he lamented. He didn't want to be without her. She made him smile again.

She came here from the future. She could go back at any time.

She was a Lancaster.

Was she here to make sure Richard died on the battlefield? Did Richard kill the princes or have them killed?

It was the same question he'd been asking himself for almost two years now.

There came a knock at the door.

Still standing in his place, he called out, "Come," hoping, praying that it was Kestrel.

Elia entered the solar and stared at him soaking wet and miserable. Her golden-hued gaze took him in and then she shook her head. "What is going on in that head of yours, Nicky? You care for her. I know you do. Will you let her go because of her name?"

"How can I not? I will not betray the House of York."

"Nicholas," she said sternly. "The House of York is about to end. You know as well as I that Richard should not be king. There are no more descendants. York is over. Henry has promised to marry Elizabeth and combine the Houses. The white and red rose together. Step aside and let him do it."

"If Richard hears you speaking like this, he could have you hanged for treason."

She looked up at him. Hers was a face he knew and loved since he was a child. The only person he could trust—until Kestrel came along.

"Are you going to tell him?" she asked him.

"Never. Just do not trust anyone else. Not even Elizabeth. She spends much time with Richard."

"I know, Nicky."

"Mayhap Kestrel."

"You are falling in love with her, that is why you are so angry."

He didn't deny it but turned away, not willing to let anyone see the pain in his eyes. He'd wanted something with her. He'd wanted to be her family and give her everything she needed. Scarborough Castle was his. He wanted to share it with her.

He closed his eyes and inhaled deeply.

"Out of all the women in the two different centuries, Elia. Two! The woman sent to me is a Lancaster!"

"Maybe it means something, Nicky," she said, going to him and putting her hand on his arm. "Maybe the good Lord does not want all this hatred in your heart. The Yorks and the Lancasters are going to join in the new king and queen. Let them be joined in your household as well."

Could he? Everything he'd fought for her? He could.

"Do not think too long, Nicky," Elia warned. "Kes has been through much in the last pair of weeks. Do not add to her woes. And dry off," she added before turning to leave the room.

He decided to take her advice and changed into dry clothes. He also didn't want to add to Kestrel's troubles. Mayhap he should try to speak with her again. Letting her leave couldn't be the right thing to do.

But when he looked for her, he found her gone. No one in the castle had seen her or knew where she'd gone. Nicholas controlled the panic rising up in him, but he knew his control wouldn't last long. It was foolish of her to leave the castle, especially on a stormy night. Where would she go?

He found the horse she'd ridden was gone from the stable. She wasn't the best rider and she didn't know which way to go, save to Old Walter's.

He saddled his horse and took off toward Walter's. It was the only place she knew. She had to have gone there. He didn't know what he would say to her, he didn't know what he would do about her being a Lancaster, but he wanted her to come back.

By the time he reached the old merchant's house, he was drenched again, for the rain continued to fall.

The place appeared deserted, but Nicholas knew better. Besides, he saw her horse in the stable.

Kestrel was here. Finding her was the easy part he found out soon enough. Seeing her was another matter entirely. She refused.

"Tell her I'm not leaving until she sees me," Nicholas told Walter, then watched him shuffle off into the corridor, leaving Nicholas at the door.

He returned a few minutes later shaking his head. "She says she doesn't want to see or speak to you tonight. She will see how she feels tomorrow. My lord," the merchant said gently. "She was very agitated when she came in. Perhaps giving her time is a good idea."

Nicholas knew he had no choice. He wasn't about to force his way upon her. He nodded. "Very well. I will see her tomorrow then."

He breathed. He had to remember to do it. Walter smiled at him. He didn't smile back.

"Good eve, my lord."

Nicholas nodded again and then left. He returned to the castle but after an hour pacing in his room then another hour pacing in his solar, he rode back to Old Walter's and slept in the stable with his horse. At least if she tried to leave Scarborough in the morning, he would hear her.

And then what? He went to sleep asking himself what would he do. Stop her? Watch her go? He hated himself for becoming so attached to Kestrel Lancaster.

He dreamed of riding through the forest.

"Pick up your hood, Nicky," Elia said beside him on her horse. He was on one too. "Listen to your mother."

His mother? He turned his head and his poor eyes beheld his mother. Tears fell over the rims of his eyes. "Mother."

She rode beside…his father. "Papa?" he cried, pulling up his hood. His sister and two brothers rode in the cart behind his father.

A cold chill swept over him and seeped into his veins. No! This was the day!

He tried to turn back, but his horse kept moving forward.

And then, like a hoard of locusts, they came out of the trees. Elia immediately grabbed for him and pulled him onto her horse. They rode away, but Nicholas could imagine it all in his mind, his family's screams painted the pictures. *Mother! Papa!*

He woke up about an hour before dawn, remembering it all. It was fresh in his mind, as if it had just happened. He sat up and leaned against a wall of the stable. He should have brought breakfast…and his good sense.

What was he doing here, making sure she didn't run away? He had to make a damned decision and he was making it now. He could never live with a Lancaster. Any Lancaster.

He rose up, leaped into the saddle, and rode away.

THE DOOR TO Walter's house opened and Kes stepped out. She looked around. The sun was shining brightly, in contrast to yesterday's dark skies "Walter," she called softly into the house, "he's not here."

"Are you sure, I thought I saw him near the stable a moment ago."

"Miss Locksley?"

She turned to the man's voice. It was Mr. Simeon behind her. It must have been him who Walter saw near the stable.

"Mr. Simeon, what a nice surprise in the morning," she greeted. "And please, call me Kes."

He offered her a wide smile. "I wasn't expecting to see you here, Kes. But I'm glad to have found you. Is Lord Scarborough with you?"

She shook her head.

His smile widened. His teeth were white and straight. "Let us go inside."

She didn't move. "Oh, is it more bad news?"

"No. No. Not at all," he reassured gently. "I have a gift for you."

"Will it help me get home?"

His smile vanished. "I'm afraid not."

Hers vanished, too. A few days ago, she would have been able to deal better with the fact that she wasn't going home and everyone she'd lost, because Nicholas was with her. She felt safe with him. And she needed to feel safe here.

Now, he wasn't with her and she was still stuck here.

"Any word on a way to get home, Mr. Simeon?" she asked as Walter ushered them inside.

"No, my dear lady. I hate to disappoint you. There has been no word. I am still hanging about in realms I shouldn't be in and keeping my ears open to any talk of you from the knights. So far," he went on as they entered the solar and sat, "I've discovered that Sir Gawaine has been severely reprimanded by Morgan for not finding Arthur. The other knights blame the brooch. I would tend to agree after where you landed."

"Yes," Kes said. "I would agree, as well. And Sir Gawaine— how severely was he reprimanded?"

"I do not know the extent of it," Simeon told her, then smiled again. "I brought you something from the chests of Queen Berengaria."

Kes blinked and looked at the velvet sack he handed her. "King Richard's wife, Queen Berengaria?"

"Do you know any others?"

She covered her mouth with her hand and looked at Walter to giggle. She took the satchel. It was soft and the velvet was thick and luxurious. "What's in it?"

"Open it and see!"

She did, like a child on Christmas morning.

With a great sigh she pulled out a sapphire blue gown made of the finest, thinnest silk. It was an A line cut with a silver filigree belt and silver stitching on the cuff. Sewn into the shoulders was a gossamer cloak of blue tulle flowing down her back.

"Oh, Mr. Simeon, I couldn't accept this. How did you…? Did you steal it?"

He waved her concern away. "She won't miss it, dear Kes. You both look to be built the same. It should fit."

"Oh, that you've seen her," Kes stood up and held the gown up to her body. She couldn't keep it. But to own something that Queen Berengaria had worn.

"Take it," Mr. Simeon insisted. "The queen has more than she could wear in a lifetime."

"No. It still doesn't make it right." She pushed the gown and its bag at him. "Thank you, but I can't accept it."

He exhaled a great breath. "Very well, I will leave her a gift in its place. Something she will actually enjoy, and I will pay for it myself. Deal?"

"What will you give her?" Kes asked, tempted.

"I'll let you know what I decide."

Jonathan, Walter's servant served them tea and something that looked suspiciously like a famous little hot apple pie.

"Walter?" she asked, turning to him and holding the rectangular pie up to him. "What is this?"

Walter looked at it over his spectacles. "You know perfectly well what it is, Child. I suggest you eat it and stop holding it up to me or I can almost assure you that *I* will be the one who eats it."

Kes cut Mr. Simeon a side glance. She knew it came from the future and he was the one who'd brought them here.

"What?" Walter asked, seeing her disapproving expression. "What are we changing by eating this delicious pie? 'Tis my favorite treat!"

"Of course." Kes feigned a smile. "So the people who created this pie in my century don't matter. If someone makes something similar now, you've changed those people's future."

Walter frowned at his pie and then at her. "Aw, very well then. Let this be the last time I ever eat one." He bit into his pie and closed his eyes with delight.

Kes looked at hers, shrugged her shoulders, then took a bite. He was right. It was delicious.

Remaining here would be difficult. Knowing Mr. Simeon would make it a temptation to have possessions from every century, every dynasty. To everything, everywhere. But nothing would be as hard as trying to live without her knight in her life. Why did he have to be such a stubborn, gentle bear?

"Tell me," Mr. Simeon said while they ate. "Where is the earl this morning?"

"He's having a hard time with me being a Lancaster."

"Pig-headed fool," the time traveler muttered then sipped his tea.

"The Lancasters murdered his family," Kes defended him. "We don't understand what it's like for him."

"Aye. She's correct," Walter muttered and set down his cup. "This is a delicate matter and must be treated so. For now, let us leave matters of their hearts to them."

Kes smiled at Walter for his thoughtfulness, and then laughed when Mr. Simeon suggested she try on the gown.

It didn't mean she was keeping it. She was just trying it on.

It was no big deal.

# CHAPTER TWENTY

S OMEONE KNOCKED ON Walter's front door. Kes' heart skipped its beats. It had to be Nicholas. He'd told Walter he would see her today. She'd admit, she hadn't known him long, but he'd never lied to her—that she knew of. Yet.

Sure she was suspicious of him and his motives. She'd had ten years of experience with boys and men—well, they'd never grown up, so, just boys. They always had ulterior motives and they always lied.

"Miss Locksley," Walter knocked and spoke through the door. "Lord Scarborough is here to see you."

She felt a little faint and rushed to the door, blue silk and feathery tulle flowing behind her. She stopped when she reached the wooden barrier in front of her and the man she'd foolishly allowed herself to love.

She shivered in her spot, though the temperature in her room was a warm eighty degrees at least.

She didn't want to seem overly eager to see him, though in fact, she was. She'd thought of him all night, hearing his deep voice at the door when he'd spoken to Walter about seeing her. She'd refused. She couldn't accept that he suddenly hated her because of her name. He needed time. He was stubborn and he needed time—

She opened the door to her room and stepped into the corridor. He'd come. She knew he would. That had to earn him something, didn't it? He was reliable.

She walked to the stairs, feeling herself in her beautiful gown. She lifted her hems and hurried down the stairs in her slippered feet.

When she reached the solar door, she took a deep breath and stepped inside.

He was sitting with Walter and Mr. Simeon. When he saw her, he stood up. She barely noticed anyone else so tall and handsome was he in his—armor. His armor. Was he leaving? Returning to the war?

"My lord?" she asked in a soft voice.

"My lady," he said just as softly.

"Ehm, come then, Roldan," Walter said and tossed his arm around Mr. Simeon, "Let us go walk outdoors."

When they were alone, Kes opened her mouth to speak, to ask him if he was leaving.

He spoke first. "Kestrel, you look…" He stopped and swallowed and started again. "You look perfect. Where did you get the gown?"

"It was Queen Berengaria's gown. She was—"

"I know who she was." He looked tired and gaunt. When had he slept last? "So, is this how 'tis to be while I'm away?" he asked angrily.

Away. The bastard was leaving.

"How what is to be?"

"Simeon will be bringing you gifts?"

"He might!" she snapped at him. "What do you care? You're leaving early!"

"I think it best."

"Explain that to me, Nicholas. How is it best?" She wouldn't shout or cry. She wouldn't let him let know how much she cared.

"'Tis best for more than one reason."

She nodded mockingly and folded her arms across her chest.

"You deceived me about something very close to my heart."

"To save my ass. Sorry." Her hands balled into fists under her boobs.

His jaw clenched and, for a moment, he couldn't speak. Good. She liked him better this way. Finally, he said in a low tone, "Had I given you reason to believe I would not keep you from harm?"

"I didn't know what you would do for—"

"Woman, I risked my life and killed every man around you, then rode you away from battle. *Before* I asked your name. You were the one who wanted nothing to do with me. And even after you reviled me, I came back for you. Telling me the truth would have angered me, but I would not have put you out with nothing. I haven't done that now. You are the one who left the castle in the cover of darkness, which is dangerous in this century."

"It's dangerous in mine, too."

His expression hardened on her. "Are you that eager to be away?"

"It's hard to be around you when you hate breathing the same air I breathe because of my name."

His scowl turned fierce. "I do not hate breathing the same air you breathe!"

"You hide in your solar and scowl when you see me," she argued. "Like now. I feel like Reg. So yes, I was eager to be away."

His gaze on her softened just a bit. "I did not mean to treat you like Reg. Forgive me."

She nodded and asked God for strength to be strong. He was leaving, garbed for war. This was who he was.

"What are the other reasons?" she asked him. "You said there were many reasons to stay away. Tell them to me.

"They don't matter, Kes—"

She turned away. She couldn't get an answer from him. He couldn't make up his mind if he cared or not and she promised herself she wouldn't stick around if he tried to string her along.

His fingers closing around her wrist stopped her from leaving. He pulled her into his arms, against his metal chest and bent to hover his mouth over hers.

"They do not matter because only this does. I'm falling in love with you, Kestrel. I feel my heart giving in to it more and more each day, every time I look at you. I cannot stop it and it terrifies me to think of you disappearing as easily as you appeared and taking my heart with you."

What? He was terrified of losing her. "What about my name?"

"I will change it," he whispered and covered her mouth with his.

She should fight him and not let him think he could be a jerk and then kiss it all away. But who was she kidding? She wanted to be ravished by Nicholas and only Nicholas. She opened her mouth to his plunging tongue and coiled her arms around his neck. She wanted him to hate leaving her, to refuse to fight for Richard.

"I do not want to leave you," he said against her.

She smiled. "Was it the dress or the kiss?"

"'Twas the heart. Mine," he confessed. "And 'twas the kiss also," he added and let his silvery gaze rake over her body. "And the dress. I don't give a damn what your name is, Kestrel. I will not lose you over it.

"Don't go back yet, Nicholas. Don't leave."

He held her by the upper arms and gazed into her eyes.

"I still have two days. I will figure something out."

He kissed her again. It was a kiss of complete possession and mastery. This is how she longed to be kissed, as if his life depended on breathing her, tasting her, holding her. She held on to his shoulders in his armor, so wide and strong. He said he would change her name. Was that a proposal? Was he willing to wed her so she'd no longer be a Lancaster? Would she wed him for such a reason?

"Come back to the castle," he urged with a gentle bite to her lobe.

"No. I think I should stay here. I don't want you to leave for battle. We have much thinking to do. I'm falling in love with you, too."

He dipped his brows over his eyes as if he doubted the good of his ears. Then his eyes brightened, and he smiled. "I was hoping you were. Part of me was," he added, almost as an afterthought.

"Which part?" she asked while he covered her in his metal embrace.

"That part that rejoices in you. The part that wants to think nothing but death could take you from me—and I will not let that happen. But what do I do against some spell that decides to hurl you into the next century? Or if you find the brooch and want to go back. I should stop us both from falling in love. 'Twill only lead to heartache."

She stared up at him, trying to ignore the burning in her eyes. "If you believe that then we're already doomed."

"Mayhap we are," he said, leaning his temple on top of her head. "Mayhap we should cherish every moment we have together."

She nodded and smiled and let him wipe a tear from her cheek. "I think that's a good way to live our lives together, Nicholas. We will deal with whatever happens when the time comes. Until then, if there even is a *then*, we will cherish our moments. Even when I want to strangle you."

"Me?" He took a step back, breaking their hold. "You are just as stubborn as me. Mayhap even more so. Let me prove it. Come back to the castle with me."

"No, I think—"

"You see?" He smiled, watching her when she laughed. "At least let me take you somewhere today."

Her smile brightened. "Where shall we go?"

"Where do you want to go? In our century, of course."

Their century. Not his and not hers.

"Swimming!" she told him. "I want to go swimming with you again."

"Very well. Let us change clothes and meet here."

"You won't change your mind?" she asked playfully, but with a serious edge. He'd taken days to realize he didn't care about her name. What if he—

"I will not change my mind about loving you, for you have taken hold of my heart in a way that no one else ever has. What choice is there when love strikes?"

Her smile on him warmed. Her gaze did the same. "You're a romantic."

He looked ill, but then it passed. "I'll return shortly."

When he was gone, she looked down at her dress and sighed. She'd given in to him. She loved him. Did she love him enough to refuse to step through the veil in time if she had the chance to go back? He'd been ready to leave her, to go back into battle. But had he truly wanted to return, or had he been running from his emotions for her? She believed it was more the latter. She didn't blame him for being afraid of it. She was, too. But more than fear, she wanted more with him. She wanted all of him. Would she give up home and marry him? She could never go back if she were his wife. She thought about it all while she changed into her white kirtle and teal overcoat, gifts from Elia.

Kes wasn't just falling in love with Nicholas, she was also beginning to love Elia and Walter. Everyone here. Claire wasn't even angry with her for taking Nicholas off the market, so to speak. They were becoming close friends.

She wouldn't give up hope of seeing her father again but until she did see him, she liked building up a new family here.

As promised, Nicholas returned to her for an afternoon at the waterfalls. They rode together on his horse. The beast was a huge warhorse and handled her weight without a problem. Besides, they traveled at a lazy pace under the blessed canopy that shielded them from the hot sun.

"Would you have gone off to fight?" she asked him, sitting on his lap, leaning against his chest.

"Aye. I felt it was the safest thing to do."

She laughed, but there was little mirth it. "Oh, great. Going off to battle is safer than staying here with me."

"No, 'twas not great," he corrected, confusing her a little and making her conceal a soft smile. "But 'tis safer," he continued. "You have the power to make me ache in my guts, my chest, my head. I have never felt the pain of being empty until you left. One day felt like a thousand. Two days, ten thousand. I felt I had to go back to the field, or I would go mad. But then I saw you." He closed his arms around her and spoke into her hair. "I saw you and I knew I would die without you in my arms."

Kes covered his forearms with hers and sighed with delight. When had any guy ever spoken to her like this? Nicholas proved over and over again that he wasn't like the men she knew. He'd been angry that she lied to him. But it also made him realize how he really felt about her.

"You are enough for me to be happy here," she told him, turning to look at him. "Never to forget the people I've loved, like my father, but able to live without them. You saved me from going nuts."

"I'm glad to hear that. Going nuts sounds painful." He smiled. He often did. She was glad he found her amusing. She loved being the one who made him smile.

"I'm sorry for not telling you the truth, Nicholas. I didn't want to be someone you hated."

"I did not want that either. But I cannot hate you."

Now that he knew and had accepted the fact that she was a Lancaster, it felt as if a giant weight had been removed from her shoulders.

She heard the waterfalls before they reached them. The flow was harder, and the basin was full thanks to the last storm. They set out a wool blanket on a large flat rock partially shaded by the trees. Nicholas had been thoughtful enough to bring wine and black bread and sweet butter. Walter packed some fresh fruit and cheese for them. Kes set out the food, but she wasn't hungry. She was nervous about being with him alone, with him probably naked again. She didn't trust herself.

"Let's swim first," he said as if reading her mind.

She nodded and straightened so she could begin undressing. Her bra and panties were clean and still holding up.

Once again, he stripped first. This time, he wore thin breeches. She had but a moment before he took off running and jumped into the water with a loud shout. But it was enough time to view him in his somewhat loose fitting, knee-high breeches. The waistline fell to below his hips, showing off his tight abs. The sensual flare of his back muscles into his pecs and deltoids made her want to climb him.

She blushed and followed him in. The water was surprisingly frigid for the early days of August. When she came up, out of breath, he gathered her in his arms and instantly warmed her. She didn't fight him or make him suffer for how he'd treated her when he'd found out that she was a Lancaster. She understood they killed his family and it had been something he'd been dealing with for years. She was happy to be with him. She loved being held in his embrace. It was where she'd woken up when she arrived here.

He kissed her with a mouth that tasted of passion and desire. His arms closed around her, one around her shoulders and the other to the slope of her behind. His tongue flicked and stroked around the inside of her mouth.

A thought occurred to her. Did he think she was a virgin? Most unmarried women in this era were, weren't they? Should she tell him she wasn't? That she was sorry she'd done it with the guy she'd done it with? He was selfish and therefore terrible in bed and out of it. He didn't deserve her.

Did Nicholas?

He released her and turned his scarred back on her. "Climb on."

*Don't tempt me,* she wanted to tell him. She looped her arms around his neck on held on when he dipped and swam with her on his back through the waterfall.

She wanted to laugh but water went into her mouth. He swam a little farther, behind one of the falls. "What is this?" she faintly heard his voice through the roar of the water. He turned a bend and swam into cave.

"Oh, Nicholas, it's huge!" Her voice echoed beneath the high rock ceiling. Sunshine coming through from the vaulted entrance faded to a golden incandescence. He stopped swimming and stood up, bringing the water with him. Kes let him go and watched the liquid flow down his body in rivulets, over hills and valleys. She stood with him on flat rocks, much like the ones outside.

"Have you been here before?" she asked him, wondering how many women had been here with him.

"No." He shook his head and looked around. "I do not swim often and when I came here with Edward and his family, we did not venture through the falls."

She liked that they were seeing it for the first time together. "Do you think there are many visitors?" Finding deserted little paradises in the twenty-first century was rare. There would be twenty other couples in here with them if they were home.

"I do not think there are *any* visitors," he said, his voice, deep and thrilling against her ear as he stepped closer. "We are alone." He scooped her hair away from her nape and kissed what he'd exposed. His arms slipped around her and pulled her close against him. He felt as hard as his armor, but he was warm, his muscles twitched and tremored when her flesh touched his.

A few rays of sunshine shot into the cave before a billowy cloud passed the sun and cast them into its soft radiance. They smiled at each other, close enough to kiss.

Instead, Nicholas bent his knee and took her hand. "Kestrel—"

Her heart thundered in her chest and felt like it moved to her throat and lodged itself there. Was he going to ask her...?

"Since you got here, you have taken over my thoughts. I think about you all the time. I want to be with you and nowhere else. I want to laugh with you and learn about your life and the people you love. I want to take pictures," he stopped to smile at her, "of us and our children. Nothing in this life would please me more than to be your husband. Will you be my wife?"

She brought her free hand to her mouth. His wife. His wife!

"Yes," she said in a dulcet whisper. She could give no other answer.

# Chapter Twenty-One

"**Y**ES, I'LL BE your wife."

Was she crazy? Marriage? This meant she couldn't leave here without him. It also protected her should anything befall him. But marriage? Her? She smiled thinking about what Lilith and Jack and the others would say.

She watched her fiancé…or betrothed as they said here, stand up. Her mouth went dry when he scooped her up to cradle her in his arms. He carried her up the next few ledges, where the water barely reached, and set her down.

"You will tell Elia whatever you wish for our wedding and celebration." He sat beside her with her between his legs and gave her an indulgent grin. "Whatever you wish. I will spare no expense."

Goodness, he sure knew what to tell a girl. "And where did you come by so much money?"

"Everything that was my father's and his father before him, is now mine. I also have the pay from my service to the king and to England, and—"

She held up her hand to stop him. Ok, he was rich I. She got it. "Well, I'm glad we won't be starving."

"I will take care of you, Kestrel, and I will provide for our children. We will never starve."

"I want to help," she told him, looking into his eyes. "In twenty nineteen, many women provide for themselves, as I did with my career as a historian."

"Very well, help then."

She almost gasped a smile at him. She never expected to hear him agree. She thought he'd beat his chest a little. But he didn't.

"Do whatever you can think of to keep yourself busy, and that will not get you thrown into a cell. I will put coin to your desire, aye? If you wish to continue your work as a historian, Walter has enough pieces of history in his house to log and keep you happy. Or open a shop at the market, with Elia, mayhap. Have your *exercise* classes, though I will have to station a man outside the door to protect you. Whatever you wish, my love."

She had to be dead and this had to be Heaven. She pinched herself. Nope. This wasn't Heaven, she felt pain.

Those were wonderful ideas. "Maybe," she said, feeling like she might cry or leap around the rocks with happiness, "I will do it all." She could help Cook cook, give some of the servants the night off, even if it meant her doing some serving. As the lady of the castle, she could get whatever anyone needed.

She stared into his lightning-colored eyes and vowed to give him whatever he wished for "that won't land us in hell."

He gave her a worried look. "Like what?"

She giggled into her hand. "I'll let you know if it ever comes up."

"'Tisn't kissing you, for you let me kiss you already."

He leaned forward and kissed her, parting her lips gently with his tongue.

All that touched her was his lips. It sparked lightning in her everywhere else. She wanted more and broke their kiss to sigh when he put his arm around her and gently pulled the back of her against his chest. She had to turn her face upward to kiss him, and she did so happily. She let him seduce her with his lips, his teeth, and one hand moving from behind her to cup her upstretched throat and then lower to her breast. His fingers disappeared beneath the lace and tugged at her nipple.

Kes groaned and he rubbed the taut nub until her knees parted.

"Nicholas, I'm not…I'm not a virgin."

He stopped for a moment, leaving Kes to wonder if he'd take back his proposal.

"Neither am I," he admitted.

Goodness, he relieved her at every turn. It was as if nothing fazed him—except her name. How would he feel about the Lancasters after the last Yorkist king was killed? Would he want her around him then? He said he'd never change his mind, but just how deeply did he hate her ancestors?

"Then there is no judgment," she whispered. "Only pleasure."

"Only pleasure," he agreed with a lazy smirk before his lips covered hers again.

This time, he used both hands to expose and cup her breasts. He kissed her upside down and spread his rough palms over her flat belly to the small triangle of hair beneath her panties.

Her legs opened with a will of their own. Beneath her, she could feel his erection in his wet breeches. She pulled free of his embrace and turned to tug the laces with her teeth. His huge, hard cock sprang forward.

He moaned, deep and guttural. The sound heated her blood. She turned her head and opened her mouth to him. He drove himself into her but stopped just before she would gag.

He pushed her down gently and pulled down her underwear. She watched him, eager for him, while he pulled out of his breeches.

Poised above her, she nearly wept looking at him. He spread her with his knees and pushed against her wet opening. When she resisted slightly, he slipped his hand under her and cupped her bottom. He heaved himself up on his knees, taking her with him. He moved her under him, and she held on, unable to do much else as he eased his way into her and they rode his deluge together.

Much to her surprise and delight, he only required five

minutes to recuperate before he was ready again. This time, she took control and made him sit up against the slick rocks. He held on with his arms over the ledge behind him and waited for her.

Did she just purr? She couldn't wait to straddle him. Coy was not in her twenty-first century vocabulary. She flung her leg over him and let him impale her.

He cried out and lifted his hips, taking her deeper, almost tossing her off. But she wouldn't let go. She felt small in his arms and lifted herself off him then back down until he had her gyrating like a flame atop him, her cries echoing through the cavern.

They rested but not for long as the water, without the sun on it, was cold and they soon began to shiver.

She let him clean her, rubbing her and licking her swollen lips.

"We need to find a priest," he ground out. "I want you in my bed tonight."

Kes wanted to be there as well. She loved being at Walter's, but she was ready to go back to Scarborough. Two hours ago, she wanted time for both of them to think about what they were doing. Now, they'd done it and she thought about it enough. She wanted to be with Nicholas.

When they were done dressing, she put her arms around his neck and looked into his eyes. "I never thought I'd find anybody like you. I'd become caustic when it came to men and cynical of love. Everything is so complicated in that century. But not you. Oh, I'm sure even here, you're still a rare kind of man. How I mean anything to you at all, I don't know."

"No?" he asked, tightening his arms around her waist. "You do not think yourself interesting and humorous, beautiful and ravishing?"

She laughed, dipping her breath to his shoulder. "No, I don't."

"You are. And surely you know how your words, your stories captivate me." He lifted his arm and held his hand as if he were holding his phone. He took a picture. She struck a pose with her head against his chest, thrilled and happy in his arms.

"I love the flare of your temper and the glint of fire it sparks in your eyes. But most of all, my beloved Kestrel, I love your humility. 'Tis very pleasing to my eyes to see the goodness of your heart, and to my ears to hear of it. Everyone at the castle has noticed it. You are well loved there already. The servants ask for you continually." He laughed shortly. "Even if I wanted to forget you, I could not."

"I love them all, too. Come on." She let go of him and took his hand. "Let's ride back and give them the good news. Of our eng…betrothal."

He agreed and followed her into the water. They swam out of the cave and through the falls. Kes lost her breath from the heavy rush of water spilling over the side of the cliff. Nicholas was there, still holding her hand. After making sure she was un-harmed, he splashed water in her face and swam off. They laughed, playing and basking in the warmth of the sun.

They returned to the food and found it being enjoyed by some forest critters. Kes squealed with delight at the chance to feed some deer and groundhogs—or gophers. She couldn't tell. She didn't care.

"Hello!" she said softly and held out her hand to one of the deer. "Do you want this apple?" She sat still and asked Nicholas to do the same. "Come now, baby, don't be afraid." She spoke softly and waited patiently for the skittish deer to come closer.

"Toss a piece of black bread to those squirrels, will you, Nicky?"

She didn't think about what she called him, but rather if the scurrying little gophers had gotten enough.

When the food was gone, along with the animals, Nicholas set her atop him on his horse and headed for home.

"This has been a perfect day!" she breathed, leaning against him. "I wish I had my journal."

"Journal?"

Her face contorted as if she were in pain. "Oh my gosh, there are no journals here. It's a notebook. Bound pages of blank paper that I write in."

"A note book. A book of notes!" he exclaimed as if he'd just figured out the secret to happiness.

"Yes," she told him with a small smile.

"We can have a bound book of papers made for you, Kestrel," he promised. "Do not be troubled by this."

"Thank you, Nicholas." She hugged his arms around her. "You are making this all so easy."

"Aye," he muttered softly, looking up at the long wall and his castle at the top of it. "I have decided not to return to Nottingham to fight, but to wait and join the army at Bosworth Field."

The Battle of Bosworth Field. It was coming. What would happen to Nicholas? Would he fight against Tudor's men?

"I'm thankful that you're not leaving right away for battle, but I still wish you would think on this."

"I will," he promised.

"Are you sure you want to be my husband when the days come?" she asked him, her cheek turned to his chest. "I won't stop bugging you about not fighting."

"What is bugging?" he asked with amusement in his voice.

"Nagging."

"I see." The amusement was gone.

"There is no reason to fight, Nicholas. You said yourself you didn't fight for Richard but for York. Maybe you saw it as some noble thing, to die with the word York on your lips. Very dramatic."

He dipped his brows and gave her a confused look.

"But things have changed. You didn't have me waiting, worried sick over you. I'll be heartsick until you return, and if you don't..." She shook her head and wiped her tears. "I don't want you to go, Nicholas. There's no reason to go. At least Elia will have a companion when she is wearing out the wood in the floors."

"You seem to have this all settled in your mind."

She sighed. "I'm being selfish, I know. But your heart isn't in this. You know that. Why risk dying over it?"

She was happy when he didn't argue but remained quiet. Let him think about it. In the meantime, she would do everything she could to keep him off the battlefield.

They returned to the castle and were met by Elia on their way from the stable.

"Richard is looking for you. Lady Elizabeth told him about Henry Tudor. He seems restless and he's quite angry with Elizabeth's mother for always siding with Henry."

Nicholas shook his head. His scowl was deep and menacing. "What does he expect when he had her marriage declared invalid and possibly had her sons killed? Should she be on his side now just because she wears a white rose?"

Kes and Elia shared a glance. Kes wanted to ask, should he?

He looked at her, stripping her of her thoughts and reading them. "I do not have to be on his side to fight for him. The princes may be found—"

"They are never found, Nicholas," Kes told him. "If Richard lives, it will change history. Let's not have any part in that."

He stared at her, his gaze going soft. "Kestrel, mayhap I die in battle, unable to find victory for the king. Mayhap whether or not I fight does not matter. Richard will die."

"No," she said, shaking her head. "The de Marres have never lost before. Why would you suddenly lose now? I fear you're killed."

"I have always been prepared for that."

"But I haven't," she told him. "It took almost five hundred and fifty years to find you. I don't want to lose you now."

"Nicky," Elia joined in. "Kes told me about some of these things. I must say I have to agree with her. You would have to be dead for the Whites to lose. I ask you not to fight. If history says that Richard must die, who are we to try to change it?"

"We will cease this talk now, ladies," he commanded, reaching the castle doors.

"Nicholas!"

They heard the king bellow the instant he heard the doors opening.

"Where in blazes have you been?" he lamented loudly at the top of the stairs. "Henry Tudor and that old rat bastard, Jasper, his uncle, have landed in Wales and have amassed an army of five thousand against me! What shall we do?"

Why hadn't Kes ever thought of these kings frightened when their time was up? She always imagined they rode out to a glorious death. Maybe some did. Richard III did not.

"We shall stay calm," was Nicholas' first suggestion. He climbed the stairs to the king with the others following. "Our men in Nottingham and Leicester await word. We have your army in York and more men in Leeds if we need them. There is no need to worry. I have everything under control."

Had he already been in contact with his men? Kes wondered. It sounded as if he'd already made a decision. Something he didn't share with her.

"Ah," the king breathed hard. He turned to look at Elizabeth stepping around the corner in the hall. "I knew you would. But how could you unless you were aware of this information before me?"

Nicholas glanced at Elizabeth. "She told me."

"Nicky," young Elizabeth said when she saw and heard him.

"I warned her against telling you," he continued. "Why set your nerves on edge when I could take care of it all? Aye? Has it not always been this way?"

"Aye," Richard admitted, letting Nicholas calm him. "As soon as you could wield a sword, you have always protected Edward and me." He looked at Elizabeth. "All of us."

"'Tis my duty," Nicholas replied, making Kes' heart falter. "Come, let us go to the solar."

The king nodded. "I would have you know that I did not murder my nephews."

*But you would sleep with your niece*, Kes wanted to bring up. She held her tongue. Elizabeth denied she'd been intimate with him when the ladies were embroidering.

"And yet," Nicholas countered smoothly as they entered the private solar. "you wasted no time going to the courts and having them declared illegitimate and setting yourself up as the next king."

"Aye," Richard agreed. "I went to much trouble. I did not need to kill them. They were my blood. I did not want to kill them. I was their protector. I loved them just as much as you did, Nicky. But I want the crown so I made certain they could never claim it, and I did it *without* shedding their blood."

Kes realized how close they must have been when Edward was alive. Nicky, as they all affectionately called him, was part of their family. A little brother who'd grown up fierce and strong. Nicholas fought for York because it had given him the family he'd lost.

The king's reasoning sounded like a valid argument. It didn't matter though. History must not be tampered with. Richard had to die whether guilty or innocent of the princes' disappearance and subsequent deaths.

"Then where are they?" Nicholas pleaded. "Who might have them and why? Tell me what you know, and I will find them."

Kes moved to go to him but Elia's arm blocking her path stopped her.

"I wish I knew the answers to your questions, Brother," the king confessed. "Sadly, I do not. But I need your help against Henry. Do I have it?"

"Aye." Nicholas told him without looking at her. "You have it."

# CHAPTER TWENTY-TWO

H E SHOULD BE in Leicester with his men, preparing for the Tudor army. Not at home arguing with a stubborn woman about the future.

"You gave your word to help him against Henry. Why?"

They were alone in the solar, sitting in chairs by the window.

When he didn't answer her, she girded herself up as if straightening her armor for war.

"He has to die, Nicholas!"

"Who says, Kestrel? God? He has not told me."

"Would you shut up and listen to Him if He tried?"

He knew his betrothed was more afraid for him than angry. He wanted to vanquish her fears and see her smile, confident in him.

"Aye," he said with the slightest of smiles. "I listen every time I want to throttle you and do not do it."

The one-sided curl of her lips made his muscles tighten.

"Who would help you live up to your fullest potential if you strangle me?"

He couldn't help but grin. "You see? He reminds me yet again not to do it and why."

"Nicholas," she grew somber again. A shaft of sunlight fell on the curve of her alabaster cheek and the glistening drop rolling down it. "Please don't go to the battle."

What was he to do? He prayed for an answer every time he

thought about it. If Richard died, it would be the end of the House of York on the throne. They had all fought so hard for it. His father, his grandfather, and father before him. How could he step over to the other side and abandon everything, everyone?

She sniffled and turned her gaze to the window.

"Will you refuse to marry me if I decide to go?"

She turned to look at him, filling his heart to bursting. Her cerulean eyes widened with hope. "Are you still undecided?"

He rose from his chair and knelt in front of hers. He wanted to marry her today. Now. "You did not answer my question."

"And you did not answer mine."

He stared at her breathless, parted lips for a moment. Then he replied, "Very well." He gave in. As usual. "Aye. I am undecided."

Her lips curled into a smile. Finally. "Yes, I will wed you no matter what."

He leaped up on his feet, took her hand, and hurried with her out of the solar. He led her to the great hall where everyone was gathering for supper.

"Everyone!" he shouted. "I have something to say!" When they settled down, he called out for the priest, Father Philip. "Kestrel and I are to be wed immediately. You will all be witnesses! To the chapel!"

Kestrel laughed and let him lead her and at least fifty others to the chapel.

"This is all so sudden!" someone in the crowd shouted out.

"'Tis truly cause to celebrate!" someone else called.

"They love you," Nicholas said as he pulled her close as they hurried to the chapel. "Just as I love you."

"Is this real?" she asked close to his ear so only he could hear her. "Are we really about to do this?"

"Aye," he said, smiling at her.

They reached the chapel. Father Philip was the first one in, Bible in hand. He was excited and happy. Everyone was. Nicholas was glad she was sent here.

"'Tis in fact like a dream," he said, taking a place before the priest with Kestrel at his side. It was like a whirlwind. They'd met just a fortnight ago and he was making her his wife. He was making a Lancaster his wife. He didn't care. He loved her. He'd kill anyone who questioned it.

He had to call for quiet so the priest could get on with the ceremony.

Nicholas watched her while they answered Father Philip's questions, candlelight falling on her face. He couldn't wait to be alone with her. Everyone would have to have a celebration tomorrow night. Tonight was theirs.

"...and do you promise to love and cherish her 'til death parts you?"

Nicholas gazed into her eyes, and with the confidence of David when he went up against Goliath said, "Death will not part us."

He wanted to ask Father Philip if there were any parts he could leave out so he could get to kissing her. But he kept quiet lest she think him an overeager barbarian.

When it finally came time to kiss her, he still needed to hold back and control himself. He was in a house of God, after all.

Everyone cheered as Nicholas and Kestrel became husband and wife and he hurried her out of the chapel.

When he had everyone's attention again—which took quite long thanks to every woman from the castle *and* the village wanting to wish her their best. The men poked and ribbed him about his good fortune and excellent choice of wife—he told them to prepare for a feast and celebration tomorrow.

"No one will work today," his wife called out. "And anyone who must work today to prepare for the feast will not work at all *during* the feast."

They began to cheer again but quieted and turned their gazes to Nicholas, who cast his wife a stormy side-glance.

They were waiting for his agreement. He gave it with a nod. "As the lady says."

The roar rose up to the turrets. People began singing and some danced.

Nicholas took the opportunity to spirit Kestrel away to the castle. To his chambers. Their chambers.

She stood at the doorway looking into the large bedchamber, the enormous bed in the center of it all. The mattress looked thick and inviting covered in woolen and fur blankets. The heavy four posts in each corner were polished and attached to a frame from whence curtains fell around the bed. For now, they were tied back. There were trunks, large and small, laid out along some of the walls. Wooden bookshelves lined a wall with colorfully bound volumes of books. She liked it. She liked that he was not only good-looking but he was smart.

Leaning on one of the bedposts, he crossed his ankles and folded his sensuous arms to be at ease while he studied her. "You can do whatever you want to it. I just ask that you remember 'tis my chamber, too."

"I think it's perfect just the way it is." She stepped inside and stopped at one of the polished tables around the chamber.

"It's very much like you in here. Polished and beautiful and untouched."

He came up behind her and rested his hands on her shoulders. "And now 'twill be lived in." He lifted a handful of her hair off her neck and bent his head to kiss her throat.

"I have been thinking of this all day," he whispered, his voice honey soft as he came around to face her.

She unlaced her kirtle and slipped it over her shoulders.

He watched her undress and pulled and tugged at his own clothes. "I have waited for you…it feels like forever."

"Here I am," she told him, helping him out of his léine then running her hands down his belly. "I'm yours."

He pulled her close and lifted her onto the bed. The rest of his clothes came off quickly, tossed here and there, along with his boots. Kneeling on the bed, he let her look and take her fill. And he did the same, basking in the sight of her round, upturned breasts, her erect nipples begging for his mouth to taste them.

He hauled her in and leaned over her when she arched her back. He held her slim waist in his hands and sucked her nipple into his mouth. Her long limbs curled around him. She weighed nothing, but fell draped over his arm like a veil. He'd thought of being intimate with her since they'd left the cave. He grew hard quickly. When she wrapped her fingers around him, he had to grind his jaw until it hurt to keep from coming. He hadn't been with anyone before her for years. He'd lost track of how many.

But he didn't want her hand. He wanted her.

He covered her hand with his and guided himself to her entrance. With one semi-forceful thrust, he pushed into her, once, twice, three times, until she grew wetter and able to take his full size.

Still on his knees, he held her by her hips and drove her over his length until she cried out. Her nub was as hard as a pebble. He rubbed himself over it. She trembled in his arms. He leaned forward and held her thighs up around him then pushed her down on the bed.

Atop her, he rode the crest of the wave, undulating his hips, wedging himself inside deeper, looking into her eyes and seeing his future, his children there.

His climax came slowly, pulsing, hot, searing his veins. He moved atop her and held her with one hand around her waist and the other holding her hand over her head. He filled her and then filled her again, while she clawed him, crying out his name until they laughed, covering each other's mouth while their release finally ended.

Nicholas had never felt this way before. She satisfied every inch of him. He didn't care if she wasn't a virgin. She wasn't coy and shy but bold and confident, taking hold of him as if she owned him. And he liked it.

"Tell me more about your life in the future," he asked when he turned to look at her, finally able to even his breath. "Tell me of your father and more of those gadgets. I want to know everything. You said you are a historian. What time period did you study?"

"Hmm? I'm sleepy."

"What?" He leaned up on one elbow.

She opened her eyes to him staring at her through a few strands of her hair. "Aren't you sleepy?" she asked.

"No."

She smiled, setting his heart to ruin. "Oh, yes. I forgot your great stamina on the field, practice and otherwise."

He laughed and moved her hair away from her face. "We will need to get you on the practice field if you are already sleepy."

"Um, no thanks." She shook her head as if to clear it. "If I know you're awake then I'm good."

He blinked. "I think I actually understood what you said."

"Good, now do you still want to hear about my life?"

"Aye." Nicholas smiled, pulling her in. Here is what he wanted more than anything else in his life. Moments like these, entangled in each other's arms, while her voice…her words filled the air.

"I think you will be a silver fox like my father—if you live that long," she whispered against his chest.

"I will live whether I go to battle or not," he promised.

"Will you fight at Bosworth then?"

"I would be turning my back on everything the de Marres fought for."

"They fought for treachery then?"

He studied her in the candlelight, taking in every perfect line of her face "Do you know something about Richard that I do not know?"

She shook her head. "I don't think so."

"Then we do not know for certain if he is guilty. If he lives long enough to father a son or two, the House of York could survive."

"Nicholas!" She pushed away from him. "You make me sorry I ever told you what happens. It was wrong and now I'm seeing the consequence of it. You would change God's plan—what has already been set into motion. The blame is on me."

When she put it that way... "My love," he pulled her back in, close enough that they shared breath. "I will do whatever you ask of me."

She tossed her leg around him and pushed him onto his back. "Commander, you give me too much power." She kissed a trail from his lips to his tight little nipple. He grew tight everywhere beneath her. She licked the muscles in his arms and rubbed her hot entrance over him until he grew thick and heavy.

"I love that you trust me with all this body," she whispered against his belly.

He groaned. "Do what you wish to me, Wife."

And she did. All through the night, proving that her stamina could match his own.

>>>><<<<

THE LOUD RAPPING on the door at around noon the next day finally woke them up.

It was Elia. She rushed into the room covering her eyes from the blanket Nicholas had wrapped around his waist.

"Oh, Nicky! 'Tis happened!" She hurried to the bed and reached for Kestrel's hand. "We must hide you, Kes!"

"What? Hide her? Why? What has happened?" Nicholas demanded, taking hold of one of Elia's arms.

"Oh, Nicky. There has been an accusation against our Kes."

"What is it?" he demanded, but he already knew.

"'Tis being said she is a witch. That she appeared out of thin air on the battlefield and has come to Scarborough to enrapture you!"

Kestrel gasped and covered her face in her hands.

"Being said by who?" he growled. He'd find out who started this rumor and then he would kill them.

"I do not know. 'Tis still unclear."

"Find out," he charged the head maid. She nodded and patted Kestrel's shoulder. "We will take care of this, Kes."

"I will be down shortly," he promised Elia and then shut the door behind her.

"Get dressed, my lovely. We shall go to Walter's. He has crypts below the cellars no one knows about."

"Crypts?" she asked, frozen in her spot in bed.

"They are filled with his most precious possessions. You will likely enjoy yourself," he told her, pulling on his pants and then his léine, "and I will come when I can. I must find Richard and speak with him about this."

"Ok," she agreed, "but I don't like it. I know how folks feel about witches these days."

He noticed her hands were shaking while she dressed in her chemise and kirtle. His anger burned hot against whoever ruined the morning of such a glorious night. Whoever made her afraid and tremble.

He wanted to go to her and sit beside her, but there was no time. Her accusers could be here at any moment, and though he wanted to kill them, he wanted to keep her safe first.

"Come, love," he beckoned gently while sheathing his long blade to the belt at his side. "I will keep you safe. Trust me."

Thankfully, she nodded, pulled on her slippers, and followed him out the door.

Most of the people they met on the way to the stable wished them well. Still, Nicholas kept his eyes honed on anyone coming too close to her. He warned her friends, of which there were many here at Scarborough, not to mention seeing her. "She is in danger of someone's evil plan," he told them. "I must protect her."

"We will help you!" they called back.

"Just deny that you have seen her if anyone comes here looking for her," Nicholas charged them.

The people gave their words and went about their business as if they hadn't seen her.

"We will have to enjoy our celebration some other time," she told him after he pulled her up in front of him in his saddle.

"'Twill be sooner than you think. I intend to squash this now."

They did no more talking and rode hard to Walter's.

The old merchant needed no prompting or monetary promises to do as Nicholas asked him. He opened his crypts to them without question and left them alone once he had her settled in.

"What now?" she asked Nicholas when they were alone. "What will you do?"

"First, go to the king and get him to denounce this."

"Do you think he will?"

"If he values his life. After that, I intend to discover who started this and kill him and any others with him."

"Nicholas," she went to him and fell into his arms. "You can't go around killing anyone who calls me a witch."

He mumbled an oath and ground his jaw. "That is exactly what I am going to do."

# Chapter Twenty-Three

N ICHOLAS THUNDERED HOME. His horse's hooves tore the ground beneath him. He cursed himself for never making friends with his men. He had many under him, but he trusted none of them with Kestrel's life. He didn't know what they would do if the king threatened them or paid them. For that reason, he would rather do this alone. She would be safe at Walter's. He would end this.

He dismounted before the horse came to a complete halt at the castle doors. He rushed inside, calling for the king. He made his way to the great hall, the solar, the king's bedchamber, but Richard was not in any of those places.

"Richard!" he called out.

"Cousin, what is this uproar about?"

Nicholas pivoted on his heel and moved his hand across his hips to the hilt of his sword.

"What are you doing here, Reg?"

His cousin looked terrified for a moment and then found strength from somewhere, mayhap his mother's de Marre's blood. "I came to see the king." He lifted his chin. "As his guest."

Nicholas cast him an angry snarl. "And you think that means I will not throw you out of my castle?"

Reg shifted from foot to foot. He looked just a slight shade paler.

"What do you know about this accusation that my wife is a

witch?"

"Only what I have heard."

"Which is what exactly?" Nicholas moved forward.

Reg stepped back. "That she appeared out of nowhere on the battlefield. Men say they saw her, and they saw you take her away. More people are coming forward."

Nicholas wanted to be sick. How many men? What else were they saying? "Who was the man who first brought this to everyone's attention?"

"I…I do not know."

"I will find out," Nicholas vowed, close to his face. "Now, bring me to where *more people are coming forward*. Who are they coming forward to? Where?"

"I…I…"

"Reg, you will no longer enjoy the privilege of living in a house I paid for if you do not start telling me what I want to know."

"They are men from your garrison," Reg told him without further provocation. "They were there at the battle. They saw her magically appear."

"Nonsense! I was there, as well," Nicholas argued, terrified that even Reg seemed to believe it. "She crawled onto the battlefield, hardly able to stand. I saw her! Now take me to where they are meeting!" he demanded and gave Reg a shove toward the stairs.

"They are your own men, Nicholas!"

"No. The king's personal guard, but not my men."

"The king's guard was not there at that battlefield," Reg reminded him. "Why bring me before them and have them hate me for betraying them?"

But Nicholas didn't answer. He dragged Reg to the gatehouse. One of his men? He would find out who.

When they arrived, none of the men appeared afraid or guilty. They greeted him as they should and continued whatever they were doing, polishing their swords, eating, talking. There weren't many men present. The absent guards were in Nottingham or Leicester fighting the Reds. Some of the king's guard was there. Where were the others?

"Which of you accused my wife of being a witch?" he demanded of them. He released Reg, who slunk away in the shadows.

"A witch?" Charlie Mayfair asked, stepping forward. "That is a serious accusation, my lord. I do not think any of the men—" he turned around to face them, all of them shaking their heads. "We are all fond of Lady Scarborough. None of us would say something that would cost her her life."

For the first time, Nicholas was happy his men loved his wife. But someone was deceiving him. "I was told the rumor started here."

"We are your men, my lord," Charlie implored.

"But someone else—!" Reg suggested. "You cannot speak for every man here. They must all be questioned."

Charlie looked at Nicholas.

"I want everyone questioned thoroughly," Nicholas agreed and turned to Reg. "Beginning with you, Cousin. Charlie, you will do the questioning. I must find the king."

He slowed down just a bit when he exited the garrison. Was Elizabeth in the castle? Where was Elia? He set out to find them and came upon Elia only. "Richard and Elizabeth left the grounds shortly after you and Kes did. They left without his personal guards. Some of them have gone off to find him."

"They let the king and their lady leave without any escort?" Nicholas asked in a low voice. "I will have their hides and their titles. Do you know where they were going?"

She shook her head. "They made no spectacle of leaving. They didn't even take the carriage. I tried to stop him. 'Tis foolish to run around the countryside unprotected, when so many do not like him. He would not listen, and you know Lizzie. She was running out the door."

"He knew about the accusations when he left, aye?" he asked

her, not really certain what it meant if he did.

"I would assume so, though 'twasn't me who told him. I suspect whoever started this terrible accusation went to the king with it first."

He told her about Reg and all the guardsmen, the king's included. She promised to give it her thought.

"I am off to find the king," he said on his way out. "Or I'll start taking heads until I find the right one."

He left Scarborough and tried to think of where Richard could be. He would not have taken Elizabeth to be alone with her. He had his own house attached to the castle to be alone with her. He hadn't run off to stop this rumor. He would have told Elia if he was trying to help Kestrel.

Nicholas' belly dropped. He had to find him. He tried to think of all the places Richard might go and why he would seemingly run away. The charge against Kestrel was very serious. She could be burned on a pike. He'd seen it before when charges were made against Agnes Barlow and Kate, the butcher's daughter, last year in Nottingham. It was torture. The screams reminded him of his mother's. He would never allow Kestrel to go through it.

He rode through the market, though he doubted the king would be out buying goods.

Two hours later, he decided to go back and check on Kestrel. He'd search for the king again later. As he neared Walter's house, his heart accelerated at the thought of seeing her. He couldn't wait. He missed her. When had his heart become so lost to her? He suspected it was when they were *taking pictures*. He had to ask her patience a little longer.

He rushed to the front door and knocked.

He heard footsteps approaching the door and knocked again.

"All right!" Walter's gravelly voice sounded from the other side. "I am coming."

He opened the door and smiled at Nicholas.

"She is all right then?" he breathed.

Walter smiled and nodded. "She has been keeping busy."

Walter led him inside and then down to the cellars. "Did you speak to the king?"

"I cannot find him."

They descended into the crypt, where Kestrel had set up a chair and a table on which sat four candles, a small stack of parchment, and an inkwell and quill.

She looked up from her writing and saw him. Her expression mirrored what his heart felt. She rose from her chair and went to him. He reached her first and gathered her in his arms.

"I could not wait to see you again," he whispered into her ear.

"Tell me it's safe."

When he remained quiet, she drew back. "How afraid should I be?"

He smiled though he felt like he'd just been stabbed in the heart. "You should not be afraid at all. I will not let anyone hurt you."

"You can only stop so much, Nicholas," she said in a soft voice. "How can you go against the law if it says I am a witch?"

"How can I not? You are my wife. I love you."

"They'll burn you, too."

His smile on her warmed. "No one is going to burn, my love. Many might die by my sword, but no one will burn. Now come, show me what you were doing. Making note of all of Walter's treasures?"

"Yes. He should have a catalogue of everything." She brought him to her table and chair. She was so brave, he thought, watching her turn her thoughts from burning to helping Walter. He sat with her for a few hours. There was work to be done. The king had to be found. But she'd been dumped here without her consent and lost everyone she loved. Now she was being called a witch. She needed his company more than ever and he was going to give it to her.

He let her teach him about a few items. He saw the passion for history in her eyes when she spoke about Cleopatra's scarab or Spartacus' sword. She knew much about history and he took pride in her while she spoke.

When it came time for him to leave, he lingered behind, holding her face in his hands, promising her the moon and the stars, kissing her until she wept in his arms.

He left with his resolve sharpened. When he returned to the castle, he found Elia and learned that the king still had not returned.

Nicholas' head maid had questioned the men, but Reg had refused to answer her questions. No matter, Nicholas would ride to his cousin's house tomorrow and see to him himself.

He took Elia to the garrison and looked for the king's men, of whom there were forty, and stood before them. "You let your king out of your sight and away from your protection. As commander of his army, I relieve you all of your duties. Leave the garrison."

Without waiting for another word to be spoken in their defense, he turned to Charlie. "Gather our men. I would have words with them."

It turned out that all the men claimed to want to protect Kestrel. They agreed that whoever started such a despicable rumor should be dealt with swiftly. It wasn't any of them, so they swore. Aye, some thought they saw her appear out of nowhere while men battled all around her. But this surely could have been a trick of the eyes. After all, swords were flying, blood was spewing, their enemies were coming at them from every angle. They didn't truly know what they saw.

Perhaps it was a Red who went to the king.

The king. The men didn't know where he was either. Had he run away? Why? Why had he taken Lizzie?

"Send your men out in groups of four," Nicholas commanded. "Spread out in every direction until you come to your area's largest town. Find them. I want answers by tomorrow night. Also, keep some men here to notify me if they return."

Hoping...praying that Charlie could be trusted, Nicholas leaned in closer to his ear. "I will be at Old Walter's. Tell only one of those men. One you trust."

"Aye, Sir," Charlie answered and turned to the men.

"How is she?" Elia asked him on their way back to the main keep.

"Keeping herself occupied. She has managed to transform Walter's crypts into a candlelit haven where she can work. But she is frightened."

The thought of her so afraid made his determination to protect her even stronger. "I must go back. I will—"

"Nicky, you must stay here," Elia told him, her golden-green gaze so familiar that he almost smiled. "You have an enemy and if he sees that you have abandoned your post, left your castle with almost no protection, he will come here—and I, unfortunately, cannot hold the castle for you while you comfort your wife."

Whatever urge he had to smile faded as the realization settled over him that she was likely correct. Let his enemy come here. But not while Elia was here with just a handful of men.

He remained awake all night, pacing the walls, waiting for some kind of word. It came just before the sun rose.

One of the guardsmen in the tower called out that riders were approaching. It was one of the groups Charlie had sent out to find the king. There were five riders. Were they his men? They were still too far away to see.

He waited with the men who were at the castle joining him on the wall.

"'Tis Charlie," one of the men called out, peering over the side. "And…the king!"

Nicholas' heart pumped wildly in his chest. He looked out over the side. Where was Lizzie?

Without another thought, he pushed off the wall and sprinted to the outer gate. He tried not to allow terrifying thoughts to creep into his head. He would find out everything soon enough.

Bursting through the outer gate on foot, his eyes searched the golden landscape for the group. When they saw him, the king broke forth and raced his mount to his commander.

"Is she here? Did she come back?" Richard called out.

"Do you speak of Lizzie?"

"Aye," the king said, reaching him. "The bitch. She tried to have me delivered to Henry Tudor."

Nicholas almost laughed it was so preposterous. Lizzie cared for Richard. She would never—would she? "Sire, where is she?"

"I had hoped she would be here. I want her found."

"You will tell me what happened over some warm mead in my solar. And then we must speak of the accusations against my wife."

"Aye. I am aware that she has been accused of being a witch."

"Who is her accuser?"

"I will not tell you that and make you guilty of murder."

Nicholas would find out. "Of course, I will kill the bastard who would try to have my wife burned at the stake. The claim is ridiculous."

"I would think so." Richard kicked his horse and the beast galloped up the long, walled pathway to the castle. Nicholas and his men followed behind.

"She told me that her mother was meeting Henry Tudor in a tavern in Huntington, outside the north wall of York."

"So you went alone?" Nicholas asked the king while he stoked the fire in the hearth. The morning was cool with fog rolling in from the north.

"I didn't bring any men because that bitch told me it might alert the Tudors."

"What did you think to do to him?"

"Kill him. What else?"

"And what happened?"

"We were attacked on the road. I was nearly killed," Richard told him, sipping his mead. "Do you not have anything stronger?"

Nicholas asked one of the servants to bring some wine to the solar, and then set his attention on Richard once again. "And Lizzie? What became of her?"

"She ran off. At first, I did not know what was going on. I was struck and dragged off the road. But then I saw her, standing a few feet away with her mother. She was watching me as stoic as her mother was gleeful. Henry was there watching as well. 'Twas his uncle, that bastard, Jasper who struck me. Henry warned me to come to Bosworth. He said he would be waiting. He did not want to kill me without a battle."

For a moment, Nicholas felt pity for Richard, but he'd been a fool to leave the castle without his guard. He was the damned king. Men…and little boys had been killed for the title.

"So, Henry wants to ridicule you," Nicholas pointed out.

"You will not let him."

Nicholas shook his head. "And then what happened?"

"I do not know. I was struck again and left for dead. I woke up when the men came upon me. Thank the Lord you sent them to find me."

"Aye. What about my wife?"

"Ah, your wife. Send for her."

"She is not here. I sent her away."

"Well, bring her back, Brother. I will give the order that if a hair on her head is touched, whoever touched it will die regretting it."

Nicholas breathed. "Thank you, Richard."

"You love this woman."

"Aye."

Richard smiled. "Finally. I began to fear you were incapable of being in love. Go bring her back."

Nicholas owed him much. He would explain to Kestrel why he couldn't allow Henry to belittle the king. She would understand. She would be happy to come home.

But she wasn't home. They had only been husband and wife for a day. Did she consider his castle her home? Would she ever? He'd finally stopped worrying about Simeon getting his hands on the brooch and her choosing to return to her time. Now, he couldn't blame her for wanting to return.

He rode to Walter's and slid out of his saddle in a hurry.

He missed her. He knew it had only been several hours since he saw her last, but it felt as if a hundred years had passed.

He knocked and then pushed the door open.

One of Walter's servants, (Walter was the only merchant wealthy enough to have servants) who was about to do the same thing from his side, was knocked several feet behind the door.

Nicholas hurried to him and grabbed hold of him before he fell. "My apologies! Have I injured you?"

The servant shook his head. He looked more shaken by speaking with Nicholas than by almost being trampled by him. The older man was afraid of Nicholas. Most people were. He was big and scarred and he rarely smiled.

He didn't smile now but spoke gently while he patted the man's shoulder. "What is your name?"

"Jonathan, my lord."

"Jonathan, I have no reason to hurt you. You must not fear me, aye?"

"Aye, my lord," Jonathan nodded. His shoulders fell from around his ears.

"My wife," he finally smiled as he turned to go find her, "would have my head if she thought I went around frightening ser—"

She stood before him, gazing at him as if he were a feast for her eyes. But it was she who ravished his soul. Garbed in her dusty dress that matched her eyes, her dark mane hanging loose around her beautiful face, she made his legs go a little weak.

Without saying a word, he went to her and gathered her in his arms. She clung to him with her face buried in his neck.

"The king has been found. He is denouncing the accusation. 'Tis safe for you to return, my love. Come home."

# CHAPTER TWENTY-FOUR

I T TOOK A bit of time to get going from Walter's, mainly because Kestrel insisted on saying *goodbye* to everyone, even the stable hand. Walter doted on her as a grandfather would dote on his darling granddaughter. She had won over everyone, especially him.

He'd known to bring one horse. They both loved riding this way, with her body relaxed, her back pressed to his chest, his nose and lips buried in her hair.

"So, Elizabeth orchestrated this entire thing with the king," she said as they headed off.

What did orchestrated mean? He shook his head. He didn't need to know. He liked all her unfamiliar words. "'Twould seem so. She won his trust and then enticed him to follow her into Henry Tudor's lair."

Kestrel shook her head and sighed. "What a badass she turned out to be."

He laughed. "Badass? What kind of insult is that.?"

"It's not an insult in twenty nineteen. It means impressive, tough and dangerous. She almost got the job done. Richard will probably kill her for treason if he wins, won't he?"

"Aye," he said. Aye, she was correct. He hadn't even thought of it yet what with Kestrel's rescue being the only thing on his mind. "She brought him to the camp of his enemy."

They both nodded. Elizabeth would not survive Richard's

victory.

"But…" He didn't want to say it, to talk about it. He couldn't stop his own tongue. "I still need to fight for him. She will have to stay away—" he stopped and looked into Kestrel's eyes. He didn't want to have this conversation.

"He saved you, my love."

Tears filled her eyes. She let them fall. "At what cost? You? Let them burn me if it will save you."

He stopped the horse and took her face in his hands. "No. Do not speak such things."

He lowered his lips to hers, letting his heart pound heavy with the desire to kiss her.

He waited another moment and then turned his horse left, off the road.

"Where are we going?" she asked with her cheek pressed to his chest.

"To be alone."

They rode around trees and bramble until they came to a small patch of grass. They'd ridden around long enough to find it and, in that time, they had seen no one.

This place was private.

He slipped out of the saddle, light on his feet. He lifted his arms to her, and she fell into them. He kissed her and then carried her to a giant tree and set her under it. "Would you have me out here in the open under the trees?"

"I'd have you anywhere," she said, kissing his mouth. "Anywhere you want me."

"I want you all the time."

She giggled as he softly bit her lip, then her chin. She lay back, pulling him with her.

"No man has ever treated me the way you do, Nicholas. I'm so glad the brooch sent me back to you."

He smiled, parting her lips with his tongue, untying the laces of her dress. He moved his body over hers, loving how she felt under him. He grew harder for her and ran his palms under her skirts…over her arse in her lacy *panties*.

He didn't want to wait. He could not wait much longer. He was hard, stretching his hose to its limit.

With a flick of his wrist, he untied the laces of his hose and released himself into his hand. He held his velvet tip to the lacy barrier between them.

He wanted to tear it away. It would have taken nothing, but he pulled them down instead. Slowly, sensually, he took her full rump in his hands while she took him into her body, snugly at first and then sleeker as she molded to him.

Nicholas looked down into her eyes and his heart melted within him. He wondered how he had ever lived in a world without her before.

"I feel as if I have been surviving from one battle to the next. Then you appeared and I began to live."

She lifted her hips beneath him and gasped softly when the full size of him filled her. She rubbed herself against him and he thrust with more conviction.

"You made the most terrifying and terrible thing in my life bearable…and then enjoyable. You saved my life and my heart right along with it. You're a man in full splendor, and I'm never letting you go."

She tightened her grip on him and he drove himself deeper and then withdrew. They both held their breath for an instant, until he sank within her again, this time with the evidence of his passion filling her.

She clung to him and cried out into his shoulder as her passion poured out onto him.

Nicholas held her in his arms, in the grass, beneath a giant tree. Birdsongs sounded from the branches above. A cool, refreshing breeze rustled the leaves and her hair.

A perfect day thanks to her. He smiled and swept a tendril of hair away from her eyes. But he didn't want the king changing his mind because they'd kept him waiting.

"We should be getting back." He kissed her and then rose up

to pull his hose back on.

She was sizing him up and smiling when he turned back around to look at her. He did the same while she pulled up her panties and let down her skirts.

They didn't talk about the king on the way back. Kestrel was still set on begging him not to fight against Henry. He understood that altering time was forbidden and dangerous, but after what Richard had done this morning, the idea of abandoning him didn't sit well with Nicholas.

"Did Elizabeth ever mention Henry to you?" he asked her. Now that the danger to Kestrel was over, Elizabeth bombarded his thoughts. What kind of clever, dangerous enemy to Richard was she? How long had she felt animosity toward him—enough to lure him to his death?

"She never did," his wife replied, resting against him. "And she only spoke of the king when she was asked about him. She mostly wanted to know what happened to me, was my memory getting any better? She asked a lot of questions about you."

"What kinds of questions?"

She shrugged and he kissed the top of her head. "Questions like was I responsible for all your smiles."

"What did you tell her?" he whispered against her ear.

"That I wasn't responsible for *all* your smiles."

"Not true," he laughed softly. "You are responsible for all of them, all my laughter, all my hopes. Everything. What I do with it all is my choice. You awakened me and now I want it all with you."

He felt her take in a long, deep breath and then let it out as if all her pain rode on the breath of that wave and left her body. "I love you, Nicholas."

"And I love you, Kestrel."

When they reached the castle, they dismounted and were on their way to their room when they were stopped by a group of his men.

"King Richard wishes to see you as soon as you return," said one of the guards. "Forgive us, my lord, but we are to escort you."

"Is something wrong?' Kestrel asked him, looking up.

"No, love," he reassured. He wished he felt the confidence with which he spoke. Had something happened? He didn't want to alarm Kestrel, so he said nothing.

They were escorted to Nicholas' solar, where the king awaited them.

Sitting in a chair beside the king, with a drink in his hand, was Reg. Why did Nicholas' blood run cold in his veins? "What is going on?" he asked the king.

He noticed more guards filing into the solar. Some of them were the men Nicholas had relieved of duty yesterday.

"Nicholas," the king said, looking forlorn. "I thought you were on my side."

"What are you talking about?" Nicholas growled.

"How could you take a Lancaster as your bride? And now, she may be a witch!"

No! Nicholas' murderous gaze went to Reg as even more guards filled the solar. Five men came at him immediately while four others took hold of Kestrel.

When they put their hands on her, Nicholas fought against his captors and prevailed, but more men came. Some of his own men, afraid to show disloyalty to the king. He fought them but there were too many holding him back.

"We will have trial in one hour," Richard informed him. "Reg tells me there are witnesses already waiting to speak to me."

"Richard!" Nicholas shouted at him. "Do not do this! You will die at Bosworth Field without me. I will not fight for you if you do not stop this!"

"'Tis out of my hands, Nicky. The people want justice. Let us have her trial and if she is found guilty, I will do nothing until Bosworth Field is over and I am safe. Then, I will let her go to you."

"Release her now!" Nicholas bellowed, shaking the walls.

Richard offered Kestrel a pitying look. "Take her away," he commanded, then departed the solar. The four men holding Kestrel left after him. Reg and fourteen others stayed behind with Nicholas.

"I am going to kill you," he warned Reg on a low growl.

His cousin's mocking laughter filled his soul. "You are nothing now, Nicholas. Soon, Richard will give this castle to me. You and your witch wife will be dead, and life will be happy without you in it once again. Take him to the great hall!" Reg commanded.

There were already people in the great hall, waiting to begin the trial. This has been planned, Nicholas realized, his wrath overflowing. He scanned the hall and found Richard sitting at Nicholas' table with Reg taking Kestrel's seat. Which one of them would he kill first?

They brought her in. Another man had replaced one of the original four. Charlie.

Nicholas stared at him and his fingers around Kestrel's upper arm. Betrayal hooked him in the guts. He cast Charlie a murderous glance and then met the gaze of his wife.

She was afraid. He could see it in her eyes. She kept it hidden and he admired her for it. He would get her out of this. She tried to see him through the group of men who subdued him. His heart thrashed against his ribs. There were too many guardsmen, the kings and his own, filling the great hall. He couldn't take them all.

The king's voice tore his attention away from her. Nicholas heard his words as if in a deep fog. *Prove…Witch…Witnesses.* No. Nicholas closed his eyes then opened them again when Reg motioned to a certain man among them to come forward.

"Your Majesty, this is John, the smith from the market."

John stared, wide-eyed at the king and rolled his cap in his hands.

"John, tell the king what you saw."

"I seen her holding her arms out to the earl. He went to her as if he had no choice in the matter. He was getting ready to kiss her! We all know the earl has not taken a woman in years."

Nicholas didn't care how he knew that. It was something else the fool had said… "I went to her as if I had no choice because I didn't. I love her. 'Twas no spell involved. 'Twas her kindness and determination to help all of you."

Reg told the guards to quiet him. One of the fourteen holding him punched him in the gut.

"Richard!" Nicholas shouted again. "Stop this. Let her go and I—"

The guard struck him again, this time thanks to the king's silent order.

His cousin called another witness against her. No one stepped forward.

Nicholas looked at Charlie. "Let her go or I will kill you."

Charlie didn't seem like he was going to defy him, despite Nicholas' poor odds of getting out of this alive if he tried—Charlie uncurled his fingers, took his hand away, and winked at his commander.

It was all Nicholas needed to unleash the thing it took four-teen men to subdue. They'd taken his sword. He didn't need it when he let out a shout and took two men down with his fists and elbows alone.

Reg and the king bolted to their feet. People started running. A woman screamed when he yanked a sword free from one of the men who went down. Armed, he cut through any guards who lifted their swords to him. There were seven. The other seven who had been holding him sheathed their blades and held up their hands in surrender.

Charlie cut down two of the guards who held Kestrel and was fighting the third when Nicholas leaped over the table separating him from them and jammed his sword into the guardsmen's back. He pushed the man away before his body hit the floor and took his wife in his arms.

"Find my cousin and bring him to me," he ordered Charlie.

"Aye, Sir."

"And Charlie."

"Aye, Sir?"

"You are now my first in command. You will sit at my table from now on."

Charlie smiled. "Aye, Sir."

"Go."

Elia hurried to them and took Kestrel from his arms. "Oh, my dearest girl, my dearest girl," she cried. "Are you hurt?" What can I get you?"

They were the same questions Nicholas would have asked her, so he waited for her reply.

"Nicholas," she said softly. "Get me Nicholas."

He hadn't wept since he was seven. And he wouldn't begin now, but he came close. He stepped forward and pulled her gently into his embrace. "I am right here, my love."

"You saved my life yet again, Sir Knight," she cried in a muffled voice, with her face pushed into his léine.

He didn't like that she had seen him kill again. It was a difficult thing to forget. And now, he thought as Charlie and his men returned with Reg, he was going to kill one more. "Come, love. Let Elia take you to our room."

"No, I wish to stay here and see what happens to Reg."

"Why would you care about such a thing? Unless you wish to see me end his life—and knowing you, I do not think 'tis that."

"It isn't. I want you to remember that he has a wife and children."

"I would be doing them a courtesy," he countered.

"That is not for you to decide, Nicholas," she said softly.

"Do you hear this?" he called out to Reg, who was the one being held back now. "My wife, the woman you brought witnesses against, pleads with me for your life. This woman, whom you were more than ready to see burned alive, asks me to remember your wife and children."

Nicholas' gaze went dark. "You are not worthy to stand before her."

In two strides, he reached his cousin and punched him hard enough to break his nose. "You were always sorry I wasn't killed along with my family. I had what you wanted. The king's favor. You sicken me. I let you live because of her. But you will take your family away from Scarborough. As far away as you can get. I will give you a fortnight to go. If I see your face after that, I will kill you. Do you understand?"

Reg nodded, holding his bloody nose.

"Get him out of here."

"My lord," Charlie said, staying behind. "We have the king also."

"Let him go. He is still your king."

He returned his attention to his wife. "How was that?"

"Very good." She smiled and moved closer to him. "Now I think I will go with Elia to our room. I would like to rest."

"Of course," he said and handed her over to his head maid with a kiss to his wife's head.

He stayed in the great hall helping his men clear it of the dead. After that, they drank to Kestrel's safety.

"I had no intention of letting anyone hurt her, my lord," Charlie told him. "I relieved one of the guards holding her. I killed him just beyond the hall. I knew it was only a matter of time before you broke free and killed them all."

Charlie raised his cup to him and seeing him, his men did the same.

"What did you do with the king?" Nicholas asked.

"He is locked in his house. I have four guards stationed at the door."

"Good. I want to speak to him."

"I thought you would, my lord."

Nicholas gave his first in command a curious look and then smiled at him. He smiled at them all. Then he left to go speak to the king.

※≫≫✕≪≪

"I WAS AFRAID Nicholas would be hurt or killed," Kes told Elia in the library. The women sat in the chairs with warm mead spiked with Scottish whisky in their hands. "I couldn't even see him there were so many man…"

"The king knows how fearsome Nicky is. And still those men were not enough."

Kes was quiet for a time, thinking about it all and how Nicholas had gone wild over her and killed seven men where they stood.

She wasn't against what he had had to do. He was the kind of man needed in the fifteenth century. If he wasn't a well-abled warrior, she would have been dead twice now.

The truth of it was that she loved that he could fight so well. She loved that though he could be a merciless savage, he was also kind and thoughtful once a person got to know him. She'd seen how he'd treated Jonathan at Walter's.

"You did well raising him, Elia," Kes told her friend. "He's a good man."

"Aye," Elia smiled. Her cheeks were pink, adding more color to her eyes. "But Edward was a good father to him. He is the reason Nicholas chose to be a knight, besides his other titles. He is an extraordinary man, and you, my dearest, are an extraordinary woman. You are meant to be together."

"He is extraordinary. You're right about that. Did you see him break free of all those men? It was like watching Samson. He fought with emotion and steadfast determination. I almost loved watching him." She smiled and Elia nodded.

"Meant to be."

"You say your father was…is like him. You had a finger pointing your way. You are fortunate."

"I didn't feel fortunate. I felt cursed. Cursed to know there was at least one good man out there and he was my father. I had

236

this great role model to show me what I wanted and there weren't many more men like him by the time the twentieth-first century rolled around."

"What made him different?" Elia asked.

"I don't know," Kes told her honestly. "But Mr. Green— hmph Sir Gawaine of the Round Table read my lineage back only on my father's side before he gave me the brooch. After my mother died, my father threw himself into his work. I didn't see him all that much. But I heard him crying some nights for my mother. He loved her. I thought that was how all men loved the women they were with. I was wrong. I was beat over the head with the truth until I lost hope of ever finding a really good man."

The door opened and Nicholas stepped inside. When he saw her, he smiled as if she were the only thing he ever wanted to see again.

"Are you well?" he asked tenderly, coming around to her chair.

"Yes. I wasn't hurt, just frightened. I needed some quiet time. Is everything under control outside these doors?"

"Aye. I spoke to the king."

"And?"

"And if I refuse to fight for him at Bosworth Field, he will not show up. Meaning he will not die there." They both said the last together.

History would be changed.

# CHAPTER TWENTY-FIVE

THEY REACHED CAMP outside of Leicester early in the morning. It had taken a sennight to get here since leaving Scarborough. Nicholas missed Kestrel and hated having to be here to fight for a man who had tried to have his wife burned for being a witch. Richard had listened to lies because her last name was Lancaster. He'd shown no mercy to Nicholas' wife and, for that, Nicholas would show him none.

But he had to pretend that he would. He trained with his men, as he did now, and sometimes ate and drank with them when they were home, while Kestrel spent time with Elia and her other dozens of friends, none of whom were stately, though she had gotten along well with Elizabeth. He wondered if she missed him.

He leaped to the right and avoided Charlie's blade *and* William's sword coming from the other side. William was Charlie's best friend and second in command—and sneaky.

Good. Nicholas liked it. He swung his sword and the force of his blade striking William's sent the soldier's blade flying.

Kestrel had told Nicholas about her friends in the future, Lilith, Kim, Constantine, and Jack. Nicholas wasn't happy that she had lived with two men, but it was over five hundred years from now. The world had changed. There were airplanes and HDTVs, and virtual reality gadgets, video games, and so much more that he couldn't wrap his head around it all. He would never have believed what she told him of her time if he didn't know her.

But he did know her. In less than a month, he'd been through more with her than with anyone else in his life. He knew how she reacted to things, what made her laugh and smile, and what annoyed her.

Charlie's sword came at him but there had been too much hesitation. Nicholas swung left then right, and then ending the session with an upper cut swing that sent Charlie's blade end over end into the dirt.

"That was very good," Nicholas told them.

"Good?" Charlie asked with an incredulous laugh. "In all six sessions, we didn't last longer than a few breaths against you."

"A few breaths is better than what the king's guard had in my great hall a few days ago," Nicholas quipped, sheathing his sword. "You both fought well, and you will not be fighting me, so I have no doubt you will both come out alive in whatever battle you fight."

They all laughed together, knowing he was correct. If they could last a few breaths with him, they could win the battle.

"You will remember to stay near me tomorrow," he told them. "All will be well."

He didn't tell them about pulling them out of the battle. He trusted Charlie but he didn't know the rest enough to trust that word wouldn't get back to the king. This had to be perfect.

"Aye, Sir," they both agreed.

They were his friends, loyal and trustworthy with much, so far. Nicholas decided he liked having friends and thought about going back home when everyone returned and inviting Lord and Lady Thomas FitzRoy, and Claire, the laundress, and her seven brothers to sit at his table. Kestrel would enjoy Claire and Lady FitzRoy's company.

When the battle was over, he expected to keep Scarborough, since he hadn't fought against the victor. But if not, he had enough to build his own castle and live comfortably with Kestrel and Elia and anyone else who wanted to join them, wherever they chose. Still, he liked living in Scarborough.

He wondered what kind of man Henry Tudor was. They were about the same age. Would the new king throw him in some dungeon and forget about him?

He saw Richard, resting on a short wall, watching him as he approached.

"You truly are unbeatable," the king told him when Nicholas reached him. "And magnificent to behold when you are at war."

Nicholas bowed his head and walked past him. Richard caught up.

"Why did you not kill Reg?"

"Because my wife asked me not to."

"She makes you weaker."

Nicholas cast him a sneer. "If you see it that way, that is your choice, Sire."

"His was the first accusation to reach my ears against your wife," the king admitted.

"I thought as much," Nicholas told him, not surprised by this news.

"Henry declared himself king today by right of conquest," Richard also informed him. "He is confident."

Nicholas looked at Richard and nodded. "He is."

"If I lose, whoever fights for me tomorrow commits treason and will lose his lands." Richard stared at him. "Swear you will not abandon me."

"I will not."

The king, a bit shorter than Nicholas, moved closer. "I will stay near you on the battlefield tomorrow, Nicky."

"Aye, stay close, but also fight to keep yourself alive."

"Of course." The king laughed a haughty laugh. "I do have skills, you know."

"Of course."

They reached the camp and Nicholas blended in with the men, eight thousand strong. Another three would be here by morning. Tents were erected in rows and the rows went on almost endlessly. If Richard couldn't win with all this, that was, as Kestrel would say, Richard's problem.

He prayed she and Elia made it safely to Elizabeth and her mother. He was thankful the young sister of his heart had contacted him. She had written that she loved him, and was sorry for betraying the House of York, but soon, both houses would be united and there could finally be peace. Aye, Nicholas wanted that for the first time in his life. He'd fallen in love with a Lancaster and joined with her. He wanted Elizabeth to know that he fully supported a union between her and Henry. He contacted her back to tell her, for she had given him her location and was but a day away. He told her he was sending his wife and Elia to her. They would explain his decision. If they continued onward to the town north of Bosworth, which was Elizabeth's plan, he would meet them when they arrived.

Richard's forces were ten miles from the battlefield. There was already word from runners that the Tudor army was also waiting and ready to fight.

Tomorrow morning then.

THEY HEADED OUT two hours before dawn. At any other time in his life, Nicholas would have welcomed the day and the passion for battle he possessed. He would have thrilled in the thought of killing his enemy.

But not anymore. He wanted to live in peace, to love his wife and raise their children. He was going to see to it today.

They arrived to find that the king's other three thousand men had already arrived and were engaged in battle with the Reds.

Nicholas needed to get the king on the field, where he would have been if none of this witch nonsense had happened. Nicholas would have fought for him and the king still would have died. Nothing would be changed.

"I do not do this for you, but for the House of York," he told the king while watching the fighting with his garrison before they rode out onto the field. "As my fathers did before me, I will fight to keep it alive."

Richard smiled genuinely for the first time in days. "You never failed Edward. You will never fail me."

"Never," Nicholas said, concealing his disgust. "For York!"

"For York!" Richard shouted and flicked his reins. Nicholas and Charlie flicked theirs as well. But the rest of the men held back. The king didn't notice when they entered the fray.

The smell of blood enticed Nicholas' senses and, for an instant, he wanted to fight the Reds and kill them all.

He saw a rider approaching. He wore gold armor including a helmet with its visor down. A yellow scarf waved like a pennant from his spear. Lizzie's. It was Henry Tudor.

Nicholas turned his horse to the king. "You no longer have my support, Richard. I will not kill you, but I will not fight for you anymore. Fight to keep yourself alive." He dismissed Charlie and his first in command retreated with the slightest of smiles.

"What?" Richard shouted, wide-eyed. "No! You betray me? You betray your fathers! I will live and find your wife, and see that every man who wants a turn—"

A thump resounded through the clash of swords around Nicholas. He stopped and turned to see Henry's spear sticking out of Richard's chest, the yellow scarf now red with the king's blood.

He looked at the new king as sunlight splashed over his golden armor. Mayhap there would be peace.

KES WAITED IN the town hall where Henry Tudor sat the night before after going over the latest plans for the war.

Kes was a bit star-struck by him. This guy started the Tudor Dynasty, which included Henry VIII, Mary Tudor, also known as "Bloody Mary", Queen Elizabeth I aka The Virgin Queen. Huge historical figures. She'd been happy to know, once she'd met him, that he was a nice enough guy, as far as kings went. He'd listened to her and Elia and when they'd told him what they knew, that Nicholas would not lift his sword on the battlefield unless it was to save his own life, he remarked how fortunate Nicholas was to have such beautiful confidants, Kes especially being odd in appearance with her hair worn loose around her shoulders and her eyes like oceans waiting to be explored. He'd spent an hour with them and appeared quite happy when Elizabeth had joined them. They seemed quite taken with each other and Kes had to pinch herself twice to believe she was watching history unfold.

He'd gone off to battle this morning vowing not to harm Nicholas. Kes prayed that her husband stayed his course.

Her husband. She'd never thought she'd have one. Never thought she wanted one. But here she was trying to save him from fighting against the wrong man.

She didn't rest but paced the floor in the town hall like a pendulum, lulling her friends to sleep.

When she heard the sound of clinking armor and mail outside the window, she knew men had returned. But whose men were they?

"We return victorious!" Henry shouted from outside.

Kes hurried to the window. When she looked out, she saw Nicholas strung to four ropes tied to his four limbs.

"King Richard is dead!"

"Long live King Henry!" the crowd shouted back.

She hurried to the king's table and told him who the man was. Henry recognized him and ordered that Nicholas be untied immediately.

His orders were carried out and Kes ran to him and leaped into his arms, home again.

"Did you do it? Did you ride away from him?" she asked, needing to know. She didn't want angry, time traveling knights after her and Nicholas.

"Aye. I did it. He was making threats when Henry's lance went through him."

"And did Henry see you walk away?"

"He did."

"And he hated it."

They both spun around at the sound of Henry's voice with his soft French tones. "I do not enjoy watching such a difficult decision being made and carried out. You stepped away from your king. Why?"

It was a fair question. Why would another king trust him?

"He did not value life," Nicholas told them "He did what he wanted and took the counsel of fools."

While he spoke, Henry nodded. "How will we mend the holes this place now represents?

"Show the people that you care for them, even the lowest born," Nicholas told him. "They have had an untrustworthy king for almost two years. Give them something new. Earn their loyalty."

They all had dinner together and Nicholas was surprised and grateful that Henry seemed to like him. He figured he had Lizzie to thank. "I told him everything about you," she said at dinner, sitting close to him, "and how much my father and my family loved you."

He pulled her in under one arm and kissed the top of her head. "Thank you, Lizzie. I am in your debt."

"Nonsense, Brother. I just want you to be happy."

"And I want the same for you."

"I am. Henry is very kind and attentive. I'm happy to say that he has won my heart."

He looked at her and quirked his mouth. "Who would have ever thought our hearts could be won?"

They smiled at each other and then laughed.

"We must come to Scarborough as Richard did and live with you and Kes for a month or two."

"We would enjoy that." He smiled and she squeezed his arm and gave his shoulder a quick kiss.

He looked at Kestrel sitting on the other side of him, speaking to Charlie. He smiled and she caught a glimpse of it. She stopped talking and turned to him. She looked as breathless at the sight of him as he was of her.

"Let's leave here soon," she purred, moving closer to him. "I want to be alone with you."

He lifted his hand. "Sire?"

Henry Tudor looked his way. "My wife and I wish to retire. It has been a trying time."

"Ah, yes. Of course," he said with a knowing smile while Lizzie giggled behind him. "You may go."

He took his wife's hand and left the hall with her. He'd paid for two small rooms at the town inn. The other for Elia. Nicholas had a tent, but he thought his wife would prefer sleeping in a bed. They walked together in the twilight.

"'Tis difficult to believe that Richard, the last Yorkist king, is dead and that I had much to do with it."

"You simply did not fight for him—"

"I led him onto the field."

"Nicholas." She stopped walking and turned to him. "Do you think he was a good king?"

"I do not think he was a good *man*. How then could he be a good king?"

"Right. It is not your fault he died. It's his fault." She smiled and he felt as if he were falling in love with her all over again. It happened often. He no longer fought it. In fact, he thrilled in it.

"Will Henry be any better?" he asked her. After all, she likely knew.

"He will do more for England than Richard in restoring the country's economical, er, financial… England will no longer be poor." She laughed softly. "I can't think right when you're looking at me."

"I cannot stop looking at you. How about Elizabeth? Will she be happy?"

She nodded. "Henry loved her very much. It's written that he locked himself in his room and wept wh—"

He stopped and looked at her. "When she died?"

"Yes."

"How? How does she die? Does Henry have anything to do with it?"

She shook her head. "She dies in childbirth."

He paled and turned away. "She was young then."

"Nicholas," Kestrel said with tears filling her eyes. "I don't want to say anything more. I've already said too much."

He nodded and stepped back. So, Elizabeth dies young. He wanted to go back to the hall and spend more time with her.

He saw two people coming toward them. Elia and Charlie. His first officer was good to escort her to the inn.

A breeze from the right brought with it the faint scent of apples and something else. Something that made the hairs on his body stand up. He turned to his wife and saw two men mounted on great warhorses appear out the shimmering air to her right. The horses were draped in trappings depicting a dragon. The men wore leather armor and had long two-edged swords dangling from their belts.

Silvery mist clung to their horses' legs. Nicholas guessed who they were, though his mind told him it was impossible.

# CHAPTER TWENTY-SIX

INSTANTLY, NICHOLAS TOOK hold of Kes' arm and pulled her behind him. He reached for his sword, but her hand stopped him.

She couldn't let Nicholas kill Sir Gawaine. And if anyone had a chance of killing Nicholas, it was this brutish knight.

Mr. Simeon had warned her about telling too much. Now they'd come after her. What were they going to do?

"Mr. Green," she said, doing her best to sound calm as she stepped around her husband, to his side. Not out of reach. "May I call you Sir Gawaine?" She cut her gaze to Luke. "Sir Lucan?"

"What do you want?" Nicholas demanded, unafraid against the legendary knights.

"We want the future telling to cease," demanded Gawain right back.

"Yes! Yes!" she held up her hands. "I'm sorry about that. It won't happen again. I think we can—"

"Do you listen to her conversations?" Nicholas asked incredulously.

He had a point. Were they listening? She gave them an angry stare and crossed her arms over her chest. "Did you plant something on me?"

They were already shaking their heads, but it wasn't in defense of them spying. "You are diverting the problem. Ms. Lancaster—"

"She is Lady Scarborough," Nicholas told them. There was a warning thread in his voice that was steadily growing. "If I were you, I would stand away from her."

Sir Gawaine flicked his gaze to Sir Lucan and chuckled softly, which produced a low growl from Nicholas.

"Let me get right to the point. Ms. Lancaster," Sir Gawaine said impatiently. "We want you to return home—to your time. The future came too close to changing with you here. We are here to make certain that you go back."

She turned to Nicholas. She could go back? Back to her father, her friends, her job? Back to painkillers and cellphones and social media. "Nicholas, would you—"

"Ms. Lancaster," Sir Gawaine said, interrupting…and perhaps reading her thoughts, "you must go as you arrived. Alone."

"Can't you send him after me?"

"No. It only works every twenty years in any century."

She was looking at Nicholas when Gawaine spoke. The alarm in her eyes was set directly on him. Alone? Leave him? "No." Her voice shook. She turned to the ancient knight. "I can't."

"You must," Sir Gawaine told her. "You will no doubt disrupt time if you remain here. It should not be too much of a concern for you. 'Tis believed that you might have been brought here by mistake. The brooch has been known to malfunction."

She laughed. "What? Mistake? Sir Gawaine, nothing in my life has been so perfect for me. Nicholas has brought love into my life, and isn't that what your king wanted for others because he never had it for himself? How can my coming here be a mistake?"

"You have said too much," Gawaine said and unsheathed his sword.

Nicholas' blade was out in an instant. Charlie's was next.

Kes leaped between them and heard Nicholas swear.

"Stop it!" she demanded. "There doesn't have to be any fighting. "I told you I won't say another word. You can listen to my words or my thoughts, or whatever it is you do. If I speak of the future, you can send me back. But give me another chance."

Gawaine was already shaking his head. "'Tis not up to me."

"Just a minute now," Kes told them. "Do you mean to tell me that you came into my life and turned it completely upside-down without thought or concern for me or my family, snatched everything away and left me to my own defenses and then you expect to waltz back into my life and do it all over again? Now, you suddenly talk about filling my place? You made mistakes, didn't you, Sir Gawaine? And I must pay for them? Should I demand to speak to Lady Morgan or Lady Viviane?"

They actually cast each other nervous looks. Good. They deserved to shake in their pants a little bit.

She wasn't leaving Nicholas and it was time these two knew it. He looked drained of color when she met his gaze, so maybe he needed to know it, too. "Now, you can go and find someone else to take to the future with you, because it won't be me. I won't leave my husband. I couldn't live without him."

They looked as if they wanted to say more—to deny her, but then they both looked at Elia, oddly, at the same time. "She may go in your place."

"What?"

"No!" Nicholas turned to her. "No."

"The ladies want her," Sir Gawaine said.

Nicholas spun around on him. "Find someone else!"

Gawaine and Luke drew their swords and Nicholas and Charlie drew theirs.

"Stop it this instant!" Elia warned them through tight lips. "Kes and I will not put up with this much longer. Now speak patiently with each other or we will leave."

The men stared at her in silence for a moment.

"I will gladly show you patience, Elia," Nicholas was the first to speak. "Please do the same for me. Do not consider this."

"But I do," she told him. "I want to go ahead and find Charles Lancaster and help him heal if I can." She looked at Kes and smiled.

"Give this until morning to decide," he allowed, "and if you do decide to go, at least you will have given me a little more time with you."

She nodded and looked at Sir Gawaine.

"Wait," Kes interrupted. "You said the brooch wasn't working right. What guarantee is there that she will go to the correct time?"

"If she doesn't," Luke told her with a handsome smile. "We will go get her and try again."

That didn't sound too promising. Kes gave Elia a worried look. Elia smiled at her in return.

"We'll talk more about this, yes?"

"Yes," Elia echoed with a tender smile.

Kes hated to lose her. She couldn't imagine how Nicholas must feel. She was sorry she had told him about Elizabeth.

"We shall meet you outside the inn in the morning," Gawaine announced. "You will give us your decision then."

They agreed, albeit, Nicholas did so sounding more like a bear than a man. He dismissed Charlie when his first vowed to keep what he'd seen and heard to himself. In fact, Charlie admitted with a laugh that he didn't understand what in blazes they were all talking about anyway.

The three of them continued on to the inn in silence. Kes felt responsible for Nicholas' pain. If she hadn't come here, he wouldn't have to give up the woman who'd been like a mother to him.

Oh, what would Elia do in the twenty-first century? If she insisted on going, Kes wouldn't let her go in blind. The shock of everything would be too much. She *had* told Elia much already. Come to think of it, Elia always wanted to hear about her century.

When they arrived at the inn, Nicholas ordered three tankards of ale to be brought up to one of the rooms.

They had much to discuss.

Nicholas and Elia sat in two of the chairs by the hearth in the room, while Kes sat at the edge of the bed.

Elia listened patiently to Nicholas' thoughts and concerns and did her best to explain to him that this was what she wanted, no matter the risks.

"I have no regrets, Nicky. Not one. But I want my own adventure now. 'Tis being offered to me. I must accept it."

"But we will never see each other again," he lamented. "'Tis like you are dying."

Kes wiped her eyes. There had to be a way to find some good in this this.

"Find my father."

Elia nodded. "I will do my best."

Kes smiled and left the bed to kneel at Elia's chair and took her hand. "I feel very happy about it. You can tell him about me. Tell him I told you about the time my appendix nearly burst when I was a baby, and how I wanted to marry a cartoon dog when I was a little girl. That should help him to believe you."

Elia laughed. "All right, but what is appendix and a cartoon?"

Kes explained both, once again realizing how terribly shocking the twenty-first century was going to be. "Listen, Elia, when you get there, depending on where you land, just keep a clear head. If you are outside, remember East Sixty-second Street. Find a way to get there even if you have to walk. You'll need money. You can ask people. There will be a lot of people. Oh, a lot, Elia."

Her friend smiled, as if to reassure her.

"When you find East Sixty-second…say it. East Sixty-second Street."

"East Sixty-second Street."

"Good. Look at the doorways on the buildings. Find the number fifty-five. Go inside. You will see a man at a desk. Tell him you're there to see Art Lancaster. If he tells you my father is away, tell him a rose by any other name would smell as sweet."

"That is pretty."

"It's a line from a Shakespearean play. It's a code my dad and I use to let the doorman know to let me in. If you know the code, you can get in. Now this is a lot to take in, so let's practice while I tell you about cars and lights and horns."

"Do you think he could have something to do with this whole King Arthur thing?" Elia asked her.

"Because his name is Arthur?" Kes laughed softly. "I doubt it, but he has always been very knightly."

"His name is Arthur?" Nicholas looked up.

"Yes. Charles Arthur.

"Oh, what an adventure that would be," Elia laughed. "But you said your father never remarried after your mother died."

"Maybe he has been waiting for you."

Elia actually blushed. Kes looked at Nicholas and smiled. He didn't smile back.

That night, when Elia went to her own room, he lay awake holding Kes in his arms while he told her stories of his childhood with Elia. They made love slowly, quietly, lost in the comfort of each other's embrace.

Morning came too soon, though Kes had to smile at Elia's contagious happiness. Even Nicholas found himself smiling.

Sir Gawaine waited alone outside the inn. When he saw them, he pulled something from a fold in his cloak. "What is it going to be, Ms. Lancaster?"

"Elia is going," Kes told him. "And you better get her to the right place. Preferably, my father's apartment."

After a long, teary farewell, and a few grumbles from Sir Gawaine, the knight handed Elia the brooch and told her what to do. She took it, waved goodbye, and opened her mouth. "Pendragon."

The air shimmered for an instant and then Elia was gone. The brooch fell to the ground.

"Hell." Kes heard Nicholas mutter and watched him walk away.

Sir Gawaine reached down and plucked the brooch into his hand then he disappeared.

Would Elia find her father? If she did, would her father believe her?

Kes had every intention of sending Mr. Simeon to find out, and she thought about sending a letter with him. Surely letters were allowed. If everything worked out well, she and her father or she and Elia could correspond.

She hurried to catch up to her husband and slipped herself under his arm. He kissed the top of her head. "You refused to go back."

"As long as I'm with you, I'm happy," she told him. "I wasn't about to go back to the future without you."

"I know what you gave up for me, my love."

"And I know what you gave up for me, Nicholas. Now come, let's go back to Scarborough and lock ourselves away for a week."

"I like that idea," he said softly and leaned down to kiss her.

She would never grow tired of the taste of him, the feel of him against her, in her arms.

When he withdrew, she lifted her hand in front of them and tilted her head to his shoulder.

"Smile!" she said and posed for a picture only their eyes could see.

# EPILOGUE

*One month later…*

K ES STOOD WITH King Henry in her dress, previously owned by Queen Berengaria, and looked around at the great hall. It had been decorated for a celebration of her and Nicholas' marriage by Claire and the rest of her friends. They were told they could go as lavishly as they wished. And they did. White lilies sprinkled with bluebells were hung everywhere and were set in vases at all the tables. There were musicians hired all the way from Wales, servers and bakers hired from the best English houses, wine from the orchards of Sicily. Before long, tongues began to wag throughout the castle about how much the earl loved his lady.

He stood beside her now in dark blue, snug fitting trousers, boots, and a short coat over his shirt. He made all her dreams come true.

He'd done everything that she asked, including providing better seeds for the farmers. The scullery maids had gloves for scrubbing and the laundresses got them, too, since their hands were frequently in lye soap. Everyone had days of rest and whatever was left over in the castle kitchen each night was given to the servants.

Kes wasn't sure it would be possible but she was happy. She worked with authentic artifacts her father would die for. Four days a week, Nicholas rode her to Walter's on his horse and picked her up six hours later. It gave them time to miss each other and it gave her time to spend with Walter, one of her dearest friends.

On the other days she had exercise classes with the girls, along with embroidery and archery. She wanted to do more, but she'd been terribly sick and could barely get out of bed...in the morning.

If the first month of her pregnancy was any indication of how things were going to be, she was in very big trouble. The worst part of it all was that Nicholas was ecstatic while she was miserable. Thankfully, just when it began to get on her nerves, the sickness subsided.

Kes was too busy being swept away by her friends to notice Mr. Simeon pop into the crowd. He found Nicholas first and then her and pulled them both away.

"They found Elia," he told them. "After more tweaks to the brooch, Sir Gawaine was finally able to find her and get her to Manhattan, twenty nineteen."

Kes threw her hands to her mouth and rested against Nicholas when he put his arm around her. "What good news! After losing her for so long, it's quite a relief!"

"Have you spoken to her?" Nicholas asked. "Is she well?"

"Yes. I spoke with her," Mr. Simeon told him. "She is as well as can be expected after surviving in ten eighty-seven for the last month."

Nicholas groaned. Kes gasped. "Ten eighty-seven!" Kes couldn't imagine the shock of going from the eleventh century to the twenty-first. "Oh, poor Elia." Kes cried.

"She's a strong woman," Mr. Simeon reminded them both. "She told me she met an ancestor of hers called Matilda of Normandy." His eyes danced with awe. "Ever hear of her?"

Kes' mouth fell open. "William's wife?"

He nodded and then threw up his hands. "I don't think the brooch is that broken after all. Where it takes people is no coincidence."

Nicholas only cared that Elia was well and being taken care of. "Sell anything you must to get her coin."

Mr. Simeon nodded. "She needs clothes—"

"Whatever she needs."

"You will give her our letter?" Kes asked, putting her hand on his arm.

"Yes, my dear, I will take her your letter. Now remember, there is no guarantee it will be allowed through. I will only know once I get there."

"I understand." She smiled at him, so thankful for him. Through him she hoped she could stay in contact with Elia and with her father.

"I helped her find your father's apartment building. Mr. Lancaster is in Egypt for the next month according to his doorman, Carlo. Elia gave him the code and he let her in." He cast them a furtive smile. "She claimed to be his girlfriend."

Kes closed her eyes, thanking God it had worked and their dearest friend had a place to live at least for the next month. Egypt. It was his favorite place to go. She knew he was there mourning her. *Soon, Dad. Soon, I'll be talking to you again.*

King Henry called to them to follow him to the head table.

He'd arrived a week ago, understandably more eager to see Lizzie than he was to see them. Elizabeth had been staying with them through the harvest for all the festivals. She stayed in Richard's old house and redecorated it as her own.

They turned to head for the table and Mr. Simeon whispered, "You look lovely in that dress."

She smiled up at him as they walked. "What did you ever give Queen Berengaria in exchange for it?"

He clasped his hands behind his back and grinned. "A snow globe."

She stopped and blinked at him. "You gave the queen a snow globe for *this* dress?"

"I most certainly did. I left it on the table by her bed and watched in secret when she picked it up. She shook it. Snow and glitter dazzled her eyes as it fell all around a tiny hamlet. She held it in her hands all night long, Kes. Think of how magical it must have appeared to her fourteenth century eyes."

"Yes, I suppose you're right," Kes let him know with a pat on his arm.

"Can you stay for the celebration?" she asked the time traveler. But he couldn't stay anyplace too long. It was part of the curse.

"I heard the brooch was sent out again. And back to the twenty-first century, no less. To a New York City detective, whom if I hear correctly—and I usually do—is at his wits' end with life and uses whiskey to get through his day. I want to follow him and see where it leads him."

"Oh," Kes gasped a little. "Will you come and tell me about it?"

"Of course." He grinned at her. "If your husband doesn't mind."

When they reached the table, he excused himself and disappeared into the crowd. Kes reached for Nicholas' hand and sat at the head of the table. She looked out at all her friends enjoying the celebration. She was glad she didn't go back to the future, glad she wasn't lost for a month somewhere in time and sorry that her friend had gone through it. She was glad she was having Nicholas' baby, even if there wasn't much for the pain. She would endure it and give him children.

She had no idea why the brooch sent her here or if it was just a mistake, but she didn't believe that it was. Nicholas was too perfect.

He leaned in to speak close to her ear. "How do you feel, my love?"

"Fine," she told him with a smile.

A baby. She wished her father were here to see it, but she would write to him and tell him all about it. She wished Elia were here to see and to be with her but, hopefully, she would be with her father in the future and finally get to live her own life. Kes would write to her, too. The less people who knew of this the better, so she had to let Kim and Jack, Lilith and Constantine go.

She wiped a tear from her cheek and let Nicholas put her other hand in his while he spoke to the king.

Oh, what she gained. Did he sense her sadness without even looking at her? When he wasn't smiling, he was menacing to behold. But, as so many of the people of Scarborough, especially his men, had told her, because of her, he smiled often. Could she truly make a man so happy? She had done nothing differently than she would have in the twenty-first century, except react to his kindness, thoughtfulness, and valor. Traits she couldn't find all in one man, at least not the ones she and her friends had dated.

And then by some act of God, or crazy twist of fate, she was sent back here. To him. She loved Nicholas, therefore it was easy to make him happy.

She waved at Claire and Hilde as they made their way to the table.

"Did you see all the food that has been prepared?" Claire asked and then gasped at her own question. "Cook is dumbfounded! There is pheasant and, oh, all sorts of fowl! Tarts and puddings and pastries—"

"This will all go straight to my hips," Hilde cried out and patted them.

"We will work it off in class tomorrow," Kes told her. "Enjoy today. When we will eat like this again?"

"And we did not have to lift a finger!" Caitlyn reminded her.

"All thanks to Kes!" Claire exclaimed.

"Aye! Thank you, Kes," the other girls added.

None of them knew she came from a time when people who did what they did were paid wages and had rights just like anyone else. Kes didn't consider Claire or Cook or any of them as lower than she. She didn't care that the king and future queen sat to her right and the castle's head laundress and a handmaiden sat to her left. It was her and Nicholas' celebration and everyone was where she wanted them.

His hand disappeared under the table. He rested it on her thigh. It seemed that touching her drew his attention away from King Henry and onto her. His lashes shadowed his deep silver eyes as his gaze rose to hers.

"I do not know how much longer I can stand to be away from you," he leaned in and said against her cheekbone.

She knew he meant something more intimate with her. She loved that his desire for her was insatiable. She loved that she drove him mad. He drove her just as mad.

She turned her lips toward his ear. "I can't wait to be in bed with you."

"With me pulling on your hair and playing with you in my mouth," he added on a low growl as he went for her neck.

Her thoughts were assaulted with images of them sweaty and coiled in each other's arms.

She remembered where she was and opened her eyes. She coughed into her hand and looked at him—too embarrassed to look at anyone else.

He was no help, smiling at her, liking her reaction to him.

She wanted to pinch him, but any kind of contact could spark their passion.

This was no mistake. This was perfect.

"Scarborough," said the king. "You barely heard me!"

"Forgive me, Sire. What were you saying?"

Henry laughed. Kes knew Henry understood what they were going through. The king could barely keep his eyes off Lizzie. History showed that he was a devoted husband and one of the few kings who never had a mistress.

"I'm going to repeal the Titulus Regius that declares Edward's marriage to Elizabeth Woodville invalid and thereby legitimize my wife."

Nicholas didn't smile. "What if the princes are found? They will be legitimized as well. Are you willing to give up the throne?"

Henry laughed and clapped him on the back. "We will worry

about that if the time ever comes. Oui?"

Nicholas stiffened and turned to look at her. His gaze said everything. He was going to worry about it now.

She knew what his concerns were. There were a handful of historians willing to come out and say that Henry wouldn't have taken the chance of legitimizing the heirs if he wasn't sure the boys were gone. And there was only one way to be sure.

She sighed. Ah, well, nothing perfect lasted forever. She smiled to herself. That wasn't true. Love was perfect and it lasted forever. It echoed through time and called to hearts that were lost.

Was one of those hearts Arthur Pendragon's? And how many others would it bring together before it found its owner?

She might not ever know. It didn't matter. She had a husband to see to and a king to watch more closely.

"Come, my darling," she cooed on their way to the castle when the celebration was over. She held his strong arm and slipped her free hand to his temple and down his jaw. "Let me see to you." She leaned up to kiss his neck.

He smiled into her hand, forgetting everything else as she ran her palm over his mouth, and then picked her up and carried her to their room.

"Do not worry, love," he said. "I do not plan to live in the past with the princes...or the future, but in the present. With you. Here and now. And not waste a single day."

She stared into his eyes and smiled as he shut the door to their chambers and bolted it.

*October 13, 2019*

*Dear Daddy,*

*I know how this is going to sound, but it's me, Kes. I'm not dead and I wasn't kidnapped. I was transported back in time to the fifteenth century. I don't know why really, except it has something to do with a brooch belonging to Arthur Pendragon. A brooch that brings us to our true love. I will let Elia tell you about Nicholas, my husband, since she raised him and knows him best. Hear what she has to say, Daddy. I think she has a little crush on you.*

*There is so much I want to tell you. I don't know where to start. The Round Table knights are real. So is King Arthur. We supposedly have Pendridge, or Pendragon blood. I know how farfetched this all sounds, believe me. But it's all true. I met Sir Gawaine and Lucan! And oh, Dad, Mr. Simeon is a time traveler. He trades with a merchant here and fills his house with ancient artifacts. The things I've seen and catalogued!*

*Of course I miss you terribly. There isn't a day that goes by when you are not on my mind. That's why I sent you Elia. She's wonderful. I think you're going to love her.*

*I wish you could be here with us as we welcome…*

Charles Arthur Lancaster finished reading the letter from his daughter. So, this all had to do with the brooch and his daughter finding true love. He could see her if he wanted to. After all, it was his spell, his brooch, but he'd have to give up his position, his freedom. Maybe one day.

Not yet. He looked over his glasses at the woman from the fifteenth century sitting in his library. Elia she said her name was.

"So Elia, tell me about my son-in-law. Does he practice courtly ways?"

# End

# About the Author

Paula Quinn is a New York Times bestselling author and a sappy romantic moved by music, beautiful words, and the sight of a really nice pen. She lives in New York with her three beautiful children, six over-protective chihuahuas, and three adorable parrots. She loves to read romance and science fiction and has been writing since she was eleven. She's a faithful believer in God and thanks Him daily for all the blessings in her life. She loves all things medieval, but it is her love for Scotland that pulls at her heartstrings.

To date, four of her books have garnered Starred reviews from Publishers Weekly. She has been nominated as Historical Storyteller of the Year by RT Book Reviews, and all the books in her MacGregor and Children of the Mist series have received Top Picks from RT Book Reviews. Her work has also been honored as Amazons Best of the Year in Romance, and in 2008 she won the Gayle Wilson Award of Excellence for Historical Romance.

Website:
pa0854.wixsite.com/paulaquinn

www.ingramcontent.com/pod-product-compliance
Lightning Source LLC
Chambersburg PA
CBHW071750190726
48292CB00003B/929